ELIJAH

by

Matt Schorr

This book contains the complete unabridged text of the original work.

A Lone Coyote Productions book published by arrangement with the author.

Copyright © 2010 by Matt Schorr.
All rights reserved.

Cover illustration by King Media Productions.
Cover layout and design by Sue Harring.

This book may not be reproduced in whole or in part, by mimeograph or any other means, without permission.

ISBN: 978-0-615-42434-7

PUBLISHER'S NOTE
This is a work of fiction. Names, characters, places and incidents are the products of the author's imagination or used fictitiously. Any resemblance to any person living or dead is purely coincidental.

Printed in the United States of America.

Third printing – April 2011.

Author's Note

What follows is a story that's bounced around in my head for almost ten years.

I realized some time ago that whatever stories I told would likely draw a lot of inspiration from religion. I first noticed this in college when I found it creeping its way into every creative writing project I had, whether I wanted it there or not.

I suppose it's because I have a tenuous relationship with religion. I appreciate how faith and religious belief can both inspire and drive so many of us, but I also struggle with its occasional, nasty tendency to breed fear, paranoia and intolerance. It's a precarious balance on which I find myself, and I believe that's reflected here.

I'm not certain which side of the religious fence this tale falls upon. I'll leave that to readers. I never set out with an agenda of any kind. I've merely told the story as it happened, and I've done so without apology.

Let the chips fall where they may.

For my friends
For my family
And for Josh (whose name I "borrowed" in this story)

CHAPTER 1

The clear glass jingled like a tiny, ancient wind chime as ice and soda filled it to the brim. The dark, bubbling liquid frothed at the top and hissed for several seconds while tiny speckles leaped and danced over it like a tiny, dying universe.

Lori Roberson smiled at the elderly gentleman she guessed had long since passed over the hill of middle age. He returned the smile, a polite smile devoid of emotion. A smile that was merely a return gesture. A courtesy for her service. Nothing more. Nothing less. *Thank you, ma'am. Now, be on your way, please.*

Lori moved on to another table occupied by a mother and her two sons. Most everyone knew each other in Antioch, but this lady could be spotted as a single mother a mile away. The tired look in her eyes as she struggled to keep her two boys behaved was the look of a parent who'd worked solo for many years.

Or maybe Lori just thought it was obvious. After all, she and Janine went to high school together. Sure, they weren't—*what was that stupid phrase? BFF's? best-friends-forever?*—or anything, but they got along well enough.

Poor Janine, once a blonde bombshell head cheerleader with long legs, bouncing breasts and perfect hair, married shortly after high school. A fresh Army recruit, John McMakelroy, had ridden in and swept her right off her feet. Right out of the small town, American life and into the clouds. Promised her trips around the world. Maybe even Hawaii? The Caribbean? Hell, he probably even promised a trip to Paris.

Of course, John *did* take those trips. Janine, however, stayed home. Then, she got pregnant. Twice. And John ended up meeting some sexy Asian dancer with an exotic name no one could remember.

Janine had shunned Lori prior to the divorce. After all, she was a badass Army man's wife then. And she was going to see the world.

Life doled out sour fruit sometimes. Janine's long legs were now cellulite-riddled stumps. Her breasts sagged just enough to be cringe-worthy, and her hair was cropped just below her ears. And to top it all off, she'd never managed to shed all of her remaining baby fat.

Lori, meanwhile, had retained her figure. She was never a bombshell in high school, but now, compared with Janine, she was practically a beauty queen. She'd managed to keep a trim figure despite the dreaded post-teen-metabolism. Her hair was an unexciting brown, which she kept in an even more unexciting ponytail.

Still, she could be cute when she tried.

Lori and Janine were never friends. Not really. At best, they'd just been acquaintances on good terms; at worst, bitter rivals on opposite ends of the high school spectrum. Now, Lori only pitied her. Who could stay mad at someone with such a pathetic story?

How long ago was high school, anyway? Ten years? Geez, she was getting old.

Still, the chances for a newfound friendship between the two were slim to none. You really can't be friends with someone you pity.

It's a shame, Lori thought with a wry smile.

Janine smiled when Lori approached and asked for her check in between scoldings of Billy and Jeremy. *Stop throwing food at your brother, Billy. Jeremy, don't blow in your straw.*

Lori nodded and headed for the register. Sure, treading water as a waitress in a small town pizzeria wasn't what she'd dreamed of as a child, but at least she wasn't in Janine's boat. Besides, there were worse jobs in Antioch, Kentucky, than J.D.'s Pizza. Plenty worse.

The electronic bell gave off its two-note song—*doo-dah!*—as the front entrance door opened. The soft sound of a slight wind gust drifted into J.D.'s, and everyone inside turned to see the new customer. Just like a classic western, Lori would later tell herself.

The man who entered the establishment was young, no more than twenty-five. An unruly mop of dark brown hair that could've really used a good trim fell over most of his forehead. Beneath that were dark, tired eyes. Eyes that seemed to have seen much and cared little for it.

His nose was long and sharp, but not quite witchy. And the beginnings of tiny wrinkles were already scurrying around the corners of his mouth and eyes, which stood out on someone so young. Crow's feet were, after all, reserved for the elderly.

He wore dark jeans, a black shirt, and a long gray trench coat that dropped all the way to his ankles. It was thick and dusty. A thicker layer of dirt and dust crept up an inch or so from the coat's hem. Hell, the only things missing were a wide-brim hat, boots, and a cigar. *What brings you to this town, stranger?* Several dozen eyes locked onto the man as he entered the dining room. Even Lori, who was watching him from a distance of less than four feet—the register was placed just to the right of the entrance—couldn't look away.

He paused a moment to look back at his newfound audience as the door swung shut behind him. He was so...*different*. So unlike anyone in Antioch. So unlike anyone who'd even passed *through* Antioch.

He regarded them all with a quiet, gentle reserve, as though he understood their inability to grant him the courtesy of not staring a hole through him. Understood and didn't begrudge them. In fact, the corners of his mouth seemed to curve ever so slightly upward in a kind smile.

This man was strange, no doubt, but Lori felt, for some reason she couldn't explain, she could trust him. That everyone in J.D.'s could trust him. All of Antioch for that matter. There were no lies, no dark secrets about this stranger. Only intriguing mystery.

At last, he turned and looked at Lori. She could only stare back, still holding Janine's bill in one hand, her mouth slightly open.

The young man's eyes trailed away from Lori to the sign posted near the door, the one that said "HOSTESS WILL SEAT YOU." He looked back at her, that same subtle smile still creeping around the corners of his mouth. He raised his eyebrows.

At long last, Lori realized what he was waiting for. She blinked and shook her head, even groaned a quick

"Oh!" of realization before marching out from behind the register.

"Sorry. Would you care for a table or a booth?"

"Booth." He answered without hesitating. And Lori could guess why he was so quick to choose one. She knew—she just *knew*—he wanted nothing more than a place to sit down. Everything about him seemed exhausted. He looked as though he'd traveled the world and bore the weight of all its woes every step of the way.

Lori guided him to a booth in the far corner. He fell hard into the seat and sighed. For a moment, he didn't move, just relishing the chance to finally, *finally* sit down. Then, he placed his arms on the table and looked up at Lori again.

That was about the time Lori realized how beautiful his eyes were. At first, she'd just seen how dark they seemed. Now, she saw what they were was a deep shade of the purest blue. His gaze was penetrating but gentle. She felt as if—cliché as it sounded—he was staring into her soul.

And yet, she didn't feel the least bit violated by that. Were this man to see every dark secret she bore, he would think no less of her. She was certain of it.

"Can I get you something to drink?" she asked.

"Coke," he answered.

"Pepsi okay?"

He shrugged and waved a dismissive hand. "Absolutely." He smiled. Really smiled. The most incredible smile Lori had ever seen.

But why? she wondered. Why was it so incredible? This stranger was no fashion model. He wasn't even thirty, but he already had wrinkles forming in the corners of his mouth and eyes. His hair was unkempt, his face unshaven. And yet, something about him was just…wonderful.

I'd run across the street to the service station and buy you a Coke myself if you asked. I'd do anything if you just promise to keep smiling at me like that.

Lori smiled back and forced herself to turn away. When she turned back to the restaurant, she realized the handful of customers were now staring at her, too. She narrowed her eyes at all of them, an expression that asked, *Well? What?*

They didn't turn away. Not at first, anyway. They only turned their attention back to the stranger in their midst. Gave him another good once-over, then finally looked back at their meals.

But they still cast sidelong glances at him.

Lori returned to Janine and delivered her bill. Janine thanked her with a voice only just above a whisper. Her boys were also quiet. They stared across the restaurant wide-eyed and open-mouthed.

Lori smiled, nodded, and headed into the kitchen to pour the man's soda. The gaggle of a kitchen crew was huddled around the doorway and order window to get a glimpse, whenever possible, of Antioch's latest visitor.

Marcus, the "senior" cook (he'd worked there the longest, anyway) met her at the soda fountain. The other two cooks, both of them teenagers barely able to drive, stayed in the window.

Marcus had become Lori's closest companion since she took the waitress gig. The two of them were pretty close in age, although Marcus didn't come to Antioch until well after high school. He was tall, with the build of an anorexic rock star despite his ability to shovel food down his gullet like a deep sea bass. He had thick, dark hair, which he loosely parted to the left, and skin that almost looked tanned even though he probably never spent more than an hour in the sun each day.

"He's cute. Who is he?"

Lori only granted Marcus a quick, smirk that bordered on a giggling smile before focusing her attention on the Pepsi.

"I only took his drink order. Didn't ask for his ID."

"Well, go back out there and get his meal order, his name, and how long he expects to be in town, then," he hissed. He didn't bother hiding his wicked grin.

The man's glass filled, Lori looked back, head tilted in that *Excuse me?* pose favored by so many women. "You want to serve his drink?"

Marcus held his hands up. "He's all yours, sweetheart."

"Thank you."

She headed back into the dining room. The remaining customers were still trying not to stare at the newcomer.

And failing. Their eyes still darted in his direction every minute or so.

The stranger leaned against the back of his seat, head lowered. His eyes were half-closed, and he took what Lori was convinced were long, labored breaths.

She placed the glass before him as quietly as possible. He looked at the soda and smiled. A long, soft sigh escaped his nostrils. He looked up at her and smiled again.

And again, he caught her off guard. *God, please don't stop. Please, just let me stay here so you can keep smiling at me like that.*

Lori closed her eyes and lightly shook her head. This was ridiculous. She was acting like a teenage girl meeting the latest pop star. She'd always rolled her eyes at the girls who swooned and squealed at their favorite teenage heartthrobs, and here she was melting before God and everyone in J.D.'s for this no-name drifter...and all because he had a nice smile.

No, it's more than that, and you know it. There's more to him than that smile. A lot more.

"So what can I get you?" she asked, pen poised over her notepad.

The stranger didn't answer. Instead, he picked up the glass and took a long swig like a man in a tavern trying to impress his pals by downing a long draught of hard liquor. He returned the glass to the table, now drained of a full fourth of its contents.

"*Aaah*," he whispered, a look of extreme contentment on his face.

"That good, huh?" Lori smiled.

He nodded. "I hope you don't mind." He looked into her eyes again. "I really just wanted to stop in from the road. Grab a seat and have a drink."

Lori shook her head. "No problem at all. So just the soda, then?"

"I know it won't make for a big tip, but if you promise to keep the refills coming, I promise I'll dance at your wedding?"

Now Lori did giggle. And not just a subtle giggle, either. Huh-uh. This was a full-on, straight-out-of-junior-high-school, girls-talking-about-their-favorite-boys, loud and obnoxious "*Teeheehee!*" sort of giggle.

She slapped her lips with the tips of her fingers, covering her smile and that humiliating laugh. Jesus

Christ, she hadn't giggled like that since she was in grade school! She felt the temperature of her entire face soar.

But the stranger never stopped smiling his gentle, knowing smile at her. There was no smug amusement or cockiness about that smile. His eyes told her that giggle was perhaps her most endearing quality. Nothing to be ashamed of. Giggle away, darlin.

She "ahem"-ed and forced another smile. "Sorry about that. I'll keep an eye on that soda for you."

"Thank you, Lori."

She nodded and started to turn back to the kitchen. Then, caught herself. She almost asked how he knew her name but then remembered she bore it on her name badge over her breast.

Perfect place, after all. A man could take a good, long look at her rack and pretend he was just reading her name.

The stranger only nodded at her name badge, indicating that, yes, that's how he knew her name.

"I'm Elijah," he said. "Just so we're even."

Lori nodded again and turned away to clear Janine's table. Janine was just starting to corral Billy and Jeremy so they could head home.

No easy task. The boys were back to behaving like all young boys. *Here, Billy, put your coat on. Jeremy, so help me…!*

She kept glancing over her shoulder at the mysterious stranger—Elijah, Lori told herself—as she ushered them toward the door.

"Have a good evening, Janine," Lori called.

Janine smiled and nodded back. "You too."

She was about to usher the boys outside when the door opened again (*doo-dah!*) and—like a bright beam of

CHAPTER 3

The harsh sound of ice jingling in an empty glass shattered the silence that hung round their conversation. It was loud, almost rude.

Lori turned toward Elijah, who was shaking his empty glass and looking at her. "Sorry, Lori," he said, "but I'm just really thirsty."

She held back a relieved smile, but not completely. She looked back at Joshua. "I should get that."

Joshua, ever the politician and saint, nodded and smiled.

Lori hurried over and took Elijah's glass. She glanced into his eyes one time. He looked back at her with the same quiet gentleness he'd shown upon his arrival. She hoped he could see the deep well of thanks in her eyes.

"Sorry to be so rude," he said. "I'm just so thirsty from the road."

"Not a problem." The relief also showed in Lori's voice, no matter how she tried to mask it from Joshua.

When she turned, Joshua was standing in her path. "Won't you introduce me to your friend?"

She hesitated. "Well, umm," she stammered, "he's just a customer, but…"

"Elijah," he called from behind her.

Lori stepped out from between them. Joshua wasted no time. Here was a potential new convert! A believer! Another number for the flock! He marched over to Elijah, hand extended.

"John Joshua Hutchinson," Joshua announced. "Pastor of ChristPoint Church. Located right on the intersection of Old Havannah Highway and Tucker Road, you can't miss it!"

Lori mouthed the words behind Joshua as he spoke them. He gave that rehearsed line to everyone he met. She waited for him to finish with the *Truth* being what they were *all* about, but it never came. Guess he was slacking that night.

Elijah shook Joshua's hand.

"My first name's John, but my friends call me Joshua." His million-dollar grin was still plastered across his face like a human billboard of happiness.

"Then, I'll call you John," Elijah answered, returning the smile.

A moment passed. Then, Lori's eyes widened. Did that just happen?

Joshua blinked. For a moment, his golden smile faltered, but he regained it and managed a "Heh" in response. Elijah kept smiling, and for the first time, there was a glint of something other than that kind honesty beneath it.

Lori couldn't help but stare at them. Was there some honest-to-God friction there?

"Heh," Joshua grunted again, and finally regained his composure. He took his hand back and stood. "Well, if you're staying over the weekend and have the time, we'd be thrilled to have you at church with us Sunday morning."

She sat down in the booth opposite Elijah. He looked back and smiled again. She didn't know what to say. Where was she supposed to start?

"So tell me about the 'good Reverend?'" he offered.

Lori grunted. "The local messiah? Not really much to tell. He inherited the church from his father when he was twenty, and he managed to grow it into some sort of super-church within a couple of years."

"Impressive."

"Yeah, I guess. You know there used to be small churches on every other street corner here? Foster Creek Presbyterian, Calvary United Methodist, Northside Baptist." She shook her head. "Not now, though, ChristPoint swallowed up all of them. Now, they're either empty buildings or antique furniture stores."

Elijah raised an eyebrow. "*All* of them?"

Lori nodded. "Every last one. Everyone in town attends *his* church now." She smirked. "Well, almost everyone."

"All but you?"

"All but me, Marcus, and a handful of others. Don't get me wrong, I believe in God and everything, but that church is just...*wrong.*" She shook her head and looked away. "I don't know what it is, but it's just *wrong.*"

She looked back at Elijah. He was silent, thoughtful.

"Am I making sense?" Lori asked.

For a brief moment, she glimpsed a hint of sadness on his face. Some deep hurt she'd called up from the depths to haunt him. But it was gone just as fast at it appeared.

Elijah nodded and said, his voice just above a whisper, "Yes."

Lori thought she could sit and talk to him all night, given the chance: listen to his voice, see his smile, just be near him.

The bitter smartass part of her personality noted he seemed like everything the good Reverend wished he was but wasn't. And never would be.

J.D.'s patrons had all gone home. It was just the two of them. Lori probably would've sat and talked with him until long after the restaurant closed. But at that moment, a shriek of exquisite suffering rang out from the kitchen. And it was coming from Marcus.

As the closing cook for the night, Marcus had the dubious privilege of cleaning the main oven and deep fryer. The night's manager had called in sick, which made him, as substitute manager, the one responsible for closing the place up for the night.

The oven was actually easy enough; it was the deep fryer that was a pain. The grease (or "shortening" as the higher-up's liked to call it, since "grease" sounded dirty) needed to be emptied into a giant filter to clean all the leftover batter and breading from countless fried cheese sticks, French fries, and onion rings.

The filter was a giant, round, stainless steel tub capable of holding several gallons of grease (Marcus never could bring himself to call it "shortening"). Fortunately, the deep fryer held only a little over a gallon.

The routine was simple enough. Empty the grease into the filter, add a cup full of cleaning solution, and let it run for a minute or two. That was the easy part. It was returning all that stupid grease to the deep fryer that was the real pain.

There was no hose to spray the grease back in; Marcus had to lift the tub with his hands and pour it back. The tub weighed about thirty pounds on its own, and it was bulky and awkward as crap. The grease added almost ten pounds, not to mention a whole new level of awkwardness since you had to be careful not to scald yourself.

The fact that the tub was nearly twice as wide as the deep fryer was just one more pain in the butt. Life's just a ditch, man. Can you dig it?

The whole process went as smooth as ever, though. Empty, clean, filter, return. And watch those hands.

Another successful cleanup. Job well done, Marcus. But of course, the managers only say something when you screw up.

He set the tub back on the floor and stood up. He leaned back, stretching and feeling his lower back crackle. He groaned and was about to roll the filter machine back to its closet when the deep fryer erupted in flames.

In the days that followed, he and management did their best to figure out just what in God's name went wrong that night. Marcus had done everything by the book: switched off the deep fryer and let it sit a few minutes to cool down. He'd followed the instructions for using the filter to the letter. He'd done everything just as he should've. It was just a freak accident.

Some random spark somehow ignited the grease.

The flames leaped from the deep fryer, curved away from the air current provided by the industrial-strength overhead fans, and rushed at Marcus like a fiery octopus from hell. He covered his face with his hands and stumbled back, caught entirely off guard.

His right hand felt like it'd been shoved into the belly of a volcano, and he tripped over the filter machine.

He landed hard on his back, effectively driving all the air from his chest. For a wild, horrific instant, his lungs clamped shut and he could only make feeble gasps while his head seemed to spin like a nightmare carousel. He clamped his eyes shut and struggled to catch his breath and find his voice. His hand, meanwhile, continued to scream at his brain like a subliminal banshee. When he finally could breathe, he opened his eyes, but the light in front of them forced him to close them again.

A tiny, white-hot furnace burned where his right hand should've been. It danced and licked at his face like an exotic demon. All the while his hand continued to cry out to his mind.

Marcus flailed his arm in desperation, the burning hand swinging like a glowing flipper, and he screamed. Panic overtook him. Screaming and flapping was all he could do.

The kitchen door crashed open, and he looked up at Lori and the stranger. Lori's eyes bulged from her their sockets, and she clamped a hand over her mouth to suppress a scream. She was panicked, terrified, but, to her credit, she still rushed to help, limited as the help of a panicked pizza waitress in that situation would be, anyway.

The stranger, Elijah, however, made no sound. He slid his coat off his shoulders and clutched it in one hand. He hurried to Marcus and gently but firmly eased Lori aside. Then, less than a second later, he'd wrapped his coat around Marcus' burning hand.

The flames were gone. But the pain was still there. It hadn't gone anywhere. His skin burned, and the startling scent of what Marcus could only imagine was his own burning flesh was starting to fill the room. It smelled like...*pork chops?*

He tried to pull his hand out of the coat, his mind filled with disturbing images of a shriveled, bubbling mass where his palm and fingers had once been. But Elijah held him still. He shook his head.

"I'll call 911," Lori gasped and tried to stand. But Elijah caught her by the arm, holding her in place as well.

He looked back at Marcus. Stared into his eyes. "Trust me."

Marcus didn't answer. What was left of his vocal cords seemed inoperable. He only watched as Elijah slid his hand into the coat with his. He felt Elijah interlock his fingers with whatever remained of his. He felt skin flake and crumble like burned paper, and he yelped as Elijah's flesh brushed rudely with his own. It hurt like a mother.

And then, they both sat, fingers interlocked within Elijah's coat, staring into one another's eyes.

The pain remained. Clawed at his fingers like tiny pin needles stabbing at him. Just what was this man trying to do?

Elijah tugged his arm once, and pain exploded throughout his fingers and raced up his wrist like lightning. But Elijah held him firm.

He said nothing.

Then, Marcus felt his hand grow warm. Not warm like before, when flames ate greedily at his exposed skin. No, this was a pleasant warmth, like being wrapped in a warm blanket on a cold day. It started in his fingers, then worked its way up his wrist and arm.

The pain eased, faded. And then it was gone. Completely gone.

Elijah's fingers loosened and slid away. He took hold of the coat with his free hand and pulled it back. Marcus still had images of a charred, flaky, malformed appendage, but he knew that's not what he'd see. He knew full well what he'd see.

His hand was fine. No scars. No ashes. No, bubbly, flaky, disfigured remains. Nothing. He clenched and unclenched his fingers, as if affirming to himself he still could. It was perfect. Not burnt. Not even singed.

Perfect.

Marcus turned to Lori. She was staring at Elijah, her mouth agape. Marcus shifted his attention to the stranger as well.

Elijah looked at Lori. He looked at Marcus.

"You okay?" he asked.

Marcus could think of no way to answer. So, utilizing what he could of his voice, he croaked, "What the hell are you?"

CHAPTER 4

Lori lived in a cozy apartment just a few miles from J.D.'s. It was part of a quaint little apartment complex called Lincoln Drive Apartments, named for the nearby street. It was a four building complex with four apartments in each one, all with one bathroom and two bedrooms.

It was located right between the low and high rent districts. Lincoln Drive served as a sort of *border* between the two sides of town.

It wasn't the Ritz, but it wasn't a rat hole, either. Kind of like the Purgatory of apartments.

Lori had taken the time to furnish her home with good furniture and an attractive painting or two on the walls. She'd also joined the ranks of every other young adult in America and purchased a futon for her living room. Hers was a typical one, too, with wooden arms, a metal base, and a solid black cushion.

Lori and Marcus sat side-by-side on this sofa staring at Elijah, who sat across and just to their left in a recliner, not looking back at them. The television was on but its volume was low, which meant it did little to break the thick, uncomfortable silence covering the room.

And so they all sat. Like characters in an offbeat, romantic comedy unable to break the ice. Except a bit more tense.

Marcus finally did the honors.

"So, how did you do that?"

Elijah turned to look at them and started to smile, but he stopped when he saw Marcus and Lori weren't going to return the favor. He looked down at the floor and remained silent for an awkward moment. Then, at last, he just shrugged and shook his head. "I don't know."

Lori frowned. "You don't know?"

Elijah shook his head again. "No. I just...do it."

"And you have no idea how?" Her voice was somewhat accusatory. She knew it was, felt guilty even. But then again, she kind of felt justified at the same time.

"No. I don't."

She shook her head and grunted. It was incredible.

"So you can just heal anyone you touch?" Marcus asked, rejoining the interrogation.

Elijah nodded this time. "So far."

"So you can heal the sick, make the blind see, the deaf hear, the lame walk?" Lori was scoffing. Still felt guilty. But still justified.

Elijah nodded.

"Can...can you raise the dead?" Marcus asked.

Elijah hesitated a moment. He blinked, then answered, "No."

Silence. Neither Marcus nor Lori cared to learn how he knew that.

"I also can't heal myself." He looked at them for the first time. "Only others. Weird little limitation."

Another uncomfortable silence. Lori scanned the room, trying to come up with her next questions. It was a tricky conversation. How do you discuss miraculous healing powers?

"So, how long have you had this—power?" she finally asked.

Elijah frowned again. Lori wasn't certain, but she could almost swear she saw his eyes glance away for just the slightest moment, as though he was recalling some distant memory, a memory she had a nagging feeling he didn't like.

"A little over a year," he said.

"And you have no idea how you got it?"

Elijah looked right at Lori and smiled. And just like that, she could feel her suspicion and fear melt away. Geez, how did he do that?

There were no dark secrets about Elijah. Just a fascinating mystery. "I said as much, didn't I?" he offered.

From any other person, that sort of comment would be laced with sarcasm. Maybe even a hint of anger and frustration. But from Elijah, it was patient and warm…and maybe just a little bit playful.

Lori reddened and looked away. "Sorry."

Elijah waved a dismissive hand. "It's okay. I understand. I reacted almost the same way at first. I guess that's why I'm on this…journey. I'm…searching."

"For what?" Marcus asked.

"Answers," Elijah said.

"Answers, huh?" This time Marcus frowned. "Like, you're looking for God, or something?"

Elijah shrugged again. "I suppose."

"You expect to find God out on the road?"

"Oh, I dunno. I don't really have any idea how I'd find Him. Or Her. Or It. I've got no preconceived notions. I'm just looking. If He's out there, maybe I can actually meet Him in person. Or maybe He'll just speak to me in that 'still, small voice' some people talk about. Or maybe it'll be something else entirely, like a tree."

"A tree?" Marcus grinned.

Elijah grinned back and shrugged

"What about church?" Lori tried.

Elijah darkened. "Already been there."

CHAPTER 5

Just over an hour later, Lori carried a sleeping bag and pillow into the living room. She dropped it on the floor at Elijah's feet, where he stood holding his coat.

"You really don't have to do this," he ventured.

"Oh." Lori waved a dismissive hand of her own. "It's the least we can do for you taking care of Marcus's hand."

Elijah smiled. Were he a cowboy in a western film, this is where he'd say, *Weren't nothin', Ma'am.*

"You have someplace for coats?" he asked. "Or is it fine just on the sofa?"

"Oh, I'll take it. There's a small closet next to the door." Lori reached for his coat but stopped short when she heard Marcus clearing his throat behind her. She looked back and saw him waiting for her, arms folded and smirking. He jerked his head in a short, quick motion. *Get over here, girl!*

"Be right back," she told Elijah, then scurried over to Marcus and hissed, *"What?"*

"Shouldn't *I* be offering him a place to stay?" He raised an eyebrow. "You know? Since he healed *my* hand?"

"You can have him tomorrow night," Lori shot back. She and Marcus exchanged a series of knowing looks.

Elijah, ignoring them, knelt down and started spreading out the sleeping bag. This done, he placed the pillow at one end, stood, and removed his coat, revealing a large hunting knife sheathed on his belt buckle.

Lori and Marcus stopped talking and stared at the long blade. It hung from Elijah's waist in a leather sheathe, and it must've been over a foot long. It was the sort of weapon Crocodile Dundee would carry.

See that? That's *a knife!*

Elijah looked up at them, noticed them staring and looked down. "Oh." He un-strapped the blade and its sheathe and held it before them. "Hunting knife." His eyes were apologetic. "Can't be too careful out on the road. And I don't like guns."

He shrugged, then set the knife on the floor beside his sleeping bag.

Marcus and Lori glanced at one another again through the corners of their eyes. *You're sure about this?* Marcus was asking.

Lori turned and opened the door for him. "Drive safely, Marcus."

Marcus nodded and hugged her. When he let go, he was grinning. "You kids behave, all right?"

Lori covered his face with her hand and shoved him out into the hall. Then, he was gone. And they were alone.

A long, uncomfortable moment, somewhat different than before, passed.

"Well," Lori said at last. "You know where the kitchen and bathroom are if you need anything. I'll see you in the morning."

Elijah nodded. "'Kay."

Another awkward moment. "Um. Okay. G'night, then." Lori smiled and dipped her hips in a sort of curtsy and retreated toward her room. Her movement was somewhere between a brisk walk and a near gallop.

"'Night," Elijah called after her.

She closed the door to her bedroom, and, alone at last, she sighed. Jesus Christ, who *was* this guy? And why in the *hell* did she offer to let him stay here?

The image of the hunting knife flashed through her brain like a forensic photograph. (*Flash! Whirrrrr!*) She pictured it hovering just under her throat, poised and ready to strike. She imagined the horrific feeling of it slicing the thin flesh of her neck, the warmth of her blood pouring down her front like a small, crimson waterfall.

And would he have his way with her before or *after?*

No. He wouldn't. Would he?

Lori grabbed a chair from a small desk opposite her bed and placed it against the door. She angled it so the back of the chair wedged under the doorknob.

Satisfied, she stepped back and slipped out of her work clothes. She took hold of her pajamas, then froze.

Elijah's smile when he first entered the restaurant flashed in her brain. (*Flash!* No, whir this time, though.) Actually, it wasn't even so much a flash as a slow, gentle illumination...almost like a sunrise. Chrissake, even when he *wasn't* in the room, he had that weird power over her, assuring her it would all be all right.

Lori looked back at the chair and sighed again. She didn't need it. She knew Elijah would never force himself onto her. She still barely knew him, but she was certain she was safe with him. Maybe even safer than she'd ever been without him.

And he wouldn't threaten her in any way. She knew that just as sure as she knew he wouldn't rape her. She didn't know how she knew; she just did.

The man was a mystery, yes. But there was nothing terrifying about him. Nothing at all.

Lori removed the chair and set it back at her desk.

CHAPTER 6

    Sleep didn't come easily that night. And what little sleep Lori did manage was restless, plagued with unpleasant images and dreams. Often, she heard the sound of an infant crying somewhere in the dark. Its cries started soft, like a babe wanting only to suckle its mother. Then, they grew into high-pitched wails. Screams.

    Lori rolled back and forth in her bed in swift, violent motions. The crying continued, no matter where she turned. It rang in her ears and rattled around the inside of her head.

    She felt moist warmth spreading between her legs, and she stopped moving. It continued flowing down her thighs and covered her buttocks.

    The crying was making her head hurt. Lori squinted in the darkness, but her vision was blurry. She reached for the lamp beside her bed, but couldn't find it. She turned, hoping to see it, but her blurred vision and the darkness made that impossible. She fumbled round the table for the lamp, coming up empty.

    And all the while the screaming continued, and the warm liquid continued spreading. It seemed to get warmer.

    Lori's fingers finally bumped into what she hoped was her lamp, and she felt her way around it for the switch, found it. She winced away from the sudden blast of light that exploded in her eyes. When was the thing ever so bright?

When her eyes cleared, Lori could see a dark stain spreading between her legs. She tore the blanket off and saw her pajamas soaked in blood.

The crimson stain spread as blood spilled from her loins. Her legs burned with it, an unholy fire that spread from her loins and slowly consumed her.

And all the while, the baby continued shrieking.

Lori gasped, a sharp sound that cut through the dark silence like a blade. Half her face was buried in her pillow. Her one uncovered eye stared out at her darkened bedroom. There were two moist spots on her pillow, one beneath her mouth and another near her eyes.

Her head hurt, the headache of someone who'd slept either too long or too little. Her skin was cold and clammy thanks to a thin layer of sweat coating most of her body. Her shirt and pajamas stuck to her skin.

She pushed herself up to a sitting position and leaned against her headboard. The headache wasn't going away anytime soon. The only remedy was to lie back down and close her eyes. But sleep wasn't coming back anytime soon. Not after that.

Lori stared at the blanket covering her. She felt no warmth anymore, but the stark image was still fresh in her mind. The sound of a crying infant still echoed there.

She closed her eyes, and a single tear squeezed its way through her eyelids and slid down her cheek. It left a tiny, chilled trail behind that tickled as it dried.

Lori shook her head and pulled the blanket away. Her pajamas stuck to her legs, but there was no blood. Not a trace.

A soft knock at the door yanked Lori's attention from her body. A soft, gentle whisper called from the other side. "Lori? Everything okay?"

How in the...?

It's not like she woke up screaming. It was just a stupid dream. How in Christ did Elijah notice that?

She climbed out of bed, wobbled for just a moment on unsteady legs not quite ready for standing, and headed for the door. When she opened it, Elijah was looking back toward the living room where his sleeping bag was. He jerked his head back toward Lori. He offered her a tiny, apologetic smile.

"I—" he started, but trailed off. "I thought—"

"I didn't wake you, did I?" Lori asked, cutting him off.

"No, not at all," Elijah quickly answered. He shook his head for emphasis. "I just—"

"Is this another power you have?" Lori gave him a tired smile.

Elijah smiled back and shrugged. "I don't know." He hesitated. "Are you okay?"

Lori sighed. "You probably already know I'm not."

Elijah chewed that over a moment. "No. I don't. I just...*guess* it? I guess?"

Lori nodded. "Fair enough."

"You want to talk about it?" Elijah asked. "Would it help?"

"Maybe."

Lori stepped into the hall with him and closed the bedroom door. She didn't want to be in there anymore. That was for sure.

She led the way back to the living room and collapsed on the futon. Elijah sat beside her, but he kept a fair distance between them.

"Bad dreams?" he asked.

"Yeah." Lori looked toward the ceiling, holding back the tears she could feel fighting their way to the surface. "One of those...what do they call them? *Recurring?*"

"I think so."

She looked down again and shook her head. The tears, it seemed, were at bay. "Well, I know where they come from."

Elijah said nothing. Just waited.

Lori smiled. She wasn't getting out of this. "I guess it was about five years ago..."

CHAPTER 7

Joshua Hutchinson's rise to prominence in Antioch was anything but gradual. The young and eager new pastor practically exploded onto the town's spiritual scene shortly after the death of his father.

When Walter Hutchinson passed away, his son inherited the pastorship of the Pentecostals of Antioch. At the time, it was little more than a quaint, country church located a few miles out of town in the middle of what used to be a modest cornfield. They averaged around fifty regular members with another dozen or so who'd show up for the occasional service, Christmas, Easter, and whatnot. Mostly friends and family of the regulars.

Walter had been content enough with his small congregation of nearly twenty years—"Better a few dozen dedicated saints than a thousand hypocrites," he'd always said—but not the newly appointed reverend.

Within weeks of his father's death, the newly appointed Rev. Hutchinson upgraded the church's sound system, installed overhead projectors, invested in better musical instruments, and more. Gone were the electric organ, the aging hymnals titled "Praise Unto the Lord," and the old ladies leading song services. In their place, Pastor

Hutchinson introduced guitars, contemporary music, and song leaders under the age of thirty.

The church's elders were staggered by the pastor's new spending plans. What in the world did this upstart think he was doing? He was going to literally *bankrupt* the church within a month!

Joshua then horrified them again when he severed all ties with the Pentecostal denomination the church had enjoyed for so long. The church elders scoffed at his proposal. Religious organizations provided support, council, finances. In the elders' eyes, casting the church's parent denomination aside was tossing away a financial safety net. And they were convinced their church would need as much safety net as possible, given the pastor's unchecked spending spree.

But Joshua had a bold, new direction for his church, and, quite frankly, he had no intention of allowing a century-old organization to dictate what steps he took.

And so, exactly two months after Walter Hutchinson's death, the Pentecostals of Antioch were no more. Joshua wanted a name that was all-encompassing, a name that welcomed everyone into the fold: *ChristPoint*.

His gambit paid off. In less than a year, attendance at the renamed church doubled. New faces. New families. And they were regulars!

Before long, the congregation had tripled. Soon, they were already making plans for a new church building in order to house the growing number of worshippers.

At the time, Lori attended Calvary Methodist Church with her parents, Martin and Lisa Roberson. She'd heard of the vibrant new preacher in town and his ever-growing church, but, as a Methodist, she didn't give much thought to it. People went to church where they wanted, after all. The name on the sign really shouldn't be that important, right?

Then, the rumors started. Word crept around town that South Street Pentecostal Holiness Church was actually going to combine with ChristPoint. *Combining* churches? Had that ever happened before?

Many people, Lori included, just couldn't believe it. Preachers were, by and large, egotistical creatures, sort of like politicians (but in a nice way). It just seemed impossible that two preachers could agree on enough doctrinal issues to share congregations. Just no way.

But it did happen. With little to no fuss at all.

Then, a month or so later, it happened again with Smith Temple Cumberland Presbyterian. And again with Northside Bible Baptist. Then, the First Church of the Nazarene. And, so it went. Like dominoes all over town. All moving toward a single point: Joshua.

It was around that time that construction began for the facility that would be Joshua's greatest achievement. Calling the building a church was almost demeaning. It was a palace. It was practically an Americanized Taj Mahal. An architectural monument to Joshua Hutchinson's spiritual conquest of Antioch. One church to serve them all...*his* church.

Joshua's flock absorbed every congregation in its metaphorical path. It seemed like another church was closing its doors almost every other month.

And then, finally, it was Calvary Methodist's turn.

Lori worked in the nursery again that final Sunday. Most people had left with a sense of euphoria, an idealistic view of great things to come. Bless God.

But Lori didn't share it. She couldn't. She didn't dread joining ChristPoint, but she felt like the only one who recognized this as the end of an age. No longer would various congregations file out of their respective churches and cross paths during lunch at local restaurants. Now they were all leaving the same place, listening to one message—*Joshua's* message—and going their separate ways.

It made her sad.

Still, Lori took up work in the new church's nursery within a matter of weeks. Sure, they already had a wealth of volunteers, but there were at least two hundred children now. They needed all the help they could get. And besides, Lori had always loved working with children.

It was after one Sunday morning service when everyone else had gone home for the day that Lori met the Rev. John Joshua Hutchinson for the first time. Until then, she'd only seen him at a distance and shaken hands in a two-second encounter. Much like the day Elijah walked into Lori's life years later, the fateful day she first met Joshua Hutchinson was shaping up like any other. She and several other nursery volunteers were busy cleaning up when he wandered into the room unannounced.

"Afternoon ladies."

Every one of them gave a collective gasp. Sonya, a doughy woman in her mid-thirties (and already on her second marriage, quite the scandal), even put a hand to her chest.

Joshua smiled that winning smile, the same smile that got him off the hook in gym class when he "accidentally" walked into the girls' locker room. Sonya made a soft sound in her throat that Lori could only guess was a sigh.

"The little munchkins keeping you all busy?"

"They always do," she told him.

Years later, Lori would like to tell Elijah she'd been immune to Joshua's charms. But she wasn't. Not by a long shot. She fell head-over-heels for him as though he was a pop star singing the latest hit love ballad. She probably sighed just like Sonya but at least had the good taste to be quieter about it. "Just like every girl in America who falls for the wrong guy just because he smiled at her the right way," Lori would've said later.

Joshua's eyes met hers. Held them for a full, tantalizing moment. "Lori Roberson, isn't it?"

"You know me? That's impressive with a church this big." She was easily charmed, sure, but at least Lori still managed to be a little spunky despite Joshua's charms.

"I do my best to know everyone in the family," he said. "That one behind you is Sonya. And that's Becky, Rhonda, Ashley, and Zina." He pointed at each one in turn.

"Very good." Lori folded her arms and smiled. Still spunky.

Joshua shrugged, holding his hands up. "Could I have a moment or two alone with Sister Lori, ladies?"

Lori frowned. *Sister Lori?* She'd never been called that, and, quite frankly, she didn't like it. Made her sound…*old.*

The other nursery workers, who were watching the conversation not unlike old ladies glued to a soap opera, started. Of course, they all agreed and shuffled out. *Oh, yes, of course, pastor. No problem. Not at all.* Some of them even cast playful grins in Lori's direction before heading out.

"You know, it's pretty impressive what you've done with this church," Lori said after the last one filed out. "How many members do you have now?"

"A few thousand, I think," Joshua answered, almost off-handedly. He put his hands behind his back like a captain in the Navy and started pacing the room, his eyes toward the ceiling. "To be honest, once you get past the first two thousand, you stop counting."

He grinned and looked back at her, which prompted a grin in return from Lori. "Well, it's quite an accomplishment," she said. "I'm sure your dad would be proud."

Joshua shrugged and shifted direction, heading back to her. "I like to think so. He worked hard while he was pastor. I guess I've updated his methods a little, but I like to think I've stayed true to the path he walked on."

He stopped in front of her, and their eyes met again. He held her gaze again, said nothing. Lori's heart quickened its pace, but she wasn't sure what to say next. Joshua also seemed to search for the right words.

It was a moment Lori would later swear should've been documented in Guinness. Joshua at a loss for words? Not a chance.

"I talk with people about the church and how far it's come a lot," Joshua ventured. "I was actually just wondering if…you'd have dinner with me someday?"

She hadn't seen that one coming. The young preacher who'd converted the entire town, who probably pastored the biggest church in the state, was asking her on a date. An honest-to-God date.

"Oh." Not the smoothest response. "Um, sure. When?"

"How about tonight? Evening services are actually canceled on account of the school fundraising drive. Are you free?"

"Umm—" Again, smooth as ever. "Okay."

Joshua's face lit up. Like a Christmas tree. Like a ridiculous, clichéd Christmas tree. He took her hand in his, raised it to his big, smiling mouth, and kissed it. "Great! Can I pick you up at six?"

"Uh, ye—yeah, sure…"

Oh yeah, he had her at hello.

CHAPTER 8

Of course, dinner was great. And why wouldn't it be? She was the town Pastor's date! Dinner at a great little Italian restaurant outside town and a movie (PG-rated, of course). Only the best.

He even kissed her when he dropped her off at home. First time out, and she'd let him get that first kiss right out of the box. Maybe things would've turned out differently if they'd waited. Maybe, just maybe, it wouldn't have ended so badly.

Or maybe getting that first kiss right away actually just helped speed things along to their inevitable train wreck. Maybe, just maybe, that was kind of a good thing. Lori had long since decided it made little difference.

More dates followed, more dinners. More movies (sometimes PG-13). More kisses.

Okay, *a lot* more kisses.

At last it was official, Lori was the pastor's girlfriend. There was even a place reserved for her and her family in the front section of pews. How's that for swank?

Then, on their one-year anniversary, Joshua popped the big question.

He didn't do it in front of the church. "This," he said when he revealed the ring—an enormous diamond—"is our moment and no one else's."

Lori agreed. Even later, she still agreed. It was probably the one thing he did she never could bring herself to hate.

Of course, she accepted. What girl wouldn't, right? He was handsome, charming, and the leader of the fastest growing church in town. He was practically running the town!

They celebrated the event with dinner and a movie at Joshua's home, a two-floor house with an automated garage door, two bathrooms, two bedrooms, and an enormous plasma screen TV in the den. He'd inherited the home from his father, but in the time since he'd remodeled and renovated so that it was clearly *his*.

They ate chicken fettuccini and watched a forgettable romantic comedy starring Sandra Bullock. And afterwards…

What happened next signaled the beginning of a downward spiral. Nothing was the same after that night. Its consequences further pressed the two farther and farther apart, until they were little more than uncomfortable acquaintances with an underlying tension everyone noticed but never mentioned out loud.

Lori's memory of the night was blurry. Sandra Bullock was crying. She remembered that much. Lori didn't know why, but Sandra was in tears and pouring her heart out to her latest quirky costar (was it Hugh Grant or that guy from Van Wilder?).

All the while Sandra gushed and sniffled, Lori and Joshua embraced one another, planting tender kisses on each other's lips, cheeks, necks, and shoulders. Sandra kept crying, and then the couch was beneath Lori, and Joshua was on top of her.

She didn't fight it, only wrapped her arms around his waist and hugged him close. His kisses became deeper, more forceful. His tongue glided into her mouth, and Lori returned the favor in kind.

And then, his shirt was off. She didn't know if he slipped it off or she pulled it off, but it was lying in the floor.

For the first time, Lori saw her fiancé's bare chest. It was slim and chiseled. He had the faint markings of a six-pack on his abdomen, which arched over her like a mediocre contortionist. Somewhere deep down, just beneath her belly, she hungered for him, hungered in a way she'd never experienced before.

Then, her jeans were unzipping. Slow. Tantalizing. Agonizing. Joshua's finger was on the zipper, and Lori's was on his hand, guiding the way. He kept his eyes down, as if mesmerized by the sight of Lori's jeans opening.

She gave a soft gasp when the zipper parted, revealing a pair of light-pink panties with lacy trim. Joshua stared at them for a long moment, then looked back at her. She lay before him, exposed in such a way to a man for the first time in her life, staring back. She rose up and kissed him again.

Joshua took over from there, sliding her jeans down to her ankles. Meanwhile, Lori set to work on his khakis, eventually exposing the white boxer-briefs he wore. The night descended into a collage filled with blurred images of Joshua's gorgeous chest muscles, Lori's slender legs wrapped around his waist, and a sofa shifted three or four feet from its original position. It was their first time. And second. And third. Their appetites for one another seemed endless. After a short intermission here and there, they'd resume once more.

And to hell with the consequences.

They slept in late the next morning. On the sofa. Lori felt Joshua stir and get up around ten. She stayed a while longer, replaying the night in her head. It had been wonderful. And terrible.

Her thoughts were interrupted at the sound of eggs frying in the kitchen. She rose from the couch, stretched, and wrapped a blanket round herself before heading into the kitchen.

Joshua was already scooping out scrambled eggs from the pan when she entered the room. He handed her a plate without a word, then set to work scooping out more for himself. Lori whispered her thanks and sat down at the table.

Joshua joined her, and they ate in silence, keeping their eyes on their plates. The tinklings and soft scrapings of their forks on their plates were the only sound.

Once finished, Joshua took up his plate and hers and headed to the dishwasher. She stayed at the table, watching him work. He never once looked at her. He kept his eyes on the plates, the sink, the dishwasher. He even looked outside at the lawn, now bright with sunlight. But he didn't look at her.

"Josh—"

"Nothing's changed." He still wouldn't look at her. He looked around the kitchen...the counter, the fridge, the microwave. "I love you. I want to marry you."

Then, at last, he looked at her. He was sincere. He had difficulty facing her, but he meant every word. Even later when she recounted the story to Elijah, Lori still believed he meant it.

He was ashamed. No question. They'd committed a sin. Christ, had they ever! Several times.

What was worse, it was a sin that couldn't be forgotten. Alcohol, drugs, porn. They could all eventually be dismissed. Mistakes washed away by the blood of Jesus Christ, and all that. Forgiven and forgotten. In later years, they'd be little more than memories of a moment's weakness.

But this— *This—*

Yes, they could ask God's forgiveness. And get it. God's forgiveness was universal. But what was done could never be undone or forgotten. Once lost, virginity could never be regained. It would be a blight they'd carry the rest of their lives. Even if they got married, it would still be a dark patch in their pasts. In the years to come, how could they preach purity and chastity before marriage when they'd failed to do so themselves?

"I love you, too." The words were hollow as Lori said them. They gave little comfort, for her or for Joshua, like strangers offering feeble condolences at a funeral.

"We'll plan the wedding sooner," Joshua said. "In a few months. Make it right. And then—then it'll be okay."

Would it? Would jumpstarting a commitment they'd planned to make anyway somehow make amends for a night of sinful passion? Forgiven and forgotten?

Lori doubted it.

She stood up, eyes on the table. Joshua watched her from the other side of the kitchen. She hesitated a moment, then said, "I need some time." She hesitated again, then said, "I need to go home."

Joshua didn't try to stop her. He stayed where he was as Lori rounded the table, eyes still downcast, and headed back to the den for her clothes. He said nothing while she dressed, stayed silent as she headed for the door.

She half-expected his footsteps behind her, rushing to beg her to wait as she opened the front door. She even paused a second-and-a-half to be sure, listening for those footsteps, hoping they could come. *Pleading* for them to come.

But they didn't. Joshua never moved from where he stood. Like as not, his eyes were now on the floor, again.

CHAPTER 9

The days ticked by, slipping by faster than Lori realized while somehow still dragging on like a prison sentence.

Her appetite increased, to the point she had to make a conscious effort of backing off at mealtimes so as not to risk some serious weight gain.

At the same time, remembering her last night with Joshua often made her nauseous. Twice in the span of three days she ran to the bathroom and spat up her dinner like a vicious fire hose. Then, she'd huddle by the toilet and cry. She'd clutch at the base and whimper while the tears streamed down her cheeks, keeping as quiet as possible to avoid worrying her parents.

And then—she couldn't remember how long till it happened, but—she was late.

Late.

She. Was. *Late.*

She did nothing at first, just went about her days as if nothing was wrong, hoping nothing was wrong. Begging for it, in fact.

Maybe her period was just a day or two later than normal. Maybe it would start by the end of the week.

It didn't.

Icy fear started to creep its way into her brain. What was she supposed to do? How was she supposed to handle this? What was going to happen to her?

One Wednesday afternoon, Lori drove to Walgreens to find a home pregnancy test. Easiest way to check, right? But there was a problem. She wasn't married, yet. And, she was "the pastor's girlfriend."

Nevermind the embarrassment. When Lori handed over the test to a cashier—with no wedding ring on her finger—it would sow the seeds of the biggest scandal in Antioch's quiet history. It could destroy Joshua, and it would probably destroy Lori's family. To say nothing of ChristPoint.

She stood staring at the different brand names and considered slipping one of them in her purse and leaving the store, but the security systems would honk like a mechanical goose the moment she reached the doors.

Sneaking into the ladies room and taking the test there also wasn't foolproof. Who knew how long she'd take? Employees might get curious. And when she was done, there was still the matter of removing the evidence. A janitor might find it in the trashcan before the day was over. It was a slim chance it would be traced back to her, but it was chance enough for worry.

Lori swore under her breath. It was the first time she had in years.

Dammit!

Then, in one smooth, swift motion, one of them was in Lori's purse. She hurried to the bathroom supplies aisle and picked up toothpaste, shampoo, some toilet paper, aloe vera, Tylenol, hairspray, and a couple boxes of Kleenex. She already had plenty of these at home, but they were necessary now, and, hopefully, they'd make up in some small way for what she was about to do.

The cashier was a slender, elderly woman with blonde hair that curled just beneath her ears. Her glasses were shaded, her skin just starting to wrinkle. Her nametag said her name was Charlotte.

Lori didn't know Charlotte, so, other than the usual pleasantries ("Hi, how are you?" "Fine, thanks. You?" Good."), Charlotte didn't talk much, just rang the items up with the speed and precision of someone who's done this for several years.

She gave the total, and Lori pulled out her credit card. "Credit or debit?" Charlotte prompted.

"Credit."

Charlotte tapped a quick sequence of buttons, then waited. Lori swiped her card, signed her name on the digital screen and took the receipt. Charlotte bagged her stuff and handed it over.

Lori took a breath and started for the door. Five feet. Four feet. Three.

HOOOONNNKK!

A lightning bolt exploded in her chest, and she froze, blinked. He arms trembled as liquid anxiety sped through her veins. She looked back at Charlotte with what she hoped were innocent, questioning eyes.

Charlotte never hesitated. She waved a dismissive hand at her. "Thing does that now and then. I know I checked you out. Just ignore it."

Lori nodded and turned for the door again.

HOOOONNNKK!

She jumped this time, but continued out the door. She held her breath all the way to the car. When she climbed in, she pulled out the test just to make certain she had it.

She did.

She even opened it to make sure the test was still in the box.

It was.

Lori released her breath in a slow, relieved sigh.

Back home, the test confirmed Lori's fears. Positive.

Pregnant. She was pregnant.

She was unmarried, she was dating the town pastor, and she was *pregnant.*

The word sent a shot of ice through her gut. It crept up to her lungs and made her breath tremble.

That night was a mistake. A sin. Fornication. Sex before marriage.

It wasn't exactly open for debate. The Bible was pretty frickin' clear on that one. It may not've been one of the original Ten Commandments (Number Seven and Number Ten only went over adultery and covetousness), but God spelled that one out pretty clear to Moses while he and the Hebrew refugees were wandering through the wilderness.

The reasons had been drilled into Lori's head her entire life:

1) God intended sex to serve as a sacramental role in bonding husband and wife together as one. Engaging in casual sex trivializes an act intended to deepen an intimate relationship.

Yeah. They blew that one.

2) Sex outside of marriage is using others for self-gratification.

And there was no denying that at the time, it'd been *real* self-gratifying. Dear God, it was like a dam had burst, and the resulting flood washed them over with feelings of ecstasy and ease. Several times.

Before, Lori feared her and Joshua's actions would forever be a black stain on their memories, but it was just *their* memories. Blowing up like a balloon over the next few months would make certain everyone else saw that stain as well.

She did nothing. *Nothing.*

For several days, Lori just worked at the church's private school—which had effectively swallowed the public school this year—came home, ate dinner, and slept. She stuck with her normal routine and said nothing.

No one was the wiser. People like to think they can tell when someone's keeping a secret, but, from Lori's perspective, that wasn't true at all. For the most part, people were blind, self-absorbed idiots too wrapped up in their own lives to care about anyone around them. Sure, they'd smile, wave, shake hands, wish you a good day, but beyond that, they really just wanted you to get out of the way. Now.

Days later, the realization hit home that the situation wasn't going away. She had to call Joshua and tell him. It was his child, too, after all. He had a right to know. Maybe, together, they could figure out some way to handle this.

At first, she paced in her room, cell phone in hand. Then, she sat on the bed and stared at it in her hand, willing herself to make the call. Her hand trembled, she saw. Finally, she dialed the numbers. Her thumb hovered over the "SEND" button for several more minutes before pressing down. She held her breath until it rang.

One ring.

Two.

Thr—

"Hello?"

Her breath caught in her throat for half a second. "Josh?"

"Lori?"

"Uh-huh."

"Hey! How are you? Long time no see. I've really missed you."

Lori smiled. He still missed her, even after the awkward moments that followed that night, even after the complete lack of communication that followed.

He still missed her.

It was a good feeling, a warm feeling. She felt the tears forming in her eyes.

"I've missed you, too."

"You want to come over?"

"Well, actually, umm…" She faltered. The words caught in her throat. "There's…um…there's something I need to tell you."

Joshua was silent. Lori couldn't be certain, but she suspected he was holding his breath. He knew. He had to.

Joshua wasn't stupid. And it wasn't like it took a genius to figure this situation out. They'd screwed one another's brains out. Then, Lori vanished for a couple weeks. And now she'd just called out of the clear blue with that old cliché: "I have to tell you something…"

No sense holding back anymore, Lori decided. "I'm pregnant."

Silence. Then, "Are—you sure—?"

She closed her eyes. "Uh-huh."

Silence again. A long silence. Both of them struggled for words. Finally, Lori said, "What should we do?"

He hesitated. Then, "I don't know."

"Should we get married?"

"That'd be a bit obvious, don't you think?"

Lori turned and stared at the phone a moment. "Obvious?"

"Suddenly, without any announcement, we just get married?"

"But, we're already eng—?"

"And then, just under nine months later, there's a baby?"

"No one would have to know?"

"People aren't stupid, Lori."

Lori started trembling. Her bottom lip quivered, and her breath caught in her throat. Joshua was her beacon just as much as he was Antioch's. She'd believed he would have words of comfort and hope, a plan that would make the best of an unfortunate situation.

He had none. For the first time, Lori was seeing him with his back against the wall. He had no platitudes, no sermons to give that would make this better, nothing to sway her fears.

He couldn't fix this, and it pissed him off.

"Josh, I love you," Lori ventured.

He sighed. "I know, and I love you, too, but we've got to think here."

"We'll just raise it like any other parents," she suggested. "It won't be perfect, but that's okay. It'll still be our baby."

"Lori, I can't have a child out of wedlock!" he spat.

It made her jump. She'd never heard him this way. Angry. Afraid. On the verge of panic. It scared her.

His voice was trembling. "I…I just…*can't!*"

There was another long silence. Then, Joshua broke it again. "Are you at home?"

"Yes."

"Just stay there. I'll be right over. And don't worry."

But she did.

CHAPTER 10

Lori's phone rang again an hour later.

"I'm in the car outside."

Lori frowned. What was this? "You're not coming in?"

"Huh-uh. Just hop in. I'll tell you on the way."

She grabbed her purse and went out to him. Joshua, like his father, drove nothing but Fords. He owned a Taurus. Cars were simply a necessity for him. He didn't need a bright red Corvette to show his status. Besides, it would've been redundant.

Joshua pulled out of the driveway and started cruising through town at the speed limit. Nothing to worry about. Just the town's most recognizable couple out for a drive. Probably on a date, or something. Isn't that sweet?

He kept his eyes on the road when he spoke, just as he usually did when talking behind the wheel. A safe driver through and through, Joshua was.

"I've been praying about this," he said.

"Me too," Lori lied, and was immediately ashamed. The whole thing had been such a whirlwind. She never once mentioned anything about it to God, not even a simple prayer of forgiveness.

Which she should've done the day after…

"And the Lord answered me very clearly." Joshua glanced at her for a brief moment, then looked back at the road.

Lori turned to look at him with widening eyes. "Really?" For a brief moment, she wondered if maybe, just maybe, things would be okay again.

He nodded. "Yes."

Then, he said nothing for a moment or two, collecting his thoughts. Figuring out how best to proceed.

"Before I say anything else, I just want to tell you that again," he said. "I prayed, and God answered."

"Okay." She was torn between feelings of relief and anxiety. Joshua was the town's preacher. He was its messenger of hope and guidance. If he felt he had an answer from on high, Lori wanted to believe him, to let him give her that hope in her time of struggle.

But she'd always been a bit pragmatic, as well. How could Joshua possibly say he'd heard a direct answer from God Almighty? She'd never known anyone who could make such a claim. Even the Pope had never tried to say such a thing. Not the latest one, anyway.

Lori's eyes caught sight of Anitoch's welcome sign—its back was to them—as it slid past the window. They were leaving town.

"We…we can't have this baby," he said, his voice flat. He drew his lips together in a tight line after saying it.

"Well, I don't think we have much choice at this point," she ventured.

"We can't." Joshua looked at her when he said it. It was the longest she'd ever seen him take his eyes from the road while driving.

"Then what…what are we going to do?" Lori's bottom lip started trembling again. She felt her hair starting to stand on end. Goose bumps were forming on her arms.

"We're going to Elizabethtown," he told her. "There's…there's a health clinic there."

Lori's mouth dropped open. *You can't be serious*, she wanted to say, but the words caught in her throat. All that came out was a sort of choked gasp.

"Trust me, Lori," Joshua went on. "The Lord was very clear on this. We'll be absolved of our sin. This is the first step. Jesus will wash away our sins with his blood, but we have to wash away sin's offspring ourselves."

Sin's offspring?

"After tonight, it will all be gone. God will forgive us. Our sins will be gone. Completely." Joshua watched the highway.

Lori looked at the floorboard. At last, she found her voice. "But," she said, her voice soft and trembling, "it's murder!"

"The child is an innocent," Joshua answered. "It'll go to Heaven, and God will care for it better than we ever could. If it came to Earth, what kind of life would it have? The—bastard son of the town preacher?" That was the closest Lori had ever heard Joshua come to swearing. "Its life would be ruined from the moment it was born. *Our* lives would be ruined."

"You're talking about our baby!" she said. Tears stung her eyes. "Not a thing! Not a curse!"

Joshua closed eyes a moment, said firmly, "God was very clear."

Lori grabbed his arm. "No! Please! Josh? Please don't make me do this." She was wailing.

Joshua closed his eyes, took a deep breath. "I have to."

Lori stared at him. Tears streaked her cheeks, but he wouldn't look back.

She sat back in her seat, brought her knees to her chest, and curled up against the door. She leaned her head against the window and wept.

And so they went. For the next half hour, Joshua drove in silence while Lori cried beside him.

"We're here."

Lori never looked at the name of the clinic. Some standard, medical-sounding name, most likely. She walked in, gave a false name—Jacquelyn Byers—and waited. Alone.

Joshua didn't go in with her. After all, as a minister, he couldn't be seen inside such a place, even if it was over an hour from home.

She expected to wait at least an hour. She'd heard the stories, of so-called "worldly girls" entering the surgical area single file, walking in bloated and pregnant, striding out slim and carefree again while somewhere in a backroom, a pile of decaying infants lay in a corner, steam rising as their warm bodies cooled and died.

Lori never quite believed such stories, but the image was there. And it sure wasn't leaving now.

The wait turned out much shorter than she'd expected. Only one other girl shared the waiting room with her, a teenager with a lip piercing, black lips, and clothes like a trampy clown from hell. But her eyes were just like Lori's: afraid...*painfully* afraid.

Little Miss Goth Queen couldn't have been more than fifteen years old. She was barely showing. She chewed her black fingernails until she was called.

She was barely here five minutes, Lori thought.

And then, five minutes after that, they called Lori. She entered a room across from the one Little Miss Goth Queen did. There was a single hospital bed in the center, the foot stirrups—or whatever you called them—already in place.

"Okay, Miss—umm—Byers," the physician seated by the bed told her. "Just change into the gown in the restroom over there, and we'll get started."

He pointed to a small room with a toilet. A gown was already hanging inside.

Lori fought back the tears as she made her way inside. After closing the door, she stood still a moment, taking deep breaths and willing herself not to cry.

She changed quickly, wanting this over as fast as possible. *I'm sorry, baby. I'm sorry. I'm so sorry. Please forgive me. Please.*

She thought of sliding out of her clothes with Joshua, of the heat and passion and excitement she'd felt. Now all she felt was cold.

When Lori came back out in her gown, the doctor was already seated before the bed, ready to gaze between her legs and get to work. He gestured toward the bed, saying nothing.

A nurse stood nearby. She also said nothing.

In the years that followed, Lori decided they both knew she didn't—or couldn't—want to make conversation.

The bed was cold. The stirrups were colder.

"Just relax, and we'll be finished in a few minutes." The doctor injected her with a local anesthetic, and the nurse offered Lori her hand, but she declined.

She kept her head back, eyes closed, barely feeling the cold instruments working around between her legs. She glanced down at one point just in time to see the doctor picking up a large pair of forceps.

Oh God. Those are going to take hold of our baby. My baby. They're going to grab his head and pull him out.

Fresh tears threatened to creep out of her eyes, but she held them back. Not here. Not now. Not until after.

After...

She felt the cold tools touch her skin, despite the anesthetic, and work their way inside. She felt only the slightest pressure.

And then they slid back out. Something wet smacked the table.

Tears attacked her eyes again, and bile was readying itself to charge up her throat like a vomit train. It stung inside her chest like acid. She couldn't breathe.

But she held it all back, managed a few choked gasps through clenched teeth. Just a little longer. Only a little.

She opened her eyes again as the doctor was walking away, carrying something in his hands, his back to her. She never saw what he held, but she would believe for the rest of her life it was their baby.

Her baby.

"It's okay, sweetie," the nurse whispered at last. "You can go now. We're all done."

Lori looked at the woman, a lady in her mid-twenties with kind, gentle eyes. She nodded to her but said nothing.

The nurse helped her climb from the table and stand once more. After a few wobbly moments, Lori headed back to the restroom to change. She expected to see a bloodstain on the front of her gown, but there was nothing. She was clean.

Clean.

The trip back outside was a blur. All she remembered was that Little Miss Goth Queen wasn't there, but whether she was already gone or still in another room Lori would never know. She also never saw the doctor again. The hallway, the lobby, the entrance, all of it blurred together in Lori's memory in a haze like an acid trip.

Things came back into focus outside. Joshua wasn't there. His car wasn't there. They were gone. Just gone.

Oh God, she thought. *He's left me here.*

Everything she'd kept inside came rushing out. The vomit train she'd held in check left the station at full speed and shot up her throat like a red-hot bullet. Lori doubled over and gagged, clutching her stomach as it wrenched everything she'd eaten back out of her. Tears squeezed through her clenched eyelids and slid down her cheeks.

She had only a moment to gasp for air after the first wave. Then, her stomach wrenched again, squeezing out whatever bits of food remained in her system. She grunted, her voice sounding like an old, dying man as she dry-heaved again and again until warm bile spilled from her mouth.

She cried. Loud wails sang out at the darkening sky like a banshee in mourning. Her face was red and hot, and every muscle in her body screamed at her in protest.

Then, as fast as it came, it was over.

Lori fell back against the building and wiped her mouth and eyes. She glanced around to see if anyone noticed, but she was still alone. All alone.

But then, like an answer to a prayer, Joshua returned. His car pulled up beside Lori just as she finished catching her breath. Her mouth still tasted like bile.

He leaned over and opened the door for her, offering his hand to help her sit. She took it.

Once inside, Lori curled up against the door again, relishing the cool glass against her forehead. She ached all over. Her head was pounding.

And she felt...*empty.*

Joshua said nothing. He glanced at her a few times, his eyes sad...and sorry. But he never said a word. He couldn't, Lori knew. Nothing he could say would help. Nothing would stop or even ease the pain she felt.

It would all be just so much crap.

Neither one spoke the rest of the way home.

CHAPTER 11

The eggs sizzled and popped, quivering like a cloth in the wind as air bubbles formed and burst beneath them.

"That's when we broke up," Lori said, and started scrambling them. She frowned.

Dawn had long since come and gone. Sunlight filtered into the room through the windows and the sliding glass door that led to a small, wooden balcony.

"I'm sorry," Elijah said. He leaned against the doorway, watching her.

Lori shrugged. "Was a long time ago."

"And time heals all wounds?" he asked, skeptical.

Lori pointed the spatula at him, winked and clucked her tongue "Bingo." Then, she went back to work.

"Not all of them," Elijah sighed.

Lori sighed, too. No, not all of them. For another moment, neither one could think of something to say.

Silence. Always back to that.

Lori scooped the eggs out and set them on a plate. She turned and handed it to her guest. "Almost as good as pizza."

Elijah smiled and took it from her. He looked at it a moment, then back at Lori.

"Oh! Geez! Fork!" Lori rummaged through a nearby drawer and pulled one out.

"Thanks."

"I don't speak much with my parents, anymore," Lori added. "We speak now and then, but that's about it. But, and I know this is stupid, they're probably the only reason I haven't left town."

Footsteps in the outside hallway signaled Marcus' impending entrance. Slow, stumbling steps like a zombie. But the knock was a bit more lively.

"Come in!" Lori called.

The door opened, closed, and the shambling footsteps resumed. Marcus appeared in the doorway beside Elijah, staring at his breakfast. He was still in his pajamas, red plaid pants and a dark t-shirt. His hair was the epitome of "bed hair." It was unruly and disheveled and standing straight up in some places. It made him look three or four inches taller.

"You never made *me* breakfast," he croaked. His eyes squinted like they were swollen.

"You never asked."

"And he did?"

Lori cracked open two more eggs.

"You mind if I use your shower?" Elijah asked, scooping out the last bit of egg from his plate.

"Sure, you going somewhere?" Lori asked, focused on scrambling her new batch. Scrambled eggs were the egg dish she knew how to make.

"I thought I'd visit ChristPoint."

That pulled Lori's attention from the stove. There was a loud pop, and a speckle of grease hit her cheek. It stung—only a little—but she ignored it.

Elijah set his empty plate down. To his left, Marcus stared, too. He still squinted, just not as much. "You're kidding," he said.

Elijah shook his head. "No."

"Didn't you hear everything I just said about what's wrong with that place?" Lori demanded.

Elijah smiled. It was that same smile that won Lori over the moment he did it last night. Gentle. Patient. "You told me what an awful man the pastor was," he said. "Other than assimilating all the other churches in town, you never said much about his church."

The eggs popped again. Louder.

"Do you have any idea what those people will do to you?" Marcus asked.

"Probably try to convince me to be a member," Elijah answered, still smiling. He looked back at Lori. "Right?"

Again, *pop!*

"Yeah." She sighed. "They're not some cult. No special Kool-Aid. No dancing with snakes. But…"

Elijah stepped forward and placed his hands on her shoulders. Lori almost trembled, *wanted* to tremble. His touch was electric.

"You say it's wrong," he said. "And I believe you. But, unlike the good Reverend, it's not something you can put into words. Am I right?"

She nodded. "Yeah."

He moved his hands up and down, brushing over her arms and the curves of her shoulders. A soft, sweet—if still kind of irritatingly platonic—caress. "I'd just like to see for myself."

"But—why?"

He smiled. Really smiled. "Why not?"

Pop! The eggs were burnt.

CHAPTER 12

The Rev. John Joshua Hutchinson called down the fires of Heaven when he preached that morning. Blessed with the sort of velvet tongue reserved almost-exclusively for conservative, Southern ministers, Joshua professed faith, virtue, and the one and only saving name of our Lord, our God, and our Savior, Jesus Christ.

"We believe in one God," Joshua declared, his voice dancing the fine line between singing and screaming. "Deuteronomy 6:4 says 'Hear O Israel, the Lord our God is one God.' Ephesians 4:4 says 'There is one body and one spirit—even as you are called in one hope of your calling. One Lord, One Faith, and one Baptism. In John 10:30, Jesus said 'I and my father are one.'"

There was a tremor among the congregation. Soft but adamant from women: *"Yes!"* *"Amen!"* *"That's right!"* With polite agreements from men: "Preach it, Pastor!" And a "Yes, sir!" here and there.

Elijah sat three rows from the back of the vast sanctuary. Its width spanned longer than a football field. The distance between Elijah and the podium where Joshua delivered his sermon was just over half of that. The place was filled to near capacity.

Joshua preached to his flock with the help of an ear-mounted microphone and an enormous projection screen. His volume was rising, and he was starting to pace around the podium. "John said 'In the beginning was the Word and the Word was with God and the Word was God.'"

Elijah offered no vocal confirmations to Joshua's words, though he was very familiar with them.

All around him, the congregation swayed in every direction. There was no unity in their motions; so their movements were akin to a sort of enclosed chaos. What was once a series of scattered tremors became an earthquake of applause and cheers: *"Thank you, Jesus! Praise your name!"*

Many jumped to their feet, hands raised, faces uplifted to the sky. A man wearing khakis and a reddish sports coat beside Elijah stood and raised one hand Heavenward. He waved it back and forth as if trying to get the attention of angels on high.

"Oooooh, Lord!" he cried. "Myyy Lord!"

Elijah sighed. Truth be told, he envied the man. He envied much of the congregation, in fact. For them, God was real, oh so very real. He wasn't just up in Heaven, either. He was here. Now. In this sanctuary, so close you could touch him. All you had to do was reach out.

"Yaaaay, Lord!" Mr. Khaki & Sports Coat cried.

So many religions mourned their faith. Pentecostals celebrated it. And although Joshua had broken away from the denomination, ChristPoint was still very much a *Pentecostal* church.

Joshua and his church apparently ascribed to the belief in a single God, a singular spirit who manifested Himself in many different ways, including (but not limited to) the Father, the Son and the Holy Ghost. In short, it professed there was one God and abandoned the Trinitarian concept. Oneness Pentecostalism.

It was a branch of Christianity fast growing in popularity. Not only for the simplified concept of God and His teachings, but for the lively, energetic services Pentecostals were known for having.

As Joshua's sermon concluded, he invited all who would to come to the altar, and, true to Pentecostal form, the entire congregation—save a handful of ushers—made their way forward. It was something that set Pentecostals apart from most other Christians. Moments after the call, nearly all of the congregation would make their way forward, flooding the altar to the point it would be standing-room-only.

And still they would come. Until it was nothing more than a formality. There was an undeniable nobility in that, almost like the Biblical story of the woman who hoped only to touch the hem of Jesus' garment. *I can't get there, but I'll get as close as I can, God. And I pray that's enough.*

And the members of ChristPoint, Pentecostal or not, filled the altar within moments. Every one of them.

Every one but Elijah.

He respected these people. Admired their faith. Even envied them. But he still wasn't one of them. Not yet. Likely, not ever.

A contemporary band consisting of an electric guitar, a bass guitar, a piano, and drums hummed a soft tune while dozens—maybe hundreds?—of audible prayers arose from the gathered throng. The resulting sound was a soft cacophony of wails and chants interspersed with the twitterings of men and women speaking in tongues.

In its own way, it was beautiful.

Elijah stood and stepped into the aisle. He cast a final glance at the gathered parishioners before turning and making his way to the exit. An usher caught his hand on the way out. "Glad to have you, brother! Hope to see you again!"

Elijah smiled back at the man, a gray-haired fellow with a large nose, a receding hairline, and thick glasses. "Thank you," he answered.

The man held Elijah's hand a half-second or so longer than he liked before letting go. Elijah offered another polite smile and hurried outside.

CHAPTER 13

"Who is it...?"

Even with a door between them, Elijah could hear the caution in Lori's voice. The fear.

And that was odd, wasn't it? Why would she be afraid?

Sure, Lori might have an inkling Joshua would've followed Elijah home to meet with them all and do a bit of evangelizing. *Can I get an "Amen?"* Elijah wouldn't have been surprised if the good Reverend's actions had once bordered on harassment, if they didn't still.

But that should merit only a twinge of annoyance, maybe even some apprehension or anxiety. Not this.

This was *fear*. Blue, icy fear. She did a hell of a job trying to hide it, but Elijah could hear it just the same. A slight tremor in her voice. Ever so slight, but there.

"It's Elijah."

There were two clicks—first the door lock, then the deadbolt—followed by the jingling of the chain latch. Then, the doorknob turned, and the door opened.

It opened partially, revealing Lori's face. She glared through the opening at Elijah for a second or two before practically throwing it open and placing a hand on her hip. "Enjoy the service?"

Elijah shrugged. Smiled. "He's no Joel Olsteen."

She smirked and rolled her eyes. "Okay. Come in."

He stepped past her into the room, and Lori glanced outside once before closing the door behind him. She recounted her previous ritual in reverse, first the chain, then the deadbolt, and then the lock. *Jingle, click, click!*

Marcus was on the sofa watching television. He was still in his pajamas. "Hey, Eli! Welcome back!"

Elijah smiled. No fear in that one. At least, not right now.

"So?"

Elijah looked back at Lori, who was leaning against the door, her arms folded. Clearly, she expected a rundown of the morning.

"Church seems friendly enough," Elijah offered.

"I bet." Her expression didn't change.

Elijah tilted his head, curious. What was she getting at? "Looks like a typical, holy-rollin' Pentecostal church, at first glance. But, one thing was a bit off."

"Oh yeah?"

"Yeah. The altar call at the end. Everyone went. *Everyone.*"

"No surprise there," Marcus chimed in. "Not praying during the altar call's pretty frowned upon. Like—*a lot.*"

"I'll say," Lori agreed.

Elijah glanced back and forth between the two. "How so?"

Both of them hesitated. They looked at one another, silently asking who should explain. The quiet standoff lasted just a few seconds and ended with Lori sighing. Apparently, Elijah mused, she lost.

"Well, Josh always said it was disrespectful not to pray during the altar call," she said. "Like it was this time of holy communion—not *that* Communion—with the Lord and Creator. Like, if we're in some corner chattering away while someone up front is really seeking the Lord, who's to say God won't strike us down?"

Elijah raised an eyebrow.

"Not that He *would*," Lori added. "But how can we really be sure He wouldn't? He's done it before, right?"

Elijah nodded. "Right." He frowned. Despite the fact Jesus Christ's teachings revolved around a benevolent and loving God, intent on compassion and forgiveness, some Christians seemed to relish the idea that God could and would be a bona fide asshole under the right conditions.

"A little more to it than that, though," Marcus said. "Joshua, he—well—he's got this—*effect* on people. If you listen to him long enough, he can just *convince* you he's on the side of right. Guy's just one helluva speaker."

"But it still throws me," Elijah told them. "How does even the best speaker in all the world convince every church in town to close its doors and transfer all its congregation over to him? Billy Graham never could've done that, not even in his prime."

Lori and Marcus glanced at one another again. Some unspoken message passed between them. They looked nervous.

Screw nervous; they were scared.

Lori started to speak, but a firm knock at the door behind her nearly sent her headfirst into the ceiling. She chirped out a quick, stifled scream before clapping her hand to her mouth and spinning around. "Who is it?"

"It's Nathan."

Lori sighed, looked at Marcus. He rolled his eyes.

She stepped back to the door and restarted the unlocking ritual. *Click! Click! Jingle!* When she opened the door, a man wearing light brown pants, a blue sports coat, and a matching tie waved back. And a great big ol' Sunday morning smile. "Morning!" He checked his watch. "Or *afternoon*, I guess?"

"Hi Nathan," Lori said. "What brings you this way?"

"Well, first and foremost," he began, "I wanted to let you know we missed you again this morning."

Lori smiled and nodded. Always with that stupid line.

"And, I see our newest guest is visiting you, too?" He smiled and marched past Lori—marched right the hell in like he owned the place—hand outstretched. "I'm Nathan Riley."

Elijah shook his hand and nodded. "Elijah."

Nathan hesitated, waiting for a last name, but Elijah only tilted his head and smiled.

"Well, Elijah," Nathan finally said. "It was wonderful having you this morning. If you're staying in town, we'd love to see you again. Are you...staying with Lori?"

The question hung in the air a moment, drawing a brief, awkward silence. *Staying with Lori? Spending evenings with her?* Sleeping *with her?*

"Well, he might be staying with me, you know?" Marcus cut in.

Nathan turned back to Marcus, and his face darkened. "I...guess he could be." He looked back at Elijah again. Lori felt a furious scowl creeping over her face.

Elijah grinned and placed a hand on Nathan's shoulder, taking on the stance of a politician. "Lori was kind enough to offer me a place to stay last night when I didn't have one," he said. "Nothing more."

"Uh-huh," Nathan managed.

Elijah looked into his eyes. *Deep* into his eyes. Much like how he'd looked at Lori last night at work.

Lori stared, thinking it was almost eerie seeing him do it to someone else.

"She's a person of great character. And I'd speak with anyone who suggests otherwise."

Nathan's mouth drooped open just a little. He didn't move. Only stared back. Lori half-expected him to giggle the way she had. *Teehee, shucks Mister. I'm sorry.*

But he didn't. He just nodded. Slow. Like he was in awe. "Right..." he breathed.

"Is there anything else she, Marcus, or I can do for you?"

Nathan shook his head. Quick, this time. Like a little kid telling Momma, *No, Ma'am!*

"Huh-uh," he said.

Elijah took Nathan's hand again, smiled once more. "Thanks for coming by, Nathan. Maybe we'll see you again."

"Oh, sure. I hope we do." Nathan smiled back. *Really* smiled. He bore the stupid grin of a thirteen-year-old boy catching a glimpse of his first set of gorgeous breasts.

He turned and headed for the door. "Good seeing you, Lori," he said as he passed her. She forced herself to smile at him.

Then, she closed the door behind him. *Jingle! Click! Click!*

"Okay, not to sound like a broken record or anything," Marcus said as he jumped up from the sofa. "But how the hell do you do that?"

Elijah shrugged. "I told you. I don't know."

"What? Did you, like, *hypnotize* him?"

"No. Of course, not." Elijah waved him off and walked over to the small table in the alcove by the kitchen that served as a dining room.

"Not to be impolite, but I'm getting hungry for lunch," he said. "Anything I can do to help with it?"

CHAPTER 14

People talked. They always did.

Plenty in the congregation saw Elijah that Sunday morning. Those who didn't soon heard about him. By the end of the night—after the evening worship service—everyone knew of the mystery man in town.

But only a handful knew he was staying with Lori. For now. That news would also make the rounds soon enough. No news spread faster in a small community like Antioch than a scandal...especially a scandal that might be *steamy*. But for the time being, only Nathan Riley and a few other deacons at ChristPoint were aware of it.

And the good Rev. Hutchinson.

Nathan, along with three other church deacons, sat in Joshua's plush office long after that Sunday evening's service had ended. The young pastor spared no expense in furnishing his large office with plush furniture: a black, leather sofa with matching loveseat and recliner that faced an enormous plasma screen television. There was also a glass coffee table and a large, marble desk facing the door so Joshua could greet his guests as they entered.

Nathan sat on the sofa along with Greg Foster, a gentleman who'd just climbed over the hump of middle age. Greg's once brown hair was starting to gray, and what were previously just hints of wrinkles were now full-blown crow's feet beneath his eyes. He also happened to be Antioch's chief of police.

Still plenty of years away from retirement, thank you very much!

Frank Hollister sat on the loveseat. Hollister was the oldest in the room, and he'd retired from a job at a tire plant years ago. His history prior to that was shrouded in mystery to most everyone, save Joshua, who was well aware of Frank's time as a U.S. marine in Vietnam. He'd seen his fair share of death, destruction, and the filthiest of mankind's underbelly. His hair was long gone, save for a smattering of white behind his ears. He wore silver glasses with round lenses over a pair intense, burning eyes.

Dean Smith was the youngest. He was fresh out of college with a business degree. He assisted with the church's finance department. He wasn't the head of it yet, but he probably would be within the next ten years. He was a lean young man with blonde hair and a friendly smile that it seems are reserved only for the white-collar community. With the seats in Joshua's office all taken, he stood facing the group.

Joshua sat in the recliner, legs crossed. He rested his chin on his right hand and listened as Nathan recounted his visit with Lori, Marcus, and Elijah.

"You say he made you feel...*good?*" Joshua asked after Nathan finished.

"Yeah, I guess so." Nathan shrugged, frowned. He looked around the room as if searching for something to help him explain. Nothing did. "I dunno. It was just...something about him."

"You sure you're not sweet on him like Marcus probably is?" Dean ventured and grinned.

"Stop it, Dean." Joshua looked up at him, his eyes firm. He pointed at him. "Such as were some of you, after all."

"I was never a *faggot*."

Joshua leapt to his feet. He stared at Dean a moment and took a deep, loud breath through his nostrils. Everyone braced themselves for the Reverend to smack the kid hard across the face. Dean, despite his efforts not to, shrank away. Like a puppy.

"I don't ever want to hear that word in here...*ever* again," Joshua said. "Marcus, for all his faults, is still beloved of God. Just like you. Just like me. We've all come short of the glory of God in our own way. We're no better than he is. You'd do well to remember that."

Dean frowned and looked at the floor. He folded his arms and *harrumph*ed.

"And," Joshua added, "even though this isn't the sanctuary, this is *still* the house of God. That sort of language has no place here."

Dean nodded. "Yeah. Yeah, you're right."

Joshua looked back at Nathan. "What did he say to you? Exactly?"

Nathan forced an uncomfortable smile. A thin, tiny one. "Well it's kinda' cheesy, but he said Lori was a person of great character."

Joshua nodded. His expression was neutral. Nathan was already uncomfortable, and the pastor's growing interest in Elijah and Lori wasn't helping. "And he said he'd speak with anyone who said otherwise," he said.

"Oh *really?*" Dean, not concealing his feelings at all, laughed.

"Quiet, Dean," Frank ordered. His voice was gruff, the voice a man who once had his fair share of hard liquor. (But, praise the Lord, those days were behind him.)

Dean waved him off and quieted. *Yeah, yeah, okay, old man.*

"He seems harmless," Greg ventured. "I mean, I can't speak for certain what's going on in Lori's apartment. Maybe nothing. Maybe something. But he doesn't seem dangerous to her or the town. I figure the worst that could happen is he breaks Lori's heart the day he leaves town."

Joshua nodded. Maybe. Maybe this man was nothing more than a drifter, a nomad wandering the roads of America in search of whatever it was nomads wandering the roads of America searched for. Maybe.

Maybe.

But something gnawed at him, a feeling he couldn't quite place. Some small notion that this man maybe—*just maybe*—was trouble. He first felt it at J.D.'s Saturday night, the way Lori reacted to him. The girl was just mesmerized. It was obvious. And Lori didn't *mesmerize* easily.

Granted, that could just be jealousy talking. Joshua knew he hadn't quite gotten over Lori. His last love. They were together for so long. And, then of course, there was that night…

"Did it look like he was leaving when you visited?" Joshua asked, trying to ignore those thoughts.

And failing.

"Hard to say," Nathan admitted. "I mean, I don't think the guy carries a suitcase or anything. So, he could probably leave just about any time."

"Tell me again about when he spoke to you."

"Again?"

"Yes. What he said. How you felt."

"But I already—"

"Tell me again." Joshua didn't yell, didn't raise his voice, but it was definitely an order.

Nathan blinked. Swallowed. "He looked me right in the eye, and he said that Lori was a person of great character, and he'd speak with anyone who said otherwise," he said. "Then, he asked if there was anything else I needed, and I said no. And, then he showed me to the door."

It was the last part of Nathan's story that bothered Joshua. The similarities of the Roman soldier's accounts to the Pharisees about Jesus weren't lost on him. *Never did a man speak like this man.*

But Jesus was the Messiah. God in flesh. The Christ come to earth. When he spoke, his words were the words of the Lord. He spoke with an authority no other person could ever have.

But this man—this *Elijah*—somehow had that very effect on Nathan, a duly appointed deacon of ChristPoint, a man saved by the grace and provisions of God.

Fact was, it made Joshua nervous. Whatever Elijah was—and Joshua certainly didn't think he was Jesus' second coming—he had some power. Something about him held sway over Lori and, no doubt, over Marcus. And, for just a moment or two, it held sway over Nathan.

What was it? Was there some sinister force at work here? Some device of the devil? Had Hell itself taken notice of Joshua's work in Antioch?

Or was he just being paranoid? Maybe Elijah was just one heck of a smooth talker? And maybe he pulled the wool over Nathan's eyes today just as he had Lori's? That made sense, didn't it?

Sure. Maybe.

Maybe.

Unfortunately, there was a problem. Joshua had felt the same thing from Elijah as well. It wasn't quite so direct, but it was there. There *was* something about this man. Something underneath. A thing you couldn't see or touch, but you could feel its impact.

And that was a problem.

"Why don't we just keep our eyes open?" Greg offered. "Ears to the ground. That sort of thing. If we hear talk of this guy doing anything suspicious, I'll look into it."

Then, he added, "We'll also make sure Lori's okay."

Joshua smiled. "Thank you."

CHAPTER 15

Lori trudged out of her bedroom the next morning like a hangover. She found Elijah already up and resting on the sofa. He greeted her with a sleepy smile.

"Eggs?" she croaked.

Elijah shook his head. "Just some fruit." He thought a moment, then said, "You know, I really should hit the road again today."

Instantly, Lori was wide awake. It was better than black coffee. "You're leaving?"

Elijah stood and stretched his arms behind him. His elbows popped. "It's not right for me to stay and eat all your food like this."

"But I don't mind!"

"You will."

"No, I won't!" Her voice leapt an octave.

Elijah smiled. He stifled a yawn and walked over to where Lori stood in the kitchen archway. "But I shouldn't. You work hard to pay for this place. For your food. Everything. I'm just some freeloader off the street."

"*Bull!*" Lori stared back at him. Her eyes were hot, angry. It startled him a little. "I... Geez, this is gonna' sound cheesy and stupid. But I've never met anyone like you. You can't leave, because...I'm—"

Lori put her face in her hands and sat down at the dining room table. Elijah started to say something, but she shushed him with a quick point of her finger. Then, she looked up at him again, and he could see she'd been holding back tears. They still clung to the corners of her eyes, just waiting to jump out and crawl down her cheeks.

"Before you came, I was afraid," she said. "All the time. And now—now, with you here—I'm not." Her eyes were swimming now. "I don't want to be afraid anymore."

"But why?" Elijah sat next to her at the table. "Why are you afraid?"

Lori shook her head and looked down, not sure how to start.

"It's Joshua, right?" Elijah ventured. That much was obvious, anyway.

She nodded. "Uh-huh." She looked toward the ceiling, still holding back the tears that still threatened to make themselves visible. "You've only been here a few days, and you've only been to the church once, but there's more to this whole thing than just a big church that everyone in town goes to."

Elijah settled back in his chair, said nothing. *Go on*, his expression said.

"Somehow—and I don't know how it all happened—Josh *controls* this town now." She looked back at him. "Everyone answers to him. Everyone. Heck, the mayor's job is just a formality, now!"

"You don't answer to him," Elijah pointed out. "Marcus doesn't."

Lori jumped to her feet and walked into the living room, toward the sliding glass door that led to the balcony. "No, and neither do several others in town," she said as she reached the door.

She would've said more, but she stopped and stared.
"*No!*" she hissed.
That brought Elijah to his feet. "What?"
"They're outside! *The pricks are outside!*"
Lori raced to the front door, unlocked it (*Click! Click! Jingle!*) and stormed outside. Elijah ran after her.
"Who's outside? Lori! What's going on?"

Once he reached the entrance, Elijah saw. There was a squad car parked outside. The letters APD were emblazoned in blue on the side in a slick, almost sci-fi font. A single officer sat inside, an older man with gray hair. His eyes widened when he saw Lori. It was, without a doubt, a true *Holy crap!* expression.

"What are you doing here?" Lori yelled. She'd been emboldened since Elijah first arrived. Whether it was him, the fear of him leaving, or just finally having *ee—frigging—nough*, neither Lori nor Elijah could tell just then.

"What are you doing, Greg?" Lori demanded, now just inches from the driver's side window.

The window was still up, and Greg was obviously considering leaving it that way. Lori smacked the window with her hand, and he jumped. The poor bastard was terrified, Elijah saw. This was *not* what he'd expected.

Neither had Elijah.

Lori stepped back from the car and put her hands on her hips. "I'm waiting," she said.

A long moment passed. Then another. And another. Greg was seriously weighing his options. Then, at last, he lowered his window.

Halfway.

"It's just a stakeout, Lori," he said, half-whimpering.

"A stakeout? At six in the morning?" Lori wasn't buying it. Elijah was new in town, and he didn't buy it.

"At *my* apartment?"

"We—we've reason to believe—"

"Who told you to come here, Greg?" Lori demanded. "It wasn't the mayor, was it?"

"It—see—!" Greg was struggling. Bad. He was like an eight-year-old who'd just been cornered.

"Josh sent you, didn't he? He sent you to spy on me!"

Greg winced when Lori cursed at him. "Come on, Lori. Don't talk that way about—"

"Oh, give me a break! It *was* Josh!" Lori was fuming. Elijah half-expected steam to shoot from her eyes, and he forced back a grin.

"You've no legal grounds to be here," Lori continued. "Which means I've every right to demand that you leave."

"Lori—"

"*Leave!*"

Greg winced again. He started to speak again but stopped. Finally, he raised his window and drove away. He cast a final look at Lori and Elijah before looking to the road ahead.

Lori watched him go, still seething. When the car turned a corner and disappeared, she looked back at Elijah. "I've never done that before," she breathed.

"I've never seen that before" Elijah answered, smiling.

"They're watching us now," she said. "Greg Foster's the chief of police. He's a prick and a pushover, but he'll be back. Actually, he probably won't. I probably scared him enough he'll just send one of his patrol officers to do it."

"Do what?"

"*Watch us!*" she hissed. "Josh has kept an eye on me ever since we broke up. At first, he just called a few times. But when I told him to stop, he'd just drive by now and then. He didn't know I saw him, but I did. And then when he took over the town, he just had other people do it. His deacons, mostly."

She pointed to where the cop drove away and added, "Greg's one of them."

And then there was silence. Lori had nothing further to add, and Elijah considered his next words.

He looked at Lori, again. Right in her eyes. Just as he had the night they met.

"Lori," he started, speaking slow. "What haven't you told me?"

"What do you mean?" she whined. "I've told you *everything!*"

"No you haven't," he replied. "Why is this happening? Why are you afraid?"

"Afraid?"

"Yes." He stepped toward her, stood just inches away. "Afraid. Just like you said earlier. Why are you afraid? There's more to this than just an obsessive ex-boyfriend. More to it than an obsessive ex-boyfriend with some serious connections. There's something even darker underneath all this. What is it?"

Lori glanced back where Greg had gone. She looked the other way. Elijah wondered if she was checking to see if anyone nearby was watching before saying more.

"Josh runs this town," she said. "He...*owns* it, along with everyone in it. They gave their souls to God, but Josh calls the shots on earth."

"Everyone?"

"*Yes! Everyone!*" Lori took a moment to catch her breath. "The police, the mayor, city hall, they all answer to him. Nothing goes on in this town unless he wants it. Look, I know how this sounds. I probably sound like some idiot conspiracy nut."

"No you don't," Elijah interrupted. "You sound...scared."

"I *am!*" Her voice cracked, and tears formed in her eyes. "He's turned this whole town against Marcus and me. Even...even our parents."

Elijah reached out and took hold of her arms. "Your parents?"

Lori nodded, keeping her head down so he wouldn't see her crying. "They're still members at ChristPoint. They can't understand why I'm not. We...haven't spoken since..."

Elijah drew her close and wrapped his arm around her. She buried her face in his shoulder and sniffled. "They don't know," she whimpered. "About the baby. I couldn't tell them."

"Okay," he said. "Okay. I'll stay."

She sniffled a couple more times. "We should get back inside," she said into his shoulder. "Greg may be a complete wimp, but not all the others are."

CHAPTER 16

Lori returned to work at J.D.'s the next morning. Word of her fascinating houseguest had yet to reach the pizzeria, so, for now, she was spared the endless barrage of questions. But they would come. Oh yes, they would come.

For the moment, it was just another day at work. Pizza. Sodas. Restless kids.

Janine and her boys didn't grace J.D.'s with their presence that day, but there were plenty of other families in town. One couple actually had *six* children, two girls and four boys. They ordered the buffet, and it was a nightmare keeping the plain cheese pizzas stocked for them.

What was it with kids and plain cheese pizzas, anyway? It's like they thought a single sausage or pepper just *stained* and *tainted* and *ruined* a whole pizza.

While Lori was out, Elijah took advantage of her washer and dryer. His clothes hadn't been washed in a few days, and they were long past due. Meantime, he paced round the apartment wearing only a towel, keeping clear of the windows, considering his options.

What was he going to do here? And how in the world was he going to do it?

"I don't suppose you'd have any insight at taking on a church like this?" he said, looking toward the ceiling. "Yeah, me neither."

His clothes took almost two hours to finish in the washer and dryer. When they were finally ready, he dressed and headed out for a walk around town. Until now, he'd only seen a couple of locales: Lori's apartment and J.D.'s Pizzeria. At the very least, he figured he needed to familiarize himself with his surroundings.

Antioch was a simple little community. A handful of fast-food joints lined the main streets along with a local restaurant here and there. There was no Wal-Mart that he could see (and all the hippies said "Hallelujah!"), just a Walgreens, a Peebles, and a handful of furniture outlets here and there. Plus, well over a dozen convenience stores. Antioch's residents would never face a shortage of gasoline or Slim Jims, that was for sure.

Those who saw Elijah all looked twice. Without fail. It was expected at this point, but a little unnerving nonetheless.

Women whispered to one another in hushed voices. Children pointed and tugged at their mommas' skirts. Men, being men, offered polite, emotionless nods in his direction.

The town wasn't that big, and it only boasted around 9,000 residents. The church was the biggest building—hell, the biggest *anything*—in town.

Elijah was passing the parking lot of a quaint, little shopping plaza when a police car pulled to a stop just in front of him. It parked in the plaza parking lot, and a young officer stepped out.

"'Scuse me, sir?" he called.

Elijah stopped and tilted his head a little, his expression saying *Me?*

"Yeah, you mind stepping over here a moment?"

Elijah nodded. Right away, he remembered the large knife he wore on his belt. He thought he could feel the eyes of vehicle occupants on him as they sped by. *Hey, Momma, that strange man's talkin' to the cops! You think he'll get arrested?*

"Yes, sir?" Elijah asked.

"Saw you in church the other day," the officer said. "Took off without talking to anyone."

"Sorry about that," Elijah answered. "I had lunch plans."

"With Lori Roberson?"

Elijah started a little. News *did* travel fast here. No point in lying, now. "Yes."

"She a friend of yours?"

Elijah glanced at the man's badge: CPL. K. BLYTHE. "You could say that," he said.

"Not meaning to make you nervous or anything," K. Blythe began, stepping away from his car, "but, you know, this is a small town. Most everyone knows everyone. And some stranger comes in and hangs around. Well, folks get curious."

He moved toward Elijah as he spoke.

"Naturally," Elijah agreed.

"So, I'd just like to ask, if I may, if you're looking to settle down here?" Blythe finished.

"I doubt it," Elijah said. "I'll probably move on before too long. I just thought I'd stay a little longer, is all."

"Plenty of hotels near the highway," Cpl. K. Blythe pointed out, finally reaching Elijah. They now stood face-to-face. "Nice ones, too. Even got a Super 8."

Elijah smiled. So this was where they were heading. "I appreciate that, but someone already offered me a place to stay."

"Lori Roberson?" Blythe's tone was getting sharper.

"Yes. Is there a problem?"

"Well, you know, it's just a small town," Blythe continued. His voice softened. A little. "And, you know, people talk. They see a stranger spend the night in a nice girl's apartment, they start to wonder."

"They shouldn't," Elijah told him, his tone flat and hard.

"But they do." Blythe's hand went to his hip, where his gun was holstered. He never looked down though. It was as if he didn't even realize he'd done it. "Maybe, for Lori's sake, for the town's sake, you should move on, soon." He paused, then added: "Maybe also for *your* sake."

Elijah looked down at Blythe's gun. He didn't bother hiding it. Then, he looked back in the officer's eyes. "You don't want to do that."

"Do what?"

"You know what. Violence begets violence. And when it doesn't, it just brings tears."

He raised his hand to touch Blythe's shoulder, but the officer's other hand exploded from his hip. It caught Elijah by the wrist and twisted with expert precision, pinning it behind the small of his back.

Pain spiked through Elijah's shoulder. He cried out and arched his back. He felt something in his shoulder pop. From behind, he heard the jingle of handcuffs. Then, he felt Blythe's breath near his ear, and the soft, slimy speckles of saliva striking his skin when the man hissed in his ear.

The cars continued speeding by.

"Did you just try to assault a police officer, sir?" Blythe spat through clenched teeth. *"Are you aware that's a federal offense?"*

He pushed up on Elijah's arm, which sent another hard spike of pain through his shoulder like a thunderbolt. Elijah grunted, his clenched teeth bared. He took a few seething breaths, then snarled, "You're not going to arrest me."

"Oh, I'm not?" Blythe sounded genuinely amused. "And why's that?"

Elijah's free hand shot beneath his coat and withdrew the hunting knife in a single, swift motion. He spun the blade round in his hand and drove it backward, sinking it into Blythe's right side.

Blythe grunted, and his grip went slack. His chin dropped on Elijah's shoulder. He tried to keep his balance but failed. A soft sound slipped through his lips like an old woman having an orgasm, and he started sliding toward the ground.

Elijah pried his hand free and spun round to catch Blythe in his arms. He returned the knife to its sheath, hoping no one noticed that part of this exchange. He leaned close and hissed in Blythe's ear, *"You're not arresting me, because any police officer worth his salt would know to make certain a suspect was disarmed first!"*

He drew back, and Blythe stared back with wide, terrified eyes. He struggled to breathe. He gasped several times, desperately trying to suck down air as much as possible. He hands quivered in front of his chest, as if they had no idea what to do next. Elijah placed his hand on the man's chest, over the wound. Already a crimson stain was expanding across the front of his uniform, and blood oozed between Elijah's fingers. He looked into the expiring cop's eyes and said, "You're not going to die today, Officer Blythe."

And then, just like that, the cold was going away. That chilled, sickly film of sweat seemed to just disappear, and K. Blythe felt his body grow warm again. The throbbing wound in his abdomen grew silent. It relaxed into a dull ache, and then that was gone, too. His body felt warm all over, like he was relaxing in a whirlpool bath with the heat turned up *just right*.

Kent Blythe's breath escaped his mouth in a long, relaxed sigh. Just at the end, it became a soft whimper.

Elijah drew his hand back, still supporting Blythe with one arm. It was still bloody.

Blythe's shirt also bore the telltale signs of a knife wound. The hole was still there, and blood soaked the area around it. But there was no puncture wound on his chest. Nothing. Just a healthy belly showing the first signs of love handles.

Blythe staggered back, slipping free of Elijah's grip. He stared down at his shirt in stunned silence. His handcuffs dropped to the ground.

"What—? How—?"

"You should probably take that home and wash it right away," Elijah offered. "Maybe your wife can sew it for you?"

Blythe stared back at him. His eyes were wide, like giant orbs bulging from his head. His mind was blank save for a single, asinine thought: *I'm not married.*

"May I go now?" When Blythe didn't respond, Elijah said, "Okay. Bye then."

He turned and made his way back in the direction of Lori's apartment.

CHAPTER 17

Minutes later, Kent Blythe sat in his squad car, staring at the front of his shirt.

"What...the hell?" he whispered. It was the first time he'd full-on swore in a year. The last time was when he was hammering nails into his living room wall to hang pictures and he'd smashed his thumb with the hammer and he—

Well, he'd let slip one or two choice words, actually. Something along the lines of *"Dammit!"*

If you don't swear much, might as well make the times you do count, right?

Kent touched his shirt again with his left hand. The blood was cold now, but still damp. The tips of his fingers were stained crimson when he pulled them away.

It wasn't possible. It just wasn't fu—*better make that make that "flip"*—ing possible. He should be in an emergency room now. He should probably have tubes attached all over and a breathing apparatus over his face. Geez, Kent didn't know what medical stuff you had to go through after someone stabbed you in the lung, but he figured it was more than just a few stitches, an antibiotic, and some ice cream. And a heck of a lot more than a simple touch from some nomad to make it all go away.

"He healed me," Kent whispered.
That was the plain truth of it. It couldn't be, but it was. It was impossible, but it happened. He was, quite literally, living proof of that. The man had stabbed him, which should've killed him, and then he'd turned around and *healed* him. Just like—
Just like—
"Jesus…"
No way. Absolutely no way. Blythe paid attention in Sunday School. He listened to sermons, even studied the book of Revelation once or twice. There was no place it said that Jesus would come back like some wandering hobo that shacked up with the first girl he met in town.
There was also nothing about stabbing a cop and then taking the wound away.
Kent looked out his driver's side window at the church. He'd come straight here and parked in the massive parking lot. He needed a few moments to himself to come to grips with what just happened.
He had to tell Joshua and the others. After all, what if the next time Elijah stabbed someone, he decided *not* to heal them right after? Or who was to say it was Elijah at all? Maybe the good Lord Himself stepped down and healed Kent, because it wasn't yet his time, and this nomad was just quick enough on his feet to take all the credit?
Okay, yeah, that was stupid.
But he still had to tell Joshua.

After relaying the afternoon's events, Elijah once again told Lori, "I want you to know, I really think I should leave."

Lori was quiet. She and Marcus sat together on the sofa. Elijah sat in the recliner, much like the first night he spent in Antioch.

"My being here is bringing you—both of you—unwanted attention," Elijah said. "And now it's only going to get worse." He paused a moment, said: "But I did promise before that I'd stay. So, if that's what you still want, I'll stay."

Lori said nothing. Quite frankly, she was kind of in shock. The once peaceful man who'd spent two nights in her apartment just admitted to stabbing a police officer.

"Will he be okay?" Marcus managed to ask.

"He'll be fine," Elijah answered. "Just like you."

Lori stood and walked across the room. She clutched her elbows as she moved. Her lip trembled. When at last she spoke, her voice was just barely above a whisper: "Stay." She turned and looked back at Elijah. "Please."

Elijah looked to Marcus for a response. He agreed. "Yes, stay. Please."

"Okay."

Joshua stared at the hole in Kent's shirt, touched it with his finger. Saw the unharmed flesh beneath.

"That's incredible," he breathed.

Nathan Riley, Greg Foster, Frank Hollister, and Dean Smith had joined both Kent and Joshua in his office. All of them stared at Kent's would-have-been injury.

"It's impossible," Frank whispered.

"So, um, what should we do?" Kent asked.

Joshua sank into the sofa and sighed. That was a good question.

"There has to be some other explanation," Dean insisted. "Like Frank said, it's just not possible."

"I'm just telling you what happened," Kent told him.

"Well, then you must've missed something. He must've done something else."

"I didn't miss anything." Kent was on the defensive now, his credibility called into question. That wasn't a good thing to do to a cop. He pointed an angry finger at Dean. "Don't tell me what I did or didn't see!"

"Enough!" Joshua called from the sofa. "Kent? I think you're required by law to bring this man in for assault. He did assault you, didn't he?"

"Well, yeah, but—" Kent glanced back at his shirt.

"He might've—*healed* you, but he still attacked you with a deadly weapon, didn't he?" Joshua asked. "What if he attacks someone else and doesn't offer the same courtesy?"

"They'll come for me," Elijah said. "I'll stay, but I can't stay here anymore."

He moved toward the door. Lori cut him off, blocking the way herself. "Wait a second! Where will you stay?"

"Let me worry about that."

"*No!*" Tears were brimming in Lori's eyes.

Elijah sighed. He took hold of her arms and smiled at her. "It's better you don't know. The less you know, the less they can press you for."

He gently but firmly pushed her aside.

"And I think I have to hurry," he added.

Joshua climbed in the squad car alongside Kent. He'd insisted on coming for this. He wanted to be there when Elijah was placed in handcuffs, to watch as he was escorted into the back of a police vehicle, and to heave a sigh of relief when he was locked away.

Elijah was a potential danger to this town. He'd already somehow seduced Lori and Marcus. With his apparent healing powers, who knew how many others he could lead astray?

The Bible spoke very clearly of false prophets who would appear in the last days, people who would cast out devils and heal the sick, but were in reality wolves in sheep's clothing. Joshua wasn't certain before, but now was beginning to be convinced Elijah was one of those.

"You should stay in the apartment," Elijah sighed.

Lori was following him outside despite his protests. She was a stubborn woman. That was certain.

Then again, did they come any other way? Elijah grinned but hid it from her.

Outside, Elijah first checked the streets for anyone who might be watching. Then, he said, "Don't worry about me. I've survived a long time on the road. You and Marcus just be careful."

He started to leave, but Lori grabbed him by the front of his coat and pulled him back. She planted a firm kiss to his lips and held it as long as she dared. When she drew back, Elijah placed a gentle hand to her cheek. "I'll be back when you need me," he promised.

He started at the sound of a nearing vehicle. Red and blue lights shone on the neighboring buildings. *"Get back inside!"* he hissed, turned, and raced away. The darkness swallowed him up in seconds.

Lori obeyed. She didn't look to see where he went, just raced back upstairs to her door, threw it open, then slammed it behind her. She sank to the floor without bothering to lock it. Tears stung at the bottom of her eyes, struggling to push their way out.

"Company," Marcus sighed, looking outside.

CHAPTER 18

It was Greg Foster who knocked at the door. He was flanked by Kent Blythe and another officer. He'd meant to bang on the door and bellow "*Police! Open up!*" But all he'd managed was a slightly louder-than-normal knock and "Umm, Antioch Police, Lori. Open the door, please?"

Beside him, Kent Blythe rolled his eyes.

Once the door was open, both of Foster's officers put their hands to their pistols and scanned the room from the doorway. Blythe's shirt was still bloody. "Lori? Is Elijah here?" Greg asked.

"Just left," Lori said.

"Any idea where he went, ma'am?" Blythe asked.

Lori snorted. *Ma'am?* "No idea, guys. He just walked out the door and went his merry way."

Greg fidgeted a moment. "Well," he stammered, "would—you mind if we checked the apartment?"

"Sure. Knock yourselves out." Lori stepped aside and let the men enter. "Just don't make a mess, huh?"

"We won't. I promise." Greg offered her a winning smile. Lori only barely returned it.

After the men passed, she noticed Joshua waiting in the stairwell. She shook her head and sighed. It figured he wouldn't be far behind.

"You okay, Lori?" he asked.

"Fine, Josh."

He stepped out of the stairwell and took a cautious step toward her. "Where'd he go?"

A sarcastic smile spread on Lori's lips. "You calling me a liar, Josh?"

"I just...wonder if perhaps you've been...influenced."

She chuckled at that. "This guy really bothers you, doesn't he?"

"I don't trust him."

"Of course not. He doesn't buy into your crap."

Joshua started a little, taken aback. Hurt. "Lori," he began, "what he can do. It—he—it's not natural. Is it true he—he can heal people?"

"You saw your crony over there." Lori jerked a thumb in the direction of the hallway.

"You know what the Bible says about that," Joshua said. "False prophets will claim to be messengers of the Lord."

Lori barked out a derisive laugh. "Are you serious? You've got some real nerve! Take a look at yourself, Josh. What the—?"

Joshua's hand shot out like lightning and blasted her across the right side of her face. Lori's vision jolted, and the back of her head bounced off the doorway. The inside of her head gonged. Crazy spots danced for a moment before her eyes. Her cheek burned.

Joshua had smacked her. The bastard had reached the out and hit her.

She stared back at him, eyes wide and furious. She wanted to leap at him and claw his eyes out, but his expression softened her.

Joshua's eyes looked almost wild. They blazed within their sockets with a lunatic fury that, although caged for now, might break out at any time. His bottom lip quivered, and he breathed heavy gasps through his nostrils.

"Nothing here," Officer No-Name called from within the apartment.

Lori looked back and saw the three men shuffling back down the hallway toward her. She glanced at Josh again and saw that red fury subsiding. But it was still there.

"I want you to call us, Lori, if he comes back," Greg was saying. "And we're going to station a squad car outside for the time being."

Lori sighed. "At least this time you're telling me before."

"That was for your protection, sweetie," Greg told her.

She looked at Joshua again. He'd managed to almost bottle up all his rage, now. Almost. "Right."

Elijah watched the lights of all but one vehicle—a police cruiser—leave Lori's apartment building. He watched from over a hundred yards away, surrounded by trees. He waited a moment longer, listening for the possible sound of footsteps. He heard none, just the ongoing sounds of evening. Crickets, birds, toads, and other such noisome creatures declaring their territory.

He hurried farther into the woods, leaving Lori's apartment and the police behind. When they were little more than a distant blue glow in the night, he folded his coat into a pillow and lay down near a large oak tree.

He hadn't slept outside since coming to Antioch. In a small way, he'd kind of missed it. The clear night sky and the cool, late-summer breeze were relaxing, despite being right smack in the middle of a pretty *un*-relaxing situation.

He was a fugitive. Granted, they weren't launching a manhunt, but they'd most certainly arrest him on sight if they found him. All of Antioch's police force would likely be watching for him.

Luckily, he was pretty sure there'd be no outside help. After all, how would they explain the situation? *We've a warrant for this man's arrest for stabbing a police officer with a hunting knife. What's that? How's the officer doing? Oh, fine, just fine. See, the perp actually healed him right after stabbing him, so there's no injury to report. Ain't that a pip?*

This was also a small town, which meant a small local police force. Elijah figured there were a dozen cops at best, but probably only a little over half of that, in fact, including Chief Foster.

Those weren't exactly comforting numbers: six or more armed men on the lookout for him. But hiding was something Elijah had become pretty good at. It was a skill he'd honed to near perfection just over a year ago when—

He pushed those thoughts aside. Now wasn't the time for past regrets. He had to figure out some way to resolve this situation. He'd promised Lori. He'd said he would stay, that he would help.

And he would. He just wasn't sure how.

One thing was certain: one way or another, someone had to take down this town pastor. Elijah just couldn't help but wish it hadn't fallen to him to do it.

"Lord, not my will but thine, right?" He sighed. Fact was, he wasn't doing this for God or any other deity out there. He wasn't doing it for himself or the town or even because it was just the *right* thing to do.

It was for Lori.

CHAPTER 19

Joshua was furious. Actually, that didn't do justice to the boiling rage surging throughout his body, but he could never bring himself to entertain such phrases as "royally pissed off" or "mad as all hell."

He threw open his front door and stormed into the house, his upper lip curled back in the beginning of a nasty snarl and his eyes blazing like white-hot furnaces. He huffed through clenched, grinding teeth, and his breaths whistled out between them like tiny locomotives.

Lori knew more than she was telling. He was certain of it. And the same went for Marcus. They both knew. They knew how to find Elijah, but they weren't telling because the snake had convinced them to keep quiet.

How could they not see? How could they not realize?

This Elijah was dangerous. He was a threat to them and a threat to the town. No one but Jesus Christ could personally heal the sick. And the only others to do so—guys like the Apostles Peter or Paul—did it through the name of Jesus Christ.

Elijah never once proclaimed the name of Jesus. Never once gave credit for his—his *gift*—to the Lord God above.

Joshua, his teeth still grinding, screamed and drove his fist into the wall. *Pow!* Again. *Pow!* And again. *Pow!* The wall, wood-paneled, shuddered but didn't give. Joshua's fist left no imprints behind. He howled again, his knuckles throbbing.

This Elijah was a false prophet. Joshua was sure of it. He had to be. There was no other explanation. No man could perform the miracles he performed. It just wasn't possible, not without divine intervention. Joshua just couldn't believe Elijah had any divine intervention behind his actions. He was no Christian. He never prayed, never sought God at the altar.

Never.

At first, Joshua suspected Elijah was a simple conman, a smooth talker with quick hands and even quicker words, like a televangelist asking silver-haired ladies to send a healthy check that would buy their eternal salvation.

Joshua had always held such preachers in mild contempt. They preached the grace and forgiveness of God from a soundstage where they never had to face people with problems and difficulties in their lives. They never once stepped down from their lofty podiums to meet with people, just professed God's love over and over in return for a healthy donation.

But no, that wasn't Elijah. He was more than that. The agony of it was Joshua still couldn't know just *how* much more.

He punched the wall again and screamed.

Lori had bought into him hook, line, and sinker!

He beat against the wall over and over. With each blow, he left behind tiny crimson stains. He knuckles stung where bits of skin had peeled away. But he kept going.

Pow!

Pow!
Pow!
Pow!
He screamed. It was a horrible cry, like a wounded, enraged beast.
Pow!
Pow!
Pow!
Pow!
The stains grew bigger. His knuckles burned.
Pow!
Pow!
Pow!
Pow!
Crack!
Joshua drew his fist back and saw a small but sizeable crack where his fist last struck the wall. It was surrounded by a thin layer of blood, which was starting to coagulate and trickle to the floor.

Joshua staggered back, gasping. A thin layer of sweat clung to his skin, and it chilled him. He stood still, panting, shivering, staring at the wall.

"My fault," he whispered, and a single tear tickled the bottom of his right eye.

He drove her away, away from him, away from the church, away from God. And now it was too late.

"Oh, God, forgive me."

Lori and Marcus—were they beyond saving now? Had God relinquished them to a reprobate mentality? Left them to wallow in their own degenerate wastefulness? No longer of any real value to Heaven?

Joshua sank onto the sofa, cradling his wounded hand. "I've lost her, Lord," he sighed. "Lost both of them."

He couldn't stand the fact, but it was so. He'd lost her to this—this *charlatan*.

Joshua closed his eyes, took a deep breath. When he opened them, the tear playing at his eye was gone. He sniffled one last time and stood.

Maybe he couldn't save Lori. Or Marcus. But he could still save Antioch. He'd be damned before he'd let Elijah destroy the greatness this town had achieved.

He picked up the phone and called Greg.

It rang twice before he answered. "Hello?"

"Greg, it's Joshua."

"Yes, pastor?"

"Has Kent talked to anyone else about what happened to him?"

Greg paused, thinking. "Just me, I think. I don't think we even got around to telling Billy—the other guy tonight—about it."

"Good," Joshua said. "Let's keep it that way. At least, for now."

"You want this kept quiet?" Greg sounded confused.

"Yes, for the time being," Joshua answered. "I'm not sure it would be good for the entire town to hear stories of some wandering healer hiding out in town. It's quite a story."

"It is that," Greg agreed. "But we can't keep the manhunt quiet for long."

"No manhunt," Joshua said quickly. "That'll arouse too much attention. Just tell the officers to keep an eye out for him."

Greg hesitated. Joshua could just imagine the uncertain thoughts darting this way and that through the man's head. *Keep it quiet? No manhunt? Can we do that?* But Greg finally said, "I will."

"And I'll let the other deacons know, too," Joshua said. "I'll call them right now."

"We'll get him, pastor," Greg assured him, confidence creeping back into his voice. "Don't worry."

"I've the utmost trust in Antioch's finest," Joshua told him, making certain his smile was audible.

They said their good-byes, and Joshua set to work calling the other deacons.

CHAPTER 20

The following days were somewhat uneventful. Because Chief Foster kept the search for Elijah quiet, very few, if any, people from town had any idea what was happening. Several figured Antioch's strange visitor had just moved on. Some—particularly those who enjoyed the juicier and steamier gossip—suggested the stranger spent two nights with Lori and, after having his fill, set out for the next woman just as willing to deliver.

Lori was the lucky recipient of many a condescending, reproachful look from older women who visited J.D's. Even her boss, Jack Crenshaw (also a ChristPoint member), asked if she was okay after...well, you know.

Fine, thanks, Jack.

Elijah never showed. Not once. By the following Friday, even Lori wondered if he was still in town. The police were watching her apartment less and less. After all, they weren't aware of Elijah's promise to still be around. With no sign of him for almost five days, why keep watching?

And without a full-blown manhunt, it was impossible to do much more than just make sure he wasn't in Antioch, anyway.

The following Saturday night, Lori returned home and collapsed on the sofa without bothering to turn on the lights. For the first time in what felt like years, she cried.

At first, the tears stung at her eyes like hot acid, but that pain eased into a simple warmth as they spilled over her eyelids. A dam had burst. Ever since the day she aborted her child, Lori kept everything inside. Now everything rushed out in a wave.

Elijah had been her first glimpse of hope. He was supposed to be the sign things would change for the better. But they hadn't. Everything was exactly as it was before his arrival. Nothing was different.

Nothing.

He was asleep when it happened. Peacefully asleep, too. Marcus wouldn't remember it later, but he was dreaming about Orlando Bloom at the time. Nothing naughty, just walking together through the streets of some big city. Walking and talking. Laughing and smiling.

Secret celebrity crush. Everyone's got one. Right?

But that dream pretty much shattered when something small and hard struck his bedroom window. *Pakk!* He inhaled through his nostrils so loud they whistled and propped himself up on his elbows. Eyes wide, he scanned the dark room but saw nothing.

What the hell was that?

Pakk!

He jerked his head toward his bedroom window. He jumped out of bed and hurried over to look out. He scanned the street outside but saw nothing. Nothing.

A dark hand reached up from beneath the windowsill and smacked the glass. *Bammm!* Marcus shrieked (he'd insist later that he didn't) and leapt back.

The sudden adrenaline rush left him feeling charged like he'd jammed his thumb in a light socket, and he panted like a big, exhausted dog. Then, Elijah's face rose up and looked inside. *Let me in*, he mouthed. After another moment or two, Marcus held up his index finger, asking for a minute. He hurried to the front door.

"*You nearly gave me a heart attack!*" he hissed.

Elijah smiled and shrugged, and Marcus softened. Chrissake, the guy had the same effect on him as he had on Lori.

"We were wondering—*Holy Christ, you stink!*" Marcus covered his face and stepped back several steps. He tried to wave away the scent of dirt, grass, and body odor with his other hand. And failed. It practically stung the inside of his head, stabbed the back of his retinas like tiny needles.

"Yeah, sorry about that," Elijah sighed. "A few days in the wilderness'll do that to you. I was kind of hoping I could use your shower?"

"Jesus, gladly! Just do it now before we do *anything* else!"

Marcus pointed the way to his bathroom with his free hand and stepped aside for Elijah to pass. Then, he groaned and hurried to the kitchen for some air freshener, which he used liberally in Elijah's wake.

"I can hear you, you know," Elijah called from within the bathroom.

"And I can still smell you! Jeez!"

Marcus kept the lights out everywhere but the bathroom, hoping to avoid suspicion. The police were no

124

longer watching him, sure, but being overly cautious never hurt anyone.

"Toss your clothes out," Marcus called. "I'll put them in the washer. And don't worry, I won't peek."

Much.

The bathroom door opened a few inches, and Elijah's clothes sailed out. They hit Marcus in the chest, and the door closed less than a second later.

Bummer.

He carried them to the walk-in closet in his bedroom that doubled as his laundry room. He started to toss the entire load in all at once, but he stopped. A grin crept over his face, and he set the clothes atop the dryer, then tossed them in one at a time.

Boxers or briefs, Elijah? Ah ho! Briefs, I see!

"Looks like I know something Lori doesn't," he sang and headed to his bedroom to pull out some more pajamas. A plaid, red-and-green ensemble would do nicely!

He returned to the restroom and knocked on the door. "You can wear my PJ's till your clothes are washed!"

He heard the water stop, and Elijah called, "Just a minute."

A moment later, the door opened and steam wafted out into the hallway. Elijah wore only a towel around his waist, and Marcus caught himself staring at the man's chest.

It was muscular, but not toned like an athlete. Nor was it slender. He didn't quite have the six-pack abs every woman drools over, but there was no mistaking the firm muscles just beneath the man's skin. He was beautiful.

"Hey, tiger," Elijah said. "Clothes, please? I'm a little shy."

"Sorry."

Afterward, they both sat on the bed in Marcus' bedroom. Elijah smelled ten times better. Amazing what a little soap, shampoo, and several gallons of hot water could do. His clothes were already in the dryer. Another fifteen minutes and he'd be on his way again.

"How's Lori?" Elijah asked.

"Not too good, honestly," Marcus said. "I think she's given up on you."

Elijah nodded. "Sorry about that. Had to stay in the woods most of the time to avoid any police seeing me. Tell you the truth, this is the longest I've gone 'in the wild.'"

"Yeah, well, you sure *smelled* the part."

Elijah grinned. "Yeah, yeah. Sorry about that. But listen, I needed more than just your shower. How much do you know about Joshua's organization? His inner circle?"

Marcus grunted. That was easy. "You mean the deacons?" He smirked. "The four stooges?"

"Yeah."

Marcus sighed. "Well, there're plenty of deacons at ChristPoint—like, 15 or so I think—but the four stooges are Joshua's most *inner* circle. Make no mistake, Joshua's most definitely the one in charge, but these guys are a big part of the decisions he makes."

"Okay," Elijah said, nodding, urging Marcus to continue.

"Well, Greg Foster, Antioch's police chief, you know already," Marcus began. "He's in his fifties. He's married. And he's a complete pushover. The guy can't even take a crap without Joshua's okay. He'll take charge with the other officers, but you'll never see him go against the pastor. Never.

"And you probably also remember Nathan Riley, the guy that visited us after you went to church last Sunday. Just past middle age, happily married, his wife, Katherine, is literally the love of his life. Bit of a schlub, though. I mean, he's not a *bad* guy or anything, and he's not a complete wimp like Foster, but he's just kinda'...*there*. Push him hard enough, which is to say, not hard at all, and he'll get out of your way.

"Then, there's Dean Smith. You haven't met him, and you'll live a long and happy life if you never do. He's young, he's arrogant, and he's mean. And I do mean *mean*. He got through college thanks to a scholarship from the church and plenty of fat checks from Daddy. He tends to think he owns the world, and he's likely to beat the hell out of anyone who says different.

"Steer clear of that guy."

Marcus stopped. Was quiet.

"That's three," Elijah prodded.

Marcus nodded. "Yeah. Last one's Frank Hollister, and, to be honest, he's the one that scares me. Dean'll eff you up, but he's just your average, run-of-the-mill, hotheaded bully. Frank's another story. He used to be in the Marines, or something. I don't know exactly. Point is, he's smart. He probably knows at least ten different ways to kill you.

"And every time he's looked at me, I'd swear he was going through them all, one-at-a-time in his head."

Elijah nodded again. He was quiet for several moments. Thinking. At last, he said, "Got a phone book?"

"Sure." Marcus led the way back to the kitchen and pulled the book out of a drawer.

Eiljah switched the light on. "Pad and paper?" he asked.

Marcus obliged, pulling them both from another drawer.

Elijah looked up all four men's names. He jotted down their addresses, scribbled a few notes, folded the paper up in his hand.

He switched the light back off and looked at Marcus again. From the bedroom closet, they heard the dryer alarm go off. "Okay," Elijah said. "I have to go again. I don't know when I'll pop up again, but I will. Tell Lori that. And I'll need the both of you to be willing to do anything I ask. Will you?"

"Well…what are you gonna' ask?"

"I don't know, yet," Elijah said. "But I'll need you both to be ready. I can't see Lori tonight; can you promise me for her?"

Marcus hesitated. Then, nodded. "Yes. I think so."

"Okay."

Elijah hurried to the laundry room, leaving Marcus alone for a few moments while he changed. When he came back, Marcus could see him jamming the addresses in his coat pocket.

He placed a hand on Marcus' shoulder when he reached him. "Be patient," he said.

Marcus, suddenly unable to speak, just nodded.

Elijah smiled and went to the door. He paused a moment after opening it and looked back. "It'll work out."

Then, he left.

CHAPTER 21

The next morning, Lori called in sick. She'd never taken a sick day before in her life. Not once. (Okay, there was that one time when Jack sent her home early after she was slammed with an incredible sneezing fit. But that was really only a half-day.)

But she called in this day. She wasn't sick. Not really. She just couldn't bring herself to climb off the couch where she'd collapsed and wept the night before. The fabric beneath her face was still moist from the previous evening's tears, but she didn't care. She didn't care about what her boss thought. She didn't care what the people in town thought. She didn't care about anything.

Not one thing.

What did it matter, anyway? Who the hell cared?

Lori lay still. Were anyone to see her, they'd assume she was still sleeping. But inside her head, strings of glorious profanities zipped along like electrical currents.

For years, Lori had stayed in Antioch because of her parents. She just couldn't leave them behind. They'd totally bought into Joshua's message, even asked when Lori might come back to church with them a few times, but she could just never bring herself to abandon them to Joshua and his ironfisted rule of this place.

And a hell of a lot of good she'd done, hadn't she? Her parents were still avid followers of Joshua and his message. Still dedicated little minions of his holiest of holy little kingdom. All she'd managed to do was slowly drive a wedge between them and become one of Antioch's most notable outcasts.

But, then—

Then, she'd seen a glimmer of hope wander into J.D.'s right off the street. Walked right in and sat down at her table and promised to dance at her wedding if she'd just keep refilling his Pepsi. And followed her home. *Followed her home!* Stayed a few days with her. Then, the dumbass stabbed a cop and left town.

What the crap? How stupid can you be?

Elijah was gone. Outta' here. Vamoosed. Hightailed it for the next town.

That glimmer of hope left. *Elijah, Elijah, why have you for-frigging-saken me?*

She giggled. That was actually kind of funny. *For-frigging-saken.*

The sound cut through the silence in the room like a herky-jerky knife, and whatever gloom hung about the apartment seemed to evaporate, slowly at first, but it soon picked up momentum.

Lori just kept giggling. She couldn't help it, and she didn't know why. It wasn't *that* funny, but it just kept coming. It grew into subtle laughter. Crazy laughter. One that'd most certainly scare the crap out of anyone who entered the room.

Geez, it wasn't *that* funny. Was it? *For-frigging—*

Tears were streaming down her face now. Still she laughed. Harder. Louder. To the point she worried the neighbors might come knocking on her door.

But they weren't home. They didn't call in sick. Unlike *some* people. Hah!

Lori cackled and finally—at long last—pushed herself up and sat upright. She took a few moments to catch her breath. Her chest hurt. The muscles screamed at her from the unending strain she'd put them through with all that maniacal laughter.

Geez-zuss, woman! Who on earth wakes up like that? What are you trying to do to us?

She giggled again but kept it at that.

Well, that was it then, wasn't it? Without Elijah, she was on her own. And after all these years, she hadn't helped her family. She hadn't helped the town. Maybe they were beyond help, what could one person do, anyway? Joshua wasn't just some raving street preacher. He was a juggernaut, a kingpin who ruled Antioch like Michael Corleone.

Then again, Michael Corleone was *Catholic*.

Lori giggled again.

Oh, the hell with it. The hell with Joshua. The hell with Antioch. (She couldn't quite bring herself to say the same of her parents, though.) She was leaving. Even if all she did was move to a town just twenty miles down the road. She was leaving Antioch.

Who knows? Maybe she'd even find a church there she'd actually like to attend. It wasn't like Lori was opposed to church. Even after all this time, she still considered herself a Christian.

She just wasn't a member of ChristPoint. Dear sweet Lord above, she was *not*.

So, her mind was made up. She was leaving. Leaving this place behind. She'd probably have to give two weeks' notice to Jack. J.D.'s had been good to her, after all. As good as any restaurant could be, anyway.

She'd have to make plans to move, to terminate her lease with the apartment building. It'd be a lot of work, but she'd do it.

She *would*.

Then, Marcus called.

In the darkness of that night, Elijah watched and waited.

By day, he stayed in the woods outside of town. He returned to the city only by night. He wasn't an expert, but he'd learned how to hide.

As soon as the sun was down, Elijah meandered through the streets, keeping a cautious eye out for police, ready to flee at a moment's notice. His heart thumped hard in his chest, kicking the inside of his ribcage like a steel-toed boot, but he pressed on.

Nathan Riley lived in a respectable, two-story home in a comfortable neighborhood. It wasn't the rich neighborhood by any means, but it was certainly several steps above Antioch's version of "skid row." Its walls were built with red bricks and occasionally lined with light blue siding. Two bedroom windows peeked out from the rooftop, but the Rileys' children had long since moved on to college.

Nathan and Katherine currently enjoyed empty-nesthood. Both husband and wife showed all the signs of a couple that had set down roots decades ago. Regular as clockwork, they ate dinner at the kitchen table, cleaned the dishes together, watched late-night television, then turned in for the night at 11:04 p.m. on the dot. Or maybe it was 11:05.

Frank Hollister, who lived in a cozy little cottage-like home near the city limits, was just as predictable. He ate dinner promptly at 6 p.m., cleaned everything nice and neat, then settled into a chair to read a book for a couple hours before turning in. Just before bed, he carried the day's trash to the can outside.

It was during this refuse excursion that Hollister paused once to scan the area. Elijah was hiding behind the shrubbery surrounding the house, and he lay flat on the ground. He held his breath while Hollister stared down both ends of the street for what felt like an hour. He couldn't tell if the man somehow *sensed* his presence, or if this was just standard military procedure. Either way it didn't matter; Frank eventually turned and went back inside.

Elijah determined Hollister was their most formidable opponent. He was battle-hardened and smart. Granted, his best days were probably long behind him, but he still wasn't to be underestimated. Even now, well past the point of senior citizenry, Frank was a formidable physical specimen. His abdomen had expanded somewhat, but he still harbored a bulky, muscular frame.

Elijah would've preferred to somehow remove the man from the playing field first. Strategically speaking, it would make the most sense. Even Hollister himself would've said so. Remove the biggest threat first, and what remains can't help but falter because they'd lost their "big gun."

But it wasn't to be.

From there, Elijah ventured into the high-rent district, to the home of Chief Greg Foster. Foster and his wife, Becky, waddled throughout their respectable, three bedroom/two-and-a-half bathroom home with no discernable direction. They never sat still. At least three televisions—that Elijah could see, anyway—remained on at all times. Used dinner plates sat on the table for quite some time before either of the Fosters came to clean them. When they did, they only stuffed them into the dishwasher and walked away.

Plenty of time to turn it on later, right?

Last on Elijah's list was Dean Smith. Dean lived in an apartment similar to Lori and Marcus. It was one home among many in a quaint little complex that included around seven or eight other apartments, all single bed and baths.

Dean's apartment was on the second floor. A single stairwell led up to the level housing his and two other living quarters. Dean's was on the far left, with a narrow balcony leading toward it and a single bedroom window near the corner of the building.

The apartment next to Dean's looked empty. That was good.

The one on the far end wasn't. That wasn't so good.

Dean was to be Elijah's first target. He desperately wished it could be Frank, but that just wouldn't work into his plans. He needed to eliminate more than one of, as Marcus called them, the "four stooges," on his first play. Frank was just too smart, too level-headed, for that to work.

Frank Hollister would require absolute attention.

Dean, however, was another story. He wore his attitude on his sleeve. There was a chip on his shoulder, a big one. And it kept him in a perpetual bad mood, which meant he might also be easily manipulated.

CHAPTER 22

At first, when she heard Elijah was still in town, Lori felt invigorated, renewed. That sense of hopelessness that hung over the town like a grim shroud was lifted. Maybe—just maybe—she'd stick around after all. And maybe—just maybe—there was hope for Antioch.
For her.
And for her parents.

But the more she thought about it, and the longer she went without actually seeing Elijah, she found herself getting angrier and angrier. By the end of Monday, it was a steady simmer. By Tuesday, it was starting to boil.

Just what was he doing? And who did he think he was, stringing her along like that? Promising to be around and then vanishing almost without a trace?

She tried not to let it show, especially around customers, but she was a bit short with someone once or twice. She was never rude or mean, but there was that subtle tinge to her attitude, an edge that people couldn't help but notice.

All things considered, though, she figured she was covering it pretty well.

But once Wednesday rolled around with still no word from Elijah, Lori was genuinely pissed. If and when he showed his face, she swore she'd smack the begeezuss out of it.

No, forget a slap. Maybe she'd just ball up her fist and deck him with a wicked right cross. *Heal* that! (Oh, right. You *can't!*)

Vietnam was a lifetime ago. Some had even lived and died in the time between the end of hostilities and today. But Frank remembered. He'd always remember.

The sun was setting outside, slowly turning the sky a deep crimson. Frank took advantage of the remaining daylight and loaded a flashlight and rope into his car. He wore old Army fatigues, which were still vivid and green after all these years.

Never forget, Joshua had told him. *Never forget.*

And he hadn't.

While America grew fat and lazy and a new generation forgot the price of freedom, Frank remembered. He remembered his platoon, a group of eight of America's finest, boys from all walks of life…Frank, Dillon, Marshal, Justin, Ted, Jessie, Stephen and Willy.

Willy…

Frank still vividly remembered the day he and Willy ventured into a town near base one day looking for dinner. Some child had wandered from across the street and asked them, "Shine?"

"No, thanks, kiddo," Frank had said.

But the kid was persistent. He tugged at Willy's shirt and repeated. "Shine?"

Willy started to answer just as the kid pulled a grenade out of his pocket. Willy shoved Frank aside a half-second before the explosion. A piece of shrapnel caught him in the leg and sent a blast of pain through the lower half of his body.

"Willy!"

Frank had raced back to find his friend and found only his upper torso. The rest was splattered on the street and buildings. "Frank?" Willy's upper torso called. Its arms flopped like a pair of fish.

Frank could only stare at him, too horrified to go near.

"Frank?" The upper torso was crying now. *"Frank!? Frank, I wanna' go home! I just wanna' go home! Please, Frank? I wanna' see my mom! Please, just let me see my mom!"*

Willy's cries for his mother were the last words he uttered on earth.

Frank carried that memory with him back home. When he arrived back in the states at the San Diego Airport, and the Flower Children lined the streets in protest, waving signs that declared him and his platoon baby-killers, he thought of Willy.

Would they protest him? A young boy who just wanted to see his mom again?

Frank returned to his bedroom and pulled out some old camouflage face paint. He went to the bathroom, looked in the mirror and began applying it.

He'd carried those memories on his shoulders for years, even when he wanted nothing more than to forget. There were nights—lots of them—when he awoke in a cold sweat, the image of Willy's entrails spilled out on the pavement and steaming still fresh in his mind from some vivid nightmare.

Frank had sought counseling, met with psychiatrists and other doctors. None of them helped. They all offered long and expensive advice which always summed up in Frank's mind as "Get over it."

Joshua, however, was another story.

By now, Frank's entire face was a mask of black and green. He washed the residue from his hands and pulled on a pair of gloves.

The Rev. Hutchinson had told him *not* to forget, *never* forget. "Take it to the Lord in prayer," he'd said. "Just give it over to him. But never forget Willy. Never forget your friend or his sacrifice."

It had been sage advice. Frank's nightmares returned less and less after he joined ChristPoint. By now, they were all but gone. When he thought of Willy, Frank thought also of the good times together, not only the bad. Like the time they'd stayed up late into the night watching Casablanca, of all things.

Joshua—*ChristPoint*—had given Frank that. He'd be damned if he'd let someone take that away.

Frank headed back outside. The sun was down. It was time to go hunting.

Marcus paid Lori a visit that night after work. He noted a police cruiser passing by as he arrived and decided it wasn't a coincidence. He and Lori might not be *officially* under surveillance, but they weren't quite out from under Joshua's scrutiny, either.

He hustled upstairs and knocked. Lori caught him off guard when she swung the door open. He jumped a little and started to laugh, but Lori's stony expression stopped him.

"Heard from Elijah?" she asked.

"Err, no. Not since last time."

Lori huffed and marched away from the door. Marcus hesitantly stepped inside and saw her standing in the living room, clutching her arms. She was fuming.

"Everything okay?" he asked as he shut the door.

"He could at least stop by and tell us what he's doing," Lori spat. She looked back at him, and Marcus could see the red-hot fury in her eyes. "I still haven't seen or heard from him since the night he vanished."

"Police are still checking up on us," Marcus told her. "He has to be careful. Just seeing me that night must've been risky."

"*I don't care!*" Lori very nearly screamed. "I'd literally given up. I was ready to make plans to leave town when you called. I didn't tell you that, but I was. It was the last straw."

"But he's still out there," Marcus reminded her. "And he always was. I don't know what he's got in mind, and I don't even know if he's got a chance in hell, but he's out there doing *something*. And, Lori, he doesn't even *have* to!"

That one quieted her. She nibbled the inside of her lip and looked down at the floor.

"Or did you forget that little fact?" Now, it was Marcus' turn to be mad. His voice raised half an octave, and he balled up his hands into fists at his sides. "He's got no ties to this place. Not to you or me. He barely even knows us. But now he's out there hiding out in the woods, doing God knows what to stay alive, just so he can try to find some way to help us. Or has that little tidbit never occurred to you?"

Lori said nothing. She leaned her head back, eyes closed, stretching her neck and back. She let out a soft, frustrated groan.

"Jesus Christ," Marcus sighed. He fell into Lori's sofa and stared at the ceiling. "You know, even if he had left, he's already done more for us than anyone else was willing to do. We know several others who don't listen to Joshua, but when did they ever stand up to him? When did we?"

"You made your point," Lori muttered.

"I sure hope so," Marcus snapped. He shook his head. "God, you're a whiny bitch sometimes."

Lori snapped her head in his direction and stared with wide eyes. Marcus looked back, grinned, winked at her. Lori tried to hold back the smile that pressed its way across her lips. Tried, but failed.

She pointed at him. "*You're* the only bitch in *this* house!"

"That right? Well—"

He was cut off by a knock at the door.

The both glanced at one another. Cop? Joshua? One of the other deacons?

"Who is it?" Lori called.

No answer.

The doorknob turned, turned only a fraction of an inch before it was caught by the lock. It jiggled in place for a moment. Then, another knock. Louder this time. More forceful.

Lori took a few wary steps toward the door. From his seat, Marcus mouthed an emphatic *No!*

Another knock. This one bordered on banging. Three hard knocks/bangs that rattled the door's hinges. Lori and Marcus both jumped.

She glanced at him again. He shook his head. *Don't you do it! Don't you dare!*

But she did. She stepped up to the door, redid the unlocking ritual (*Click! Click! Jingle!*)

The moment the chain was removed, the door swung open on its own. Whoever stood outside knew the routine and wasn't waiting any longer to come in. He shoved the door open, rushed inside, and closed it himself.

It was Elijah.

And he stunk, Marcus noticed. Again.

"Long time no see," Marcus ventured after Elijah turned to face them.

He smiled. "Sorry, but I wanted to get out of sight quick."

Lori stared at him. Just moments ago, she was ready to tear into him, to verbally rip him to shreds and slap the taste right out of his mouth. Oh boy, was she ready! But not now.

Not now.

"Are you okay?" Elijah asked her.

Lori nodded.

He stepped over to her. Christ, he stank. The smell hit her like a crap-covered tomahawk, probably left scars along the inner linings of her nostrils. *Gee-zuss!*

But, and this was the hell of it, she didn't care. When he reached out and placed his hands on her shoulders, she didn't want to be anywhere else in the world but where he could touch her. When he looked in her eyes, all her fear and anger melted away.

But it still didn't mask the stench. Christ in Heaven! "You *really* need a shower," she said.

Elijah grinned, nodded. "I know. And I will. But I need to ask a favor?"

He looked over at Marcus. *You remember what we discussed?* his eyes said. *What you promised?*

"Anything," Lori said.

He looked back at her. "Good. I don't know what time exactly, but I'm gonna' take action tonight. And when I do, things are going to start happening really fast. You need to be ready for them." He hesitated a moment. "And I need you both to still be committed, then."

Lori raised a quizzical eyebrow. "What'd you have in mind?"

"I'm still working that out," he answered. "And it's probably best you don't know. At least, for now. I want you to promise me you'll both stay home."

"But—"

"*Promise me!*"

Lori blinked. So did Marcus. Elijah hadn't yelled, but he'd come close. The sound didn't fit, coming from him. It was frightening.

Finally, Lori nodded. "Oh—Okay."

Elijah nodded back. He looked at Marcus, smiled, then looked back at her. "Okay then, mind if I use your shower now?"

CHAPTER 23

Soft, blue light filled what Elijah could only assume was Dean's bedroom. He was probably watching television before bed.

Elijah snatched up a rock lying near the road. He stared at it a moment, took a deep breath. He'd already committed to this. So had Lori and Marcus. But he'd arrived at another crucial moment. There'd be no turning back after this. Now, he was in till it was finished, however that turned out.

"So be it." He fired the stone as hard as he could at Dean's bedroom window.

It crashed dead center, shattering the night's silence with a chaotic symphony. The window imploded, sending shards into the bedroom and drawing a squawk from the man inside.

Elijah ducked behind a nearby car, a red Beretta, manual transmission. He peered through the car's windows and watched Dean stumble through the remains of his bedroom window. Shirtless, he glared out at the surrounding streets, searching for whoever smashed his window. His furious eyes shot in all directions. Even from this distance, Elijah could hear his breaths shooting through his nostrils like tiny steam engines.

He waited. It was several more moments before Dean gave up his search and left the window to clean up the mess. He heard the man curse once when he stepped on a glass shard.

Elijah checked the streets again—all clear—and hurried to the stairwell, climbing two at a time as quietly as possible. Whether or not the other tenants were asleep or didn't care, Elijah couldn't tell. Either way, it didn't look like he'd have any uninvited guests. He slid forward along the wall. The only sound he made was the occasional scrape of his shoes on the balcony's cement floor.

He stopped at Dean's front door, took a deep breath, then knocked. Hard. He pivoted to the side and stood just to the left of the doorway, hidden from sight whenever Dean came storming outside.

Dean was certain to bring a weapon with him when he answered. That was one variable Elijah hadn't been able to figure. Would it be a bat? A gun? A knife? Regardless, Elijah figured the best course of action was the quickest one: attack before Dean had the chance to get the first shot and disarm him as fast as possible.

Elijah heard footsteps. Angry ones. They thumped across the floor like a rhino, hurrying through the hallway to the living room, toward the front door. Elijah resisted the urge to hold his breath. He balled his right hand into a fist and held it up by his left shoulder. And waited.

But not for very long.

As it turned out, Elijah needn't have worried about Dean's weapon of choice. The guy was too furious to be bothered with the possible danger he faced. He'd stormed from his room, still wearing only his boxer shorts, with his fists clenched so tight his knuckles almost glowed white. He threw the door open and marched outside.

Elijah swung his fist hard and connected with Dean's mouth.

Dean's vision flared white, then red, then eased its way back to normal as spots danced and swirled in front of his eyes. The impact caused his front teeth to slice open the back of his upper lip (which would swell up like a clown by the next day), and warm, copper-tasting blood filled the inside of his mouth. He howled, a scream intermingled with both agony and fury.

Dean felt a pair of hands press against his chest and push him back into the apartment. He staggered, unable to keep pace as the intruder forced his way inside. Then, the man threw him to the floor and slammed the front door shut. He turned back and stared down at him.

Dean's vision finally started to clear, and he made his attacker. Elijah. The wandering prick.

Dean scrambled back to his feet. Blood was already dripping from his lip, and his teeth were stained with red. He snarled and charged forward, head down, and slammed his shoulder into Elijah's abdomen. He pressed forward until the prick's back slammed into the door.

Elijah grunted, then managed to say, *"Catch you at a bad time?"*

Dean roared and slammed his fist into Elijah's side, which drew a satisfying squawk of pain from the man. He went for a second blow, but Elijah caught him by the wrist. He then wrapped his other arm around Dean's head, shifted Dean's arm to grip it in the crook of his own arm, and pivoted his feet. He spun a full circle away from the door and threw Dean across the room.

Dean had no way to control his momentum. He tilt-a-whirled, crashed onto the floor, and rolled into the wall. The windows rattled with the impact.

But he wasted no time getting back to his feet and charging again.

Elijah couldn't help but notice the erection bouncing around inside Dean's shorts like a crooked seesaw. *Bad time, indeed.*

Elijah focused on Dean's eyes, daring the man as he shot across the living room like an animal. He then sidestepped at the last moment and thrust his knee into Dean's path. It caught the charging man in the chest, which knocked the wind out of him, and he flipped over it like a broken marionette.

Dean's erection jabbed into Elijah's shin, which hurt like hell. It felt like having the blunt end of a screwdriver driving into his leg. Dean squeaked out a horrified grunt, and Elijah guessed it probably hurt him even more.

For one crazy instant, Dean was almost convinced his dick would break in half. He landed hard on his back and gasped for air. He couldn't breathe. His balls ached. And his erection was throbbing.

He looked up and saw Elijah step back to catch his breath.

Elijah's chest hurt, and his lungs burned. No doubt he'd have a nice, purple bruise across his abdomen the next morning.

"*I'll kill you!*" Dean snarled, and he leapt to his feet again. "*I'll kill you!*"

He charged. Elijah caught him, but Dean managed to push him into the television set. The corner jabbed into his back, which yanked a painful squeak from his throat. The impact toppled the set off the table, and it thudded on the floor.

Dean pressed forward, forcing Elijah onto the table where the television previously rested. "*Kill you!*" he screamed.

Elijah felt his back hit the wall. He grunted, then brought his hands up, and dug his thumbs into Dean's eyes. At first, Dean ignored it—long enough, in fact, that for one, agonizing second, Elijah worried it wouldn't work—but then he screamed and leapt back. He staggered backward several steps and clutched at his eyes with both hands.

Elijah seized the opportunity, leapt forward from the table, and kicked Dean as hard as he could between the legs. Dean jumped in surprise and grunted loud, then sank to the floor, clutching at his wounded balls with both hands.

Despite his efforts not to, Dean groaned as the pain ate its way from his groin to his chest. His thighs burned, and his breath caught in his chest. He gasped several times, and, for just a moment, he was certain he would vomit.

But he didn't.

He tried to move, but his legs remained locked in place. He didn't dare release his throbbing balls. He gritted his teeth, wanted to scream, but couldn't.

Elijah left him and hurried into the bedroom. A frozen image of Jessica Biel in a spaghetti-string top and striped panties was on the television. A clump of used Kleenex rested on the bed.

That explains Dean's little battering ram.

He spotted the cell phone on a nearby table and snatched it up. He returned to the doorway and saw Dean, his hands still planted firmly over his groin, had managed to force himself upright and leaned into the wall for support. He pushed himself forward, baring his bloody teeth and seething furious breaths in and out. Long strands of red spittle billowed from his lips like party streamers.

Elijah came back in the hallway and smiled at him. "Round two?"

Dean roared. He still couldn't stand. He could breathe, but his legs felt like lead. He released his balls and clawed at the wall, forced himself to stand. He got halfway up, then fell again in a heap.

He screamed, got on all fours, and pushed himself forward. He ignored the numbness still clinging to his legs and forced himself onward, charging like a bull. Once again, he collided with Elijah's midsection, drawing out another pain-filled squeak from him.

Elijah staggered backward with his arms wrapped around Dean's shoulders. He backed through another doorway into the bathroom. He hit the countertop hard and tried pivoting again to throw Dean aside.

Dean proved to be a quick learner, though, and he maintained his grip around Elijah's waist. Both men spun crazily and fell into the shower curtain, which snapped and fell beneath them. Elijah, Dean, and the curtain fell into the bathtub with a deafening thud. Both men released each other.

Elijah, a little less worse for wear than Dean, managed to climb out first. He coughed a few times and turned just in time to see Dean stagger back to his feet.

He swatted Dean's balls with the back of his hand. Dean, his balls still unbelievably tender, felt his midsection explode with another bout of pain. He stumbled back into the wall, fell to one knee in the bathtub, and roared through clenched teeth.

He tried to take a step forward, but his legs were completely off balance. He stumbled over the edge of the tub and spilled onto the floor.

Elijah stepped back and caught his breath for a brief moment. Then, he switched the bathroom light off, left the room, and shut the door—leaving Dean alone in complete darkness.

The pain ate its way through Dean's body like the teeth of a rusted saw. He groped around in the dark until he found the toilet and used it to push himself back to his feet. He staggered back to the door and threw it open.

The entire apartment was dark now. Elijah had switched every light off. The only illumination in the place came from street lamps outside. Even the TV in his bedroom was off.

Dean limped into the hallway, bracing himself against the wall with one hand and clutching his aching balls with the other. He felt the pain all over his body now. The muscles in his stomach groaned because of it.

He looked everywhere for Elijah but couldn't see him. Had he left? Had the prick just come to attack him and run?

Dean checked the bedroom. The TV was off, but it was otherwise undisturbed. No one was there. He looked back into the living room, and he saw the front door was open.

He must've left. Hit and run.

But he'd find him. One way or another, he'd—

And then, Elijah was there again. He stood in the doorway, a black silhouette against the night sky. Daring Dean to come at him one more time.

Dean howled and raced forward. He didn't aim low this time. No, this time he swung his fist high and connected hard with the side of the prick's face. He heard a pop as the jaw disconnected and allowed himself a half-second of pleasure before continuing his assault. He pushed his way out and onto the balcony, throwing an endless barrage of blows. The first ones connected, shattering bone and cartilage. Afterward, his fists met with hands desperate to defend against the deadly onslaught.

Dean heard the prick scream, and he swung low at his ribcage. Something inside snapped, and the scream became a howl. Then, Dean brought his knee up and connected with the man's groin.

"How do you like it, huh?" he screamed, and he scooped him up and threw him off the balcony. A final, horrified wail filled the night sky as the body tumbled down and smashed onto the grass below.

Dean gripped the railing, huffing for breath. He leaned forward and looked down at Elijah's broken body spread out below, an arm and a leg at awkward angles.

But it wasn't Elijah. It was Nathan. Nathan Riley. His face was a bloody, distorted mess, but there was no mistaking it. His head lilted on his neck to one side and lay with the right side of what remained of his face to the sky. He struggled to suck in painful gasps of air through torn, bloody lips.

And just ten or so yards away, a police car had parked, red and blue lights blazing. The door had opened, and an officer had stepped out. He demanded that Dean did not move.

Dean's balls still hurt. A lot. Like they'd scurried up into his abdomen and burrowed their way underneath his kidneys. But that didn't seem too important.

Not anymore.

CHAPTER 24

Marcus was dozing in his chair—hadn't even changed from his work clothes, in fact—when the police banged on his door. The sudden thunder blast jolted him from sleep like a rocket, and liquid electricity coursed throughout his body.

"*Police! Open up!*"

Marcus jumped up and hurried to the door. He tore it open fast, terrified they might kick the thing down if he wasn't quick enough.

"Evening, Marcus," Chief Foster greeted. He was flanked by two grim-looking officers. "Mind if we come in?"

"Mind if I ask why, first?" Marcus countered.

"We're looking for this Elijah," Foster answered. "And that's all we care to say right now."

"He's not here," Marcus said.

"All the same, we'd like to look for ourselves," one of the officers stated, cool as ice.

"Uh-huh." Marcus sighed. "I guess I can't stop you, but I'd appreciate it if you didn't tear the place up?"

"That's at our discretion," the same officer said and pushed his way inside, followed close behind by the other.

"No, it isn't," Foster snapped at them. "It's my discretion. Search the place, but leave it intact. We clear?" The two men grumbled and trudged through the hallway.

"You see, Marcus? We're not the bad guys," Foster said, trying at a little smile. And failing. "But, now, one man's been hospitalized and another's in jail. And it all stems from this man, Elijah, showing up in town."

"Hospitalized?" Marcus' eyes widened. "What happened? Come on, Greg."

The police chief sighed. "We just arrested Dean Smith about an hour ago. He nearly killed Nathan Riley—beat the man senseless and tossed him off a balcony. But he swears this Elijah broke into his home and attacked him, and then he mistook Nathan for Elijah and, well, I think you get it."

Marcus stared at him. "Holy crap."

The officers returned from the back rooms. "Nothing," one of them called.

Greg Foster nodded and gestured for them to head back out. He looked back at Marcus one more time. "I'm begging you, Marcus, if you know *anything*, tell me now."

Marcus sighed. Shook his head. "I can't help you. Whatever Elijah might be up to, I'm not in on it."

Greg nodded, disappointed. "Okay. Well, don't go spreading this around. It doesn't reflect well."

He turned and stepped out into the hall. He paused and looked at one of the officers, an unspoken order passing between them, and moved on. The officer, a tall man with a broad chest (*He must work out*, Marcus thought), stepped inside and closed the door.

Marcus would've asked what this was all about, but he didn't get that far. With all the movement and precision of a martial arts master, the man's hand withdrew his nightstick and swung it hard into Marcus' belly. Pain racked his body, and all the air was driven from his lungs in a single instant. He fell to his knees, trying to gasp for air. His lungs burned, and his eyes watered.

"We know full well you know more than you're telling us," the officer said. "Trouble is, we don't know how much. And, with the chief wanting this kept quiet, we can't exactly take you in."

He placed his foot against the side of Marcus' head and pushed him onto his side. Marcus continued trying to gasp for air, but his chest refused to budge. Tears streamed down his cheeks, and his head felt like it would explode.

"Just think of this as us letting you off with a warning," he said. "Next time, you may not be so lucky."

Marcus finally managed a cough and a gasp. He curled into a fetal position and clutched his burning chest. He could feel the temperature of his face rising and was certain he had the complexion of a ripe tomato.

The officer, Marcus never did see his name badge, opened the door and left.

Lori didn't hear the police in time. She'd barely rolled out of bed when they kicked the door open and marched inside. She screamed and yanked the sheet from her bed to wrap round herself. (Her sleepwear for the night consisted only of white, cotton panties and a matching tank top.)

One officer (Cpl. Blythe, though Lori didn't know it) strolled in, followed by Joshua. "*Lori?*" he bellowed.

Josh? Oh Christ. "What?" she yelled, still in the bedroom.

Blythe continued searching the living room while Joshua made his way down the hall. He stopped in the doorway, and already Lori could tell he was furious.

"Where is he?" Joshua demanded, his voice hard.

"Who?"

"*Don't play games with me!*" He spoke through clenched teeth. A small speckle of saliva shot from between them. It arced and fell just in front of his feet.

"I don't know," Lori told him, shaking her head. She could feel herself starting to tremble, and she hated herself for it.

Joshua stared at her, silent. His eyes were wild again, just as they'd been the night he slapped her.

"Living room and kitchen are clear," Blythe hollered and headed to the bedroom. Joshua stepped aside to let him pass. He and Lori stared at each other in silence as the officer searched the room, checking beneath the bed and in the closet before declaring it empty.

He paused a moment on his way back into the hallway to look Lori over. What looked like a wry grin was playing at his lips, but he held it in check. He looked to Joshua, said, "I'll be outside."

Joshua nodded, his eyes still locked on Lori. Blythe moved past him and headed for the door. He waited until the front door closed before speaking again. "Nathan's in the hospital, Lori."

Lori said nothing. Tried to stop trembling. Failed.

"Dean's in jail for assault," Josh continued. He waited for an answer, but Lori couldn't find her voice to give him one. "Is this what you wanted?"

Still, Lori refused to speak. She couldn't. Much as she hated herself for giving Joshua the satisfaction, she was scared of him right now. Scared to death.

Joshua stepped into the room with all the aura of a predator. He slid his hand across the bed as he moved past it, clutched the blanket in his fingers a moment and lifted a foot or so, then dropped it on the floor. He stopped in front of Lori and stared into her eyes.

Lori only stared back. She gripped the sheet around her hard. No doubt her knuckles were white as paper. Her breaths came in little, ragged gasps.

For a moment, Joshua did nothing. Only stared. Clearly furious.

Lori finally managed to muster up her voice.

"Jo—"

His left hand shot out, seized her bed sheet, and yanked it away. Lori stifled a scream and balled her hands into fists at her sides. The sheet sailed across the room and drifted to the floor like a cloud, and Lori stood exposed to Joshua for the first time since their engagement.

He moved forward again, forcing her back until she met the wall. He slammed his hand onto the wall beside her head, and she stifled another scream. She turned away from him, eyes shut, tears threatening to creep into her eyes.

Joshua's breath came through his nostrils like two hollow wind tunnels. He stared at her, and when Lori finally looked back at him, she saw up close the wild rage behind them.

"This is how people are talking about you," he hissed, and his breath was hot against her cheeks. "Like you're some kind of whore. Have you been sleeping with him?"

Lori opened her mouth to speak, but her throat seemed to close up. She shook her head desperately.

"*Don't lie to me!*" Joshua yelled, baring his teeth. "He spent two nights here, just the two of you. Do you think I'm an idiot? You think I didn't notice how you looked at him the night he showed up?"

Lori shook her head again, but she was pretty sure it wouldn't matter.

Joshua looked down at her, as if taking advantage of this opportunity to see the treasure he could no longer possess. He stared a long time at her bare legs.

A voice in Lori's head screamed at her. *Hit him! Hit the bastard! Right now! Just bring your knee up and nail him right in his balls!*

But her legs didn't move. Couldn't move. Dear God, what would happen after she did that? What would he do?

At last, Joshua looked up again. His expression, though still half-crazed, was softer. "You know, I still think you're beautiful," he whispered.

Lori, again, said nothing. Only stared back at him. Whatever adrenaline surge she might've felt moments ago was now replaced by cold, paralyzing fear.

"The most beautiful girl I've ever known." He brought his other hand up and tried to touch her hair. He also leaned in closer, his lips drawing close to hers. But when Lori shied away, he sighed, dropped his hand to his side, and leaned back. He looked down again, no doubt taking another longing glance at her legs.

After several more agonizing moments, he backed away, turned, and headed for the door. He stopped just after entering the hallway. He looked back and said, "I'd love for you to come back to me, you know? And we could put all of this behind us."

Then, he walked away. Lori didn't dare move. She stayed right where she was against the wall as Joshua's footsteps thumped their way down the hall. The door opened, closed, and then there was silence.

Lori sank to the floor. She wrapped her arms around her legs and buried her face in her knees. This time, she didn't stop the tears from coming.

CHAPTER 25

Elijah's limbs felt like lead when he woke the next day. His joints creaked and popped when he moved. The muscles in his legs protested any motion and threatened to cramp up. His abdomen was a ball of fire that exploded when he tried to sit up.

"*Uhhnnn!*"

With all the grace and agility of a ninety-year-old man, Elijah rolled onto his stomach and tried to push himself up. Pain bit at his arms and shoulders with acid-tipped fangs, but he clenched his teeth and pushed. He worked his knees forward and beneath his belly—also one beast of a painful chore—until at last he could sit back on his legs. The muscles in his thighs and buttocks protested, but it wasn't quite so bad as—well, everything else.

He remained that way for a long time, head down, eyes closed, breathing soft whispers to the damp, morning air. "You know, God," he sighed, "or whoever might be up there…it sure would've helped if I could use this healing thing on myself."

He placed both hands on the tree he'd slept beneath and pulled himself to his feet. He grunted in pain as his arms shouted painful cries into his brain, and when he was finally upright, he still had to lean most of his weight against the tree trunk for support. It felt like he could collapse at any moment.

God, a hot shower would be lovely right now. Anything to relieve this—this *hurt*.

Elijah pulled his shirt up to examine his belly where Dean had tackled him. An angry, purple bruise had already reared its ugly head just above his right hip. On the plus side, though, it wasn't as big as he'd feared it would be. He'd envisioned a gut that was entirely purple and black, just ready to cry out in pain at the slightest touch.

Of course, there was probably another bruise that was just as nasty on his back where he'd hit that TV set. Geez, but that had hurt.

Last night's plan had worked, but it had cost him. Dearly. In hindsight, he felt pretty lucky Dean had Nathan's cell phone number stored in his own. He'd been pretty sure the little fireball had stored all the other top deacons' numbers, but, until he'd seen it when he scrolled through the stored names, there'd still been that lingering doubt.

He'd sent a text message to Nathan that said "COME QUICK, I NEED YOU" while Dean was still making his way down the hallway.

Timing had been tricky. He'd gauged the distance between Dean and Nathan's homes at less than five miles apart a night or two before. He'd figured he wouldn't have to wait long, and he hadn't. He could see the lights of Nathan's car outside as he was shutting all the lights off and dialing 911—again with Dean's phone.

He'd run in the opposite direction without looking back. By then, his presence was no longer necessary. Things were going as they would, and Elijah could do nothing more than get in the way. He'd told dispatch there was a break-in and an assault at Dean Smith's apartment, returned Dean's phone to the table in his bedroom and ran for the woods.

He also couldn't stay anywhere near the area to see if his plan had worked. However things turned out, Dean was sure to tell police someone else had been in the apartment. And, of course, they'd search the surrounding area.

Elijah had to be far away. *Far* away.

He just hoped Marcus or Lori heard what happened and could fill him in on the outcome.

"*Aoww!*"

Christ, his body hurt. When he finally tried to walk, every step was a thunderbolt of agony. Every swing of his arms, no matter how slight, was like its own miniature torture rack.

He stretched his arms out to try and loosen them up a bit. Both of his elbows popped like shotgun blasts. It hurt like hell, but it helped. He stretched his legs in a similar manner (and his knees also popped in a similar manner...*POW! POW!*).

He'd have to wait until sunset to see Lori or Marcus. Daytime was always too risky to return to town. Then again, nighttime wouldn't exactly be easy now, but he needed to know what happened after he fled Dean's apartment. It was vital to the next step.

Alone in his office, Joshua prayed. He knelt on the floor and rested his arms on the coffee table. He buried his face in his hands and beseeched the Lord God Almighty.

"This man—*this one man, Jesus!*—threatens all that we have worked for in Antioch," he said aloud. "In only a few weeks' time, he's shaken this church to its very foundations."

Nathan was still in intensive care. His wife was hysterical, and Joshua couldn't really blame her. He'd tried telling her that Antioch's strange visitor was to blame, but she just kept railing. Against Dean. Against him. Against the other deacons. She got so bad the doctors had to sedate her.

Dean's father had bailed his son out of prison just moments before. Dean only spent one night in jail, but that was enough. There would be rumblings amongst the congregation. Oh, yes, indeed, there would be rumblings.

Did you hear? One of the deacons was arrested last night.

No! Are you serious?

Oh, yes! Police took him just before midnight. And it was because he attacked another deacon!

No!

Yes! Poor man's still in the hospital in intensive care. Some doctors wonder if he'll even make it!

And it was all Elijah's doing. All of it. Joshua was certain. He'd sat with Dean in his cell for nearly an hour as he recounted everything that happened. The man's face was bruised and cut. His lip had swollen, and dried blood was creeping from the corner of his mouth.

"I swear to you, Pastor," he'd said, "I *never* meant to hurt Nathan."

Dean's eyes were swimming when he spoke. He'd clutched at the prison bars, squeezing them hard enough his knuckles were growing white.

Joshua had touched those hands and tried to be soothing. "I believe you, Dean."

Unfortunately for Dean, Nathan had still yet to regain consciousness, and so couldn't give his account to Joshua or police, which left them with nothing but Dean's account of the night.

When doctors came back with Nathan's injuries, it was like a grocery list:
- 3 cracked ribs
- 1 broken nose
- 4 skull fractures
- 1 dislocated shoulder
- 1 sprained wrist
- 1 broken leg

Until Nathan could awaken and say otherwise, the charges against Dean had to remain. His first court date was already scheduled in two weeks. And it was all public record. Right there for all the world to see. With it being such a violent, high-interest incident, the local newspaper had plastered it across the front page right away, along with area radio stations recounting the entire thing. To say nothing of the local television news media.

It was a nightmare. A bona fide nightmare.

Joshua was certain he'd have to make Dean step down from his position, something he'd never done since becoming pastor in Antioch. Not once. And it would be the biggest black eye the church had ever suffered, the biggest *he'd* ever suffered.

"I have to stop this man, Jesus," Joshua prayed. "I must, before he undermines this entire ministry. Grant me the strength, Lord. Grant me the wisdom I need. Please, Lord. *Please.*"

Nothing. No answer.

Joshua raised a clenched fist and pounded it against the chair. *"Please, Lord!"* he screamed.

Still nothing.

Tears trickled through his closed eyelids, and he sniffled. "Please," he whispered, his voice a gentle sigh. "Please."

And then, the answer came. Clear as crystal. It was so simple. So obvious. In fact, it should've been obvious from the start.

Which, Joshua supposed, was probably how every other disciple felt when Jesus offered His divine direction.

CHAPTER 26

That night, Marcus ventured to Lori's apartment. She'd asked him to while they were at work. And, truth be told, he was grateful to her. Neither of them wanted to be alone that night. They were scared.

Hell, they were terrified.

They sat together in silence on Lori's futon. She flipped through the channels; he only sat. Nothing caught their interest. Nothing sparked any conversation.

Just silence. Like a thick, invisible fog permeating the room. Filling every nook and cranny and pore.

And then it broke with a knock on the door. Both of them jumped, shot glances at one another, then looked to the door. "Who is it?" Lori called.

"Me." Elijah.

Lori hurried to the door (*Click! Click! Jingle!*) and let him in. He limped into the room quickly and let her shut the door behind him. He staggered across the room and collapsed on the recliner while Lori redid the locks.

He sighed, and both Lori and Marcus heard the pain behind it. "You guys okay?" he sighed.

"No," Lori said. She turned to face him. "We're pretty far from okay."

Elijah raised an eyebrow, looked to Marcus.

"The police paid us a visit after your little stunt with Dean and Nathan," Marcus said. "I got a whack in the gut, and Lori had the hell scared out of her by the good Reverend."

Elijah leaned forward. He winced, then groaned/asked, "What happened?"

"Dean's in jail, if you haven't heard," Lori said (she'd yet to hear of his recent bailout). "And Nathan's in the hospital. Turns out Dean beat the crap out of him, and police took him in on assault charges."

"I guess that was your plan?" Marcus ventured.

Elijah nodded, but said nothing.

"And was Joshua cornering Lori in her bedroom afterward also part of the plan?"

Elijah looked to Marcus, his expression unreadable. Then, he uttered a little sigh and looked to Lori. He forced himself back to his feet, which she could see was hard on him, and went to her. She looked away as he came near.

"What happened?" he asked.

Lori took a moment to respond. When she did, she still didn't look at him. "Joshua stormed in my apartment while I was still in bed. Demanded to know where you were. He…" She trailed off, a knot growing in her throat.

"And some ape in a uniform clubbed me in the stomach with his nightstick," Marcus added. "Said it was a warning. They want us to tell them where you are."

Marcus pulled his shirt up, revealing a hideous bruise beneath. It was smaller than Elijah's, but it was a hell of a lot darker.

Elijah looked back to Lori, but she could say no more. She kept her face away from him as she struggled to maintain her composure. He stared at her, and tears began stinging his own eyes.

166

"Joshua barged into her bedroom before she could get dressed," Marcus told him. "Backed her against the wall and screamed at her. Probably came close to raping her." He sighed, then added: "Called her a whore."

Lori still wouldn't look at Elijah. Not even when he said, "It's not true."

Marcus was silent, then. They all were. Thick silence once more dominated the room.

Lori broke it. "Yes, it is."

"What? No, it's not," Elijah insisted.

"It is so." Lori looked back at him. Her eyes were red and swollen. "Don't you remember? I humped his brains out. Humped his brains out, and I *liked* it!"

"Lori—" Marcus tried, but she cut him off.

"*Shut up! I'm a whore and a murderer! I killed my baby! Remember? Never gave it a chance! Never even found out if it was a boy or a girl! Just let them yank it out of me and destroy it!*"

Tears streamed from Lori's eyes, and she went wild. She balled up her fists and pounded at Elijah's chest. He didn't stop her, just withstood the onslaught and let her drive him back. He grunted only once at the first strike, but he kept quiet from then on.

Marcus jumped to his feet and rushed over to her. Elijah tried to signal with his eyes to stay back, but Marcus didn't see. He wrapped his arms around her waist and yanked her into the air and staggered back. She screamed and flailed her arms like a raving cat, and they both tumbled to the floor with a bang.

Lori curled into a fetal position and wept. Marcus caressed her shoulder and cooed, "It's okay, Lori. It's okay."

Elijah knelt beside them and brushed a few strands of hair from her face. Reluctantly, she looked up at him. She sniffled.

"You're not a whore, Lori," he said. "And you're not a murderer."

She looked back at the floor. Elijah hesitated, afraid to venture further. Then, he said, "I'm hardly a saint, myself."

She brought her head up to face him again. So did Marcus.

"I very nearly killed someone not too long ago," Elijah went on. "And I can't claim it was because some lover or preacher convinced me it was the right thing to do. I did it because I was angry. Because—I hated him."

Lori and Marcus stared up at him a moment. Then, they both managed to pull themselves up, sitting cross-legged on the floor. Lori dragged her arm across her nose and snorted. "Tell me," she croaked. "Please?"

Elijah smiled. "You want some Kleenex first?"

"No. Tell me. Tell me who you are. What you are. And…and I'll deal with whatever's ahead. Whatever it is, I don't care."

"I can't ask you to do that."

"Yes, you can," Marcus cut in. "We've already asked just as much. Geez, we've asked *more* from you. Yeah, what happened to us last night sucked, but it's because someone finally made Joshua squirm."

Elijah looked from him to Lori. She nodded.

"But look at you two," Elijah said. "You can't continue like this?"

"Yes we can," Marcus shot back. "Hell yes, we can. We've lived under Joshua's thumb for years. And now, even though it's hard, it looks like we might have a way out."

"We'll do whatever you need," Lori agreed. "Anything. But first—please—tell us what happened to you?"

Elijah sighed. Smiled. "All right. All right…"

CHAPTER 27

Jeremiah Lockhart was a true man of God, a man-mountain with haunches and forearms like a bear and a barrel chest carved out of stone. He maintained a thick, brown beard over his face, which often turned beet red whenever he preached.

And he preached a lot.

Jeremiah was a fire-breathing, holy-rolling, tongue-talking, born-again believer of the liberating power of Jesus' name. He was a conservative man of conservative means with conservative values. And proud of it. Bless God.

For Jeremiah, God was the great Judge and Ruler. The Almighty made mankind, and mankind only continued to exist because it was still the Almighty's will. He firmly believed the Almighty spoke to His people. He believed it as surely as he believed the grass was green. You just had to be willing to stop and listen. Just listen, and He'd speak.

And the Lord *had* spoken to him. Of that, Jeremiah had no doubt. God spoke to him one evening as he knelt in prayer beside his bed. Whispered in that still, small voice. Just as clear as day.

Jeremiah would have a son.

And not just any son, either. Oh, no. No, sir. This son was destined for great things. *Great* things. Jeremiah's son—his firstborn son—would be a great prophet for the modern era. In a time when man had long since turned his proverbial back on his Creator, God would raise Jeremiah's son up as His chosen vessel, to reach out to the lost and condemn the sin and abominations running rampant in today's societies.

Jeremiah had very nearly cried when he heard those words. *My son*, he'd thought. *My son! My firstborn!*

But there was a slight problem. Jeremiah Lockhart was a single man. And he had been for most of his life.

But that didn't matter. No. God's word was true. And God had promised.

So, that meant Jeremiah would have to take a wife.

Truth be told, until that time, Jeremiah hadn't looked very hard for a mate. He was just never comfortable with close, personal relationships. As a traveling preacher—and a Southern spitfire traveling preacher at that, thank you very much—he kept pretty busy. He didn't tend to stay in one place for very long. He'd visit various towns and communities, preach at whatever churches would have him, then move on.

It was a Spartan existence, yes, but Jeremiah was happy with it. God always provided, after all. Always.

But having a son—and a wife—meant setting down roots. He couldn't demand that they accompany him on his continual treks across the countryside from one church to the next. He needed a permanent home.

So, after much prayer, Jeremiah settled on a tiny hamlet right smack dab in the middle of Missouri. It was a quaint little village that looked like a Norman Rockwell painting, dotted with a handful of high, white church steeples, and a single downtown road lined with local drug stores, antique shops, and the like.

Greenburg. It was named for its founder, Arthur Green, who'd set his plow to the ground there, along with a handful of other farmers, in the year of our Lord, 1820.

Jeremiah rented a room above an elderly couple's garage and found a humble job as a mechanic's assistant. He joined Hope Tabernacle, this time strictly as a member, and kept an eye out for the woman who would bear his son. His prophet.

His promise.

God's promise.

It took a few months, but Jeremiah at last met a sweet country girl named Susan Friedman. She was a plump, but cute, little blonde with a bright smile and glowing eyes. She and Jeremiah had a whirlwind courtship that lasted all of four months before they walked down that rosy aisle.

As a couple of meager finances—Susan helped at the local library—they couldn't afford a fancy honeymoon. No, they celebrated the occasion with little more than a proper church ceremony and a long weekend together.

It took almost a year for Susan to finally get pregnant. By then, Jeremiah was already working full-time, and Susan had recently been promoted to Assistant Librarian.

But this was all God's will. All part of His plan. Both Susan and Jeremiah had steady incomes and a roof over their heads. It was as good a home for God's chosen as any.

When Susan suggested an ultrasound, Jeremiah said there was no need. It was a boy. He knew. He wouldn't tell her how he knew, just told her to trust him.

He'd been promised.

And then, before you knew it, it was time to give birth. Jeremiah rushed Susan to the hospital, and they spent ten agonizing hours in labor—Susan screaming and pushing for all she was worth and Jeremiah holding her hand and offering support as best he could. Susan, exhausted, leaned her head against Jeremiah's chest in between contractions, panting. He clutched her hand with his own and brushed her hair with his free one.

"You're doing wonderful," he whispered to her. "Just wonderful. Not long now."

"Thank you," she whimpered. The pain was obvious in her voice. Tears trickled from her eyes, and sweat covered her face.

Then, just after sunset, the doctors showed Jeremiah his firstborn. "Congratulations, Mr. Lockhart," the head doctor said. "It's a girl!"

Jeremiah froze. The bright smile on his face quickly faded. In an instant, all the air had left the room. He couldn't breathe. Couldn't move.

No! No! This wasn't right! This wasn't what he'd been promised. God spoke to him clearly. So very clearly. His firstborn would be a son, a son who would rise up and take his place as God's chosen prophet for today's society.

It was God's word! And God's word was true! God's word was law!

Jeremiah refused to touch the child. He leaned back when the doctor offered it to him. His bottom lip trembling, he glanced down at his wife with her pale, glistening, and exhausted face. Not comprehending, she smiled and asked, "What's wrong?"

What was wrong? *Everything* was wrong! *Everything!* But he couldn't tell her that! Couldn't!

Jeremiah pried his hand out of Susan's grasp and staggered out of the room. She called after him, but he ignored her. He stumbled through the halls, pushing aside bewildered nurses.

When his legs stopped feeling like jelly, he ran. He ran as hard as he could. As fast as he could.

He burst through the exit and charged into the night. Jumped into his truck—purchased just two months after marrying Susan—and drove. Tears stung at his eyes, but he wouldn't let them out.

He left Greenburg behind, and he never went back

Jeremiah continued on from Greenburg until he finally had to stop and rest.

He pulled into a seedy hotel and managed to get a few hours of sleep. The next morning, he hopped back in his truck and drove onward, making his way south.

How could this happen? This couldn't be God's plan. God promised that Jeremiah's firstborn—his firstborn SON—would preach to the masses.

But then, he knew. Just *knew.* He'd taken the wrong wife. That was it. It had to be. Much like when Abraham had lacked in faith and lay with Hagar, his maidservant. That hadn't been God's will. Abraham and Sarah convinced themselves it was, but they were wrong. Susan wasn't meant to bear God's chosen prophet. It was someone else. It *had* to be.

Jeremiah eventually settled in a town called Carlton, a humble community somewhere in the northern portion of

Arkansas. He never did find out where that name came from, because he didn't stay long enough.

This time, rather than waste his time underneath cars, Jeremiah stuck with what he knew—preaching. He visited various churches each week, always offering his services as a traveling preacher, and he made a decent living doing so.

He met Abigail Beaumont within a month. Abigail was a sweet, if rather plain-looking, woman. She had shoulder-length brown hair and a friendly smile.

Jeremiah, now going by the name Frederick Smith, convinced Abigail to marry him in just two months' time. Also, unlike Susan, Abigail became pregnant just another month later.

Abigail insisted on an ultrasound, and Jeremiah (or Frederick) was eager to oblige this time. The results came back almost ninety-five percent conclusive: a girl.

When they left the doctor's office, Jeremiah's legs once again felt like jelly. He drove Abigail home without saying a word. Abigail tried teasing him, saying he'd have his little boy to play ball with soon enough, but he still said nothing.

He floated into the house, a cozy little cottage on the outskirts of town, in silence, followed close behind by his increasingly nervous wife. He told himself this was wrong. *Had* to be wrong. He'd been promised. *Promised.*

Perhaps the ultrasound was wrong? Yes, that was possible, wasn't it? It wasn't one hundred percent certain?

But ninety-five? That was almost conclusive. There was no way it could be wrong, save some error in the equipment, and the nurses were pretty sure it was in perfect working order.

No, it was a girl. *A girl!*

Both wives had failed him. Failed to give him the son God said he would provide. And now, his wife was making light of the whole thing. Like nothing could be wrong. Like all the world was wonderful and she hadn't failed to deliver what God had meant for him.

There was a framed wedding picture on their wall in the living room. It pictured Jeremiah and Abigail hand-in-hand, smiling for all the world like the happy couple they were.

Jeremiah took it down and stared at it a long time. Abigail stood close behind, still asking if he was okay. It was maddening. She just chirped on and on like a cursed chickadee. Just kept on and on and on. Over and over. She'd failed him, and she was too wrapped up in herself to even *comprehend* what had happened.

Honey? What's wrong? Talk to me. Please? Sweetie?

And then he was screaming. Eyes shut, mouth wide, he bellowed his rage at the picture in his hands. And before his wife could react with more than a petite jump, Jeremiah was swinging round with the picture in his hand. It made a wide arc and struck the left side of her head with a loud crack.

The glass spider-webbed but didn't shatter, and Abigail crumpled to the floor and wailed like a wounded seal. Like she wasn't to blame for this at all. Too slow and stupid to understand she brought this all on herself.

Her! Her fault! Her failure! Her shortcoming!

And then the picture with the fresh cracks was swinging down upon her. Again and again. It cracked on the second blow. Shattered and fell apart on the third.

Abigail wailed and cried and pleaded, but Jeremiah would have none of it. He struck her in the face until it was

a bruised and bloody mess. Then, he took the largest glass shard he could find and, in one ugly swipe, slit her throat. She coughed and sputtered. Gurgled. Managed a choked whisper: *"Why?"*
And was still.
Jeremiah stood. His feet straddled Abigail's body. Apart from his heavy breathing, the room was silent. Dead silent. Abigail lay still, empty eyes staring at nothing.

Jeremiah glared down at his dead wife for several moments, then went to the bathroom. He showered while she continued bleeding out on the living room floor. Afterward, he put on clean clothes, walked outside to his truck, and drove.

He drove east for the rest of the night. He didn't stop until daybreak. Then, he rested—leaning back and closing his eyes to catch what sleep he could inside his truck—and drove further.

At last, he entered the great state of West Virginia. It was there that Jeremiah—now under the assumed name of Phil Jackson—met the woman who would be Elijah's mother: Linda Williams.

Linda was a beautiful woman—dark hair, blue eyes, and athletic. She was also a sucker for hard cases, and Jeremiah/Phil was as hard a case as she'd met.

When Elijah's father (and Linda's would-be husband) first visited Linda's church, a country chapel called Fellowship Ministries, she noticed him right away.

It was the first place he'd stopped, and he didn't even have a place to stay.

Linda offered to buy his lunch that afternoon and help him find an apartment in a small town nearby called Faulkland. Jeremiah/Phil used up the last of his spare cash on the deposit and set to work once again seeking churches to spread the gospel.

Linda was impulsive, and she agreed to elope within just a few weeks of Jeremiah/Phil's arrival. So, they were married. He continued preaching at whatever churches would have him, and she continued working as a waitress at a local diner called Fred's.

Linda took longer to get pregnant than Abigail had—almost five months—but it was worth the wait this time. She gave him a son.

At long last, God's promise was fulfilled. Jeremiah had his son. His prophet. His promise.

God's chosen.

He'd prepared for this moment for years, and when Linda asked what to name their baby, Jeremiah/Phil didn't hesitate. "His name is Elijah."

And this time, he didn't stop the tears from sliding down his cheeks.

CHAPTER 28

As soon as Elijah could talk, Jeremiah set to work preparing him for the great work God had planned. He read Bible stories to Elijah every night before bed. He taught him to pray before every meal.

God is great. God is good. Let us thank Him for our food. Amen. It was as good a start as any for a child.

When Jeremiah believed Elijah could truly comprehend, he set to work explaining what great things were in store, what God had promised.

Linda hadn't been privy to God's promises, and her husband had never mentioned them until now. Jeremiah's continued talks with their son about great things ahead as promised by the good Lord above made her—well, they made her nervous. One night she told him so.

Jeremiah assured her it was fine. He then told her just what God had promised, a son that would be raised up as a great prophet, destined to lead mankind back to its Creator, a light in this ever-darkening world.

Unfortunately, his words did little to sway Linda's fears. In fact, they only made things worse. Her husband was talking like a crazy man. God had *spoken* to him? Personally? And specifically told him he'd have a son? Who'd grow up to be a great prophet?

She tolerated it for a while longer, but by the time Elijah was five, Linda had had enough. She was afraid—genuinely afraid—of her husband now. He was adamant about their son's supposed divine destiny, and any suggestion to the contrary would send him into silent, brooding fury.

Linda was terrified what her husband would do to their son if he didn't grow into the great prophet his father expected.

One Wednesday evening, while Jeremiah (Linda still only knew him as Phil) was preaching at a revival, Linda had packed several sets of clothes for both her and Elijah. She meant to go to her mother's and set to work on filing for a divorce.

Meant to, but didn't succeed.

Jeremiah returned home early. Why in the world he was early, Linda would never know. Revivals *always* lasted until late at night. *Always.* After a round of songs, an offering, a Jeremiah (Phil)-exclusive sermon, and an altar call, it was usually almost eleven o'clock.

But due to astronomically bad luck, he came home a good hour sooner than expected, roughly 9:45 p.m. And when he saw Linda packing up, he knew just what was happening.

He flew into a rage.

He muscled Elijah—who was nearing five years old at this point—back into his bedroom and ordered him to stay put. Elijah stood in the center of the room, watching with uncomprehending eyes as his father slammed the door and marched back into his own bedroom where Linda, trying her best to look defiant, waited for him.

He dumped her clothes from the suitcase and threw it at her as hard as he could. It struck her in the chest and knocked her into the wall.

From his room, Elijah heard the loud impacts, heard his mother cry out, then moan in a pain-filled voice he'd never heard before. He heard his father screaming. And he felt the walls tremble ever so slightly as his father's fist connected with his mother's face, which knocked her head into the wall. Over and over.

Bamm!
Bamm!
Bamm!

After a while, his mother's screams stopped. But the walls continued shaking.

Bamm!
Bamm!

For several minutes, the walls trembled. Hanging pictures rattled. Until at last, there was silence.

It lasted for several minutes. Nothing but empty silence.

Then, Jeremiah opened the door and ordered Elijah to pack his things; they were leaving.

"Is Mom coming?"

Jeremiah took a few deep breaths, his red face softening. "No. She's staying here."

"Are we coming back for her later?"

His father shook his head. "No, boy. Get your things."

"But—"

"*Get your things!*" His face flared dark red again, and he bared his teeth.

Elijah jumped, and tears threatened his eyes, but he fought them back. He was a big boy now. Big boys didn't cry. Nuh-uh. No, they didn't. He got to work gathering his things and followed his father into the hall.

He tried to go to the bedroom, but Jeremiah blocked the way.

"But I wanna' say bye?"

"No, son. Just go now. Do as I say."

And he did. They climbed into the new Ford truck Jeremiah had purchased just a few months ago and drove out of town.

They drove for days. Elijah never asked where they were going, and his father never told him. He just drove, stopping only for gas, food, or rest for the night.

Somewhere in Indiana, Jeremiah revealed his real name to Elijah and reminded him that God had promised him a son that would be a great prophet. He even admitted to two mistakes he'd made—*his* mistakes, not God's—along the way with the wrong women before meeting Linda, his mother. But his mother had lost faith and didn't believe in God's promise.

"But we do. Both of us. Don't we, boy?"

"Uh-huh."

They settled down in a quiet burg called Linden, located right in the middle of the flat farmlands of Illinois. They had to have new names here, Jeremiah had told him. They couldn't tell people their real names; they had to pretend. Jeremiah was Robert Ackers, now. Elijah had to be David Ackers.

Linden, Illinois, was their home for the next thirteen years. Elijah—or David, as his classmates knew him—attended the local schools and made the usual childhood friends. After class, as per his father's orders, he studied the Bible over and over, one book each night. He'd have to know it front-to-back if he ever hoped to be the prophet God intended.

After graduation, Jeremiah sent Elijah to a Bible college in Missouri to continue his theology education, but something happened there that Jeremiah hadn't counted on. Elijah, for the first time, experienced *freedom*.

He didn't have to study the Bible every night now because his father was a whole state away. None of the professors kept any strict watch over him. Sure, he kept his grades up and studied what he needed, but he also relaxed his workload quite a bit.

Elijah, still going by the name of David, experienced his first party, his first beer, his first marijuana joint (even Bible colleges weren't safe from that), and his first kiss…with a young woman named Emily Saunders.

Sweet Emily.

Emily didn't attend the school. She lived in a nearby subdivision. She crossed paths with Elijah at one of the weekend parties. A friend of a friend had invited her, or something like that.

Emily lived at home with her parents. She attended a nearby community college and was seeking a business degree. She was a beautiful redhead, with long, flowing hair that reached midway down her back. Her features were sharp, but not too sharp. Her smile was to die for.

She also had a killer figure. She was slender, with long legs, hips that curved just right, and firm breasts. They were the first breasts Elijah ever laid his hands on, and he laid hands on them as much as he could get away with.

Emily spent several nights with Elijah in his dorm whenever her parents were away. It was an unorthodox adventure each time, sneaking her inside without school officials finding out. (This was a *Christian* school, after all. That sort of behavior wasn't permitted. Bless God.) Both of them were relative newcomers to sexuality. Emily was, perhaps, a little more seasoned, but not by much. She'd had a few boyfriends before, but nothing serious. Nothing close to a *physical* relationship, or whatever you called it.

Her last boyfriend had wanted one, though. Christ, had he ever! The horny little bastard had tried pinning her on a bed one night and pulling her clothes off with all the grace of an elephant having a seizure.

Emily had grabbed hold of the prick's balls—first time she ever laid hands on a pair of them—and squeezed as hard as she could. He'd screamed and thrashed and kicked and, finally, rolled off her. She'd pretty much dumped him after that, and he was the last guy she'd gone out with.

Elijah, on the other hand, hadn't so much as gone on a single date. The last thing he ever wanted to do was bring a girl home to meet Jeremiah. God, no.

But that wasn't a problem, anymore. Now, Elijah didn't have to worry about his father. He could bring Emily "home" as much as he wanted. So long as the dorm monitors weren't looking.

The two of them took their time walking the path of adulthood. They didn't jump in bed together the first night. They spent several evenings embracing, watching television, even just sleeping. In fact, Emily spent almost a dozen nights in Elijah's dorm room without even taking her socks off.

One evening, however, they were embracing yet again on his bed, and Elijah found himself brushing his finger across the waistline of Emily's panties, which was only just visible above her jeans. At first, he wasn't certain just what he was touching. Then he looked down, and a tiny gasp escaped his lips.

They were light blue, cotton. With tiny, lacy trim. They'd slid up her right hip about a fourth of an inch. Only four inches or so had escaped the confines of Emily's jeans. The rest dove back inside.

Elijah looked up at Emily, guilty as charged. But she only smiled and kissed him. She kept her lips against his and pulled him closer.

Elijah kept his fingertip on the line of her underwear and traced it around to her belly. His thumb crept beside his forefinger and unbuttoned her jeans, then ever-so-slowly tugged down the zipper.

Emily pulled away a moment, breathing heavily. She stared into Elijah's eyes, then leaned in and kissed him again.

Elijah pulled her jeans open and caressed his fingers across the soft fabric inside. He slid his hand in round her hip, then slid in the other.

He felt a soft tugging at his own jeans, and, before long, Emily was unzipping them and reaching inside. He pulled away for a moment to stare at her. This was it, the moment of no return.

In answer, Emily pulled away from him and stood up. She pulled off the sweater she wore, revealing a light blue tank top that matched her panties underneath. There was a tiny, pink heart stitched on the front. She set the sweater aside, then slid out of her jeans and returned to him.

Elijah started to remove his own shirt, but Emily did it for him. She slid it over his head and threw it aside.

Then, she pulled his jeans off, and—not quite gently— pushed him onto the bed.

They both lost their virginity to one another. Emily spent all of that night with him and most of the next morning. They spent almost a dozen hours in bed together, exploring the boundaries of their newfound sexual prowess or simply enjoying one another's embrace, lying together, sleeping, waking.

CHAPTER 29

 Elijah's unique talents manifested themselves over the Thanksgiving holiday. There was no great happening to signify the event. No angel came down and promised him the power to heal people. He wasn't exposed to gamma radiation or mutated spiders or bolts of lightning. Nothing like that. One day, he just...*had them*.
 His discovery of those powers however, was quite an event. It happened late at night when he was working at the convenience store across the street. He'd taken a job as a cashier to cover additional expenses like food and clothing. His father was footing the bill for school, but he was on his own for the rest, and he'd opted to stay for the holiday weekend to earn some extra spending money.
 He didn't tell his father about it, either, something he was doing more and more. He even gave the storeowner his real name to avoid any...problems.
 He was ringing up a middle-aged man's items when a lone gunman wearing a hoodie charged in, pointed a gun at his face, and screamed, *"Gimme' everything in the register! Now! Now!"*
 Elijah could only raise his hands and tremble. It wasn't quite the heroic image he would've liked. The middle-aged customer did the same.

The gunman pointed the gun at the window and fired. The noise blasted the room like an explosion. The glass didn't shatter, but there was a hole roughly an inch wide where the bullet struck. Cracks spider-webbed out from it. *"I said now! Open the register!"*

At last, Elijah's limbs started working, and he did as ordered. The register *cha-ching'ed* and popped open. He turned it to the gunman and let him scoop all the bills out and into a bag.

Two twenties spilled over the bag and drifted to the floor. For whatever reason, and Elijah could never figure out why, the middle-aged man stooped to pick them up. Did he expect to just hand them to the gunman? *Here ya go, son. I think you dropped this.* Or did he expect to keep them?

Whichever it was became a moot point when the gunman panicked and shot the man in the chest. Dead center. *Blamm!*

The man staggered back several steps, and a crimson stain exploded across the front of his shirt. He lurched once, then fell to the ground.

The gunman grabbed the two twenties and raced from the building.

Elijah pressed what his boss called "the panic button" to call the police, and he raced to the man's side. He pressed against the wound, hoping to stop the bleeding, but blood still gushed through his fingers. The man's face was already losing its color, and his skin seemed to get colder with each second.

"No!" Elijah ordered him. "Stay with me, man! Okay? Come on. Stay with me."

The man's eyes rolled in his direction, and he sighed out what Elijah knew was his last breath. His eyes started the slow, horrible transition from doorways to the soul to empty, hollow tunnels. Whatever consciousness, whatever intelligence was behind them—*whatever it was that was* him—was departing. Never to return. They rolled upward, slipping into unconsciousness.

He was dying. He was going to die in Elijah's arms, never to see his wife again, his children, his friends. He was destined for nothing more than a large box and six feet of dirt.

But then, everything changed. Elijah didn't know why, but he closed his eyes and lowered his head, as if to pray. What good it would've done, he didn't know, and he still didn't. He just *did it*. Maybe his actions were guided by some divine hand, and maybe they weren't, but that didn't much matter.

What mattered was what happened next. Elijah kept one hand over the man's wound. And then…he *did it*.

He never could explain how he *did it*. He just…*did.*

Elijah felt the wound close under his hand. The flesh came together, sealed itself closed. The bleeding stopped. The man grew warm again. Color returned to his face, and his eyes regained their focus. They were once more windows to his soul.

After several moments, the man blinked and looked up at him. His eyes were wide, amazed. "H—How—?" was all he could say.

Elijah, also at a loss for words, just shrugged. Then, he smiled and said, "Does it matter?"

The middle-aged man smiled back. "No. I guess not."

And he laughed. Tears brimmed in his eyes, but still he laughed. Elijah laughed with him. The most wonderful sound they'd ever heard.

Elijah convinced Middle-Aged Man to keep what happened between them, and they worked up a story about the gunman shooting himself in the foot (to explain all the blood on the floor). The police didn't buy it, but there were no security cameras. The owner operated the store practically on a shoestring budget. So they didn't have much choice.

Elijah decided he'd tell Emily when she came over that night. Her parents weren't out of town, but she could still visit for a few hours. Elijah's floor in the dormitory was deserted; everyone else was home for Thanksgiving. In fact, he even thought he'd reveal his real name.

When Emily did come, she wore a pair of light blue, cotton panties—a favorite of his, especially when she wore them with that matching blue tank top with the heart in the middle. Elijah could tell she was wearing them the moment she arrived; a sliver of the hem was just visible above the waistline of her jeans, and he recognized the tank top strap beneath her sweater.

Had she done that deliberately? Just to tease him?

Yeah, probably. And he *loved* it.

The two of them sat together on his bed and kissed while he traced his hands in slow arcs around the curves of her waist. Unable to wait, Elijah unzipped her jeans and slid them from her legs. He dropped them to the floor and traced the curves of her thighs with his fingertips—up, up, up, until at last they brushed across the soft fabric of Emily's underwear, cupping the smooth curves of her buttocks.

Emily, meanwhile, caressed Elijah's chest for several moments before creeping down toward his—

And *that's* when, like a righteous ball of fire, Jeremiah Lockhart kicked—yes, *kicked*—the door open and stormed inside. He wasted no words; he struck Emily with the back of his hand, sending her sprawling to the floor, and he seized Elijah by the throat. He squeezed—hard—and Elijah felt himself beginning to lose consciousness when Emily leapt at Jeremiah and caught hold of his arm. Her right eye was already starting to bruise. She screamed and clawed at him like an outraged tiger.

Jeremiah dropped Elijah and turned his attention to Emily. While Elijah coughed and wheezed, trying to get precious air back into his lungs, his father seized Emily by the throat and started pummeling her face with his fist. She cried out with each blow.

Bamm!
Bamm!

The walls shook. The windows rattled.

Elijah, his bearings regained at last, jumped onto his father's back and tried to snake his arm around the man's thick neck. But Jeremiah, his body seemingly saturated with adrenaline at this point, tossed Emily across the room like a broken doll and backed into the wall, effectively crushing his son. He turned and planted both arms on Elijah's shoulders.

"This isn't why I sent you here!" he snarled through giant, clenched teeth. "*You have a destiny!*"

He tossed Elijah with ease onto Emily. She yelped again when his weight crashed over her belly, fell forward and draped over his like a mother protecting her child.

Jeremiah marched over, yanked both of them to their feet, clamped their heads under his arms, and dragged them outside. His car—now, he drove a rusted old boat of an Oldsmobile—was parked near the dorm's rear entrance, and the trunk was open. Both Elijah and Emily struggled, but his father's grip was like iron. He tossed them in—first Elijah, then Emily—and slammed the lid shut.

Then, he drove home. Four hours. Without stopping.

CHAPTER 30

Jeremiah's violent appearance at school was the result of pure, youthful carelessness on Elijah's part. He'd decided against going home, and, in an act of what he'd later call "young, stupid arrogance," he'd decided not to tell his father. With no word from his only son, coupled with the recent police contact about a robbery his son had witnessed (again, with no word from his son), Jeremiah had traveled to the school to check on him.

He'd been terrified. Had Elijah been hurt? How would such a thing affect him? *Had the police learned his real name?*

Those fears were replaced by righteous fury when he arrived just in time to witness Emily sneaking into the dormitory.

The couple clung to one another in the cramped dark. She wept and buried her head in his shoulder. *"Why is he doing this?"* she sobbed. Her voice was cracked and hoarse. *"Why?"*

"He's angry with me," Elijah told her. "This is all my fault."

He revealed his real name to her. He revealed his past, his heritage. Everything. But it was too late. Too late for her to have the chance to avoid all this.

She said no more, only cried.

After a couple of hours, he told her he was sorry for getting her into all this. He should've warned her. Maybe even told her to stay away.

At this, Emily sniffled and, after a long moment, said, "I wouldn't have been able to stay away."

It was small comfort.

So they clung to one other, both holding tight before facing whatever awful future lay ahead. It was an old vehicle, a beat-up vehicle that was at least twenty years old. The backseats rattled but wouldn't budge, and there was no emergency release.

Jeremiah returned to Linden, Illinois, but he didn't go home. He drove into the county on an old, winding road. He continued into a patch of forest that was almost a dozen miles from any local residents' homes. Then, he turned off the paved road and followed a dirt path a few miles before shifting gears to park.

Inside the trunk, Emily gasped. *"We've stopped!"* she whispered. They both waited, shivering, for whatever would come next. They heard the door open and shut, heard Jeremiah's footsteps rounding the car.

The sun had almost set when Jeremiah threw the trunk open, but after four hours of total darkness, it was still enough to make both Elijah and Emily wince. Jeremiah moved fast, catching hold of Emily's arm and yanking her out. Elijah tried to come after her, but Jeremiah just shoved him back with ease and closed the trunk.

Elijah screamed and kicked at the trunk's lid. Outside, he could hear Emily screaming, her voice growing fainter and fainter as his father dragged her from the car. He kicked over and over, but the lid remained in place, and his legs were starting to ache. He gave another defiant cry, but no one heard it.

He was alone.

The minutes dragged by. *Tick*... ...*Tock.*

Elijah heard nothing outside. Nothing. No screams. No threats. Not even footsteps. Just...*nothing.*

What had Jeremiah done to her? Had he killed her? Just as Elijah suspected he'd killed his mother? Had he brought a butcher knife and sliced open her belly, so that her intestines spilled onto the ground? Or carved out her heart to show him later? His mind raced through dozens of morbid scenarios—beheading, dismemberment, or simply beating her to death, smashing her skull against a tree trunk?

All these images and more shot through his head like a grotesque horror show, but they were cut short when his father returned and threw the trunk open. He only heard one footstep before he was blinded once more by the outside light.

Elijah tried to lunge at him, but Jeremiah caught him by the throat and held him in place. "You've done this," Jeremiah said, his voice now eerily calm. "You and you alone."

He yanked Elijah from the trunk and let him spill onto the ground. He closed the trunk and turned to pick him up again, but Elijah charged and drove his shoulder as hard as he could into his father's gut.

Jeremiah grunted and staggered into the car. Then, he laughed. "Think you're big enough to take down the old man, huh?"

He shoved Elijah to the ground and stood over him. His smile was gone.

"But you forget," he said, "I have God on my side. And if God be with me, who can be against me?"

It was right at this moment that Elijah noticed his father's hands were bloody. The crimson stains on his fingers caught his eyes and held them. The blood crept up his fingers to his palms.

"Where is she?" Elijah demanded, unable to mask the terror in his voice.

Jeremiah pointed ahead. "Move."

Elijah staggered back to his feet, his legs wobbly. He stared back at his father a moment longer. "What have you done?"

"Move," Jeremiah repeated.

Elijah glared at him. The man was still almost twice his size. He couldn't take him down like this. He could crush him like an insect, and he probably *would* if he weren't convinced Elijah was part of some divine promise.

So, with no other options, Elijah did as he was told. He turned and stumbled through the brown and withered grass. Dead leaves, fallen from branches overhead long ago, crunched beneath his feet. There was still no sign of Emily. No sound.

"You were supposed to be chosen of God," Jeremiah said to him as they continued onward. "A vessel meant to carry God's word to the masses."

"God never promised *me* anything," Elijah spat at him.

"He didn't have to," Jeremiah answered, his voice casual. "He already promised *me*. Which *should've* been enough, since the Bible commands us to honor our parents."

"What about loving your wife?" Elijah asked, not looking back.

Jeremiah's fist smashed against his back like a sledgehammer, effectively knocking the wind out of him and sending him sprawling to the ground. He gasped for breath, his insides burning, as his father screamed.

"*Your mother was interfering with God's plan,*" he bellowed. "*No one has a right to do that. Not her. Not me. Not you.*"

He stood silent as Elijah gasped precious air back into his lungs and, despite the near-crippling pain, stood up again. He coughed a few times and glared at his father.

Jeremiah just pointed ahead again. "Move."

The sun had long since passed below the horizon. The sky, a beautiful cacophony of purple and red, was already darkening.

"Other side of that tree," Jeremiah said.

At that, Elijah quickened his pace. He hurried forward, probably would've run if his legs weren't still so sore from being crammed into the trunk. He shot round the tree and saw, at last, what his father had done to his girlfriend.

Emily's arms were spread wide, and her feet dangled about three feet from the ground. There were two spikes planted in both of her hands, and rope was fastened around both wrists, binding her arms to two tree branches that extended from a large trunk. Emily's shirt and underwear were stained with streaks of crimson that trickled from her hands, along the lengths of her arms, and down her body. Her hair was soaked with sweat and clung together in thick strands like slender tentacles over her face, which hung low. Her legs—once long, soft, and sexy—

glistened under a fresh coat of cold sweat, pale and sickly. Her head hung low, and her glistening hair covered her face.
    For a moment, Elijah couldn't move, couldn't breathe. But his stomach forced him to. With a sudden wrench that sent fresh bile up his throat like a torpedo, he hunched over and retched, and the contents of his stomach shot out and splattered on the ground into a steaming pile.
    He'd crucified her. *He'd nailed his girlfriend to a tree and crucified her!*
    Emily lifted her head and gasped. She made a terrible noise as she did so, a hideous wheezing sound that made Elijah think of death and coffins. For one crazy moment, he even imagined Bela Lugosi as Dracula, emerging from his crypt while rats and spiders scurried around his feet, a stark, black-and-white visage of mortality.
    To be dead—really dead—would be glorious.
    Emily looked at him for an agonizing moment, held his gaze as if trying to speak. Then she dropped her head low again.
    Elijah started to run toward her, but his father caught him by the arm. He whipped back round and punched the man in the gut. His fist thudded against his father's thick abdomen but had little effect. It only served to jam at least two of Elijah's fingers and send a sharp bolt of pain through his wrist and up his arm.
    But he kept punching anyway. *Thudd!*
    Thudd!
    Thudd!
    "*You bastard!*" he screamed. "*You bastard!*"

Jeremiah said nothing. He grasped Elijah's other arm and dragged him forward. Elijah cried out, wailing his pain and sorrow at the sky.

His father slapped a pair of handcuffs on his wrists. Where in the world Jeremiah Lockhart got his hands on a pair of handcuffs, Elijah would never know. Then, he used a padlock to attach them to a chain wrapped low around the base of a tree beside Emily and forced his son to his knees.

When Jeremiah stepped back, Elijah looked up at him with wide, tear-flooded eyes. "Let her go. Please. I'll do anything. *Anything*. I'll be the prophet you were promised. I'll preach to people every day. Just let her go."

"Oh, you'll do that, son," Jeremiah answered. "I've no doubt of it. But this has to happen. You've strayed from God's plan for you."

"No! God wouldn't want you to kill her!" Elijah struggled against the chains. He only managed to rattle them.

Jeremiah pointed a shaking, accusing finger at him. "You never spoke that way until you left for college, boy." He looked up at Emily. "Until you met *her*, I'd wager."

Emily gasped in another painful breath, pulling herself up with what strength remained in her arms in a feeble attempt to allow air into her lungs. "Please don't do this," she croaked. "My parents—"

"The wages of sin are death, child," Jeremiah told her. "Right now, you'd best make your peace with God. Ask His forgiveness for leading his chosen astray."

He turned his attention back to Elijah.

"I'll be back," he said. He glanced at Emily once, then back at Elijah. "After."

He turned and walked away, heading back to the car. Elijah screamed after him.

"*No! Stop! Come back! I promise I'll do what you want! I promise to preach and reach millions! I'll bring them all to God, Dad! All of them! Just let her go! Please! Pleeeaaaase!!*"

But it was useless. The course was set. There was no alternate route. Jeremiah continued on his way.

"*Bastard! What kind of a monster are you?*" Elijah planted his feet against the trunk of the tree and pushed as hard as he could, pushed until his arms felt like they'd rip from his sockets. The cuffs bit into his wrists, drawing blood. He screamed. "*Aauurrgghh! I'm going to kill you! You hear me? I'll kill you!*"

The sound of the car's engine was faint and distant. It was gone within just a few seconds.

CHAPTER 31

Darkness set in, and with it came the sounds of nocturnal creatures. Crickets. Birds. Toads. And other wild things neither Elijah nor Emily—who was growing less and less aware with each passing moment—could recognize. The moon glowed high overhead, but darkness covered the landscape.

Elijah struggled and fought against his bonds for hours. He planted his feet against the tree again and pushed. The cuffs bit further into his wrists until blood lined his hands in tiny, red strands. His back and shoulders burned. For one crazy moment, he was certain his hands would snap from his arms. *Pop!*

But he remained bound to the tree. He leaned back and screamed, an angry cry directed at the heavens.

Then, Emily whispered, "Elijah?"

Elijah was still huffing, but in between gasps he managed to say, "Yeah?"

"I love you."

A knot grew in Elijah's throat, and fresh tears brimmed in his eyes. He blinked, and they trickled down his cheeks. "I love you, too."

Emily pulled herself up and gasped for breath again, which brought more tears to Elijah's eyes. Her voice was a small, agonized whisper, and her breathing was no better.

In just a few short moments' time—far too short—Emily stopped speaking altogether. Either crucifixion somehow had ill effects on her larynx, or she just couldn't think of anything else to say. She just pulled herself upright with her arms to suck in another breath, which Elijah could tell was growing harder and harder. Each breath was a drawn out, high-pitched hiss that sounded less and less human.

"It's going to be okay, Emily." Elijah was also exhausted, and it showed in his voice. "You'll—you'll see." He sniffled, sighed. "You'll see. I promise. I'll—we'll—we'll find a way out of this. Someone'll come along. Some—something."

He sighed and leaned against the tree. The bark scraped against his cheek. Like gruff sandpaper. And rocks.

But nothing happened. No one came.

Night gave way to morning. Elijah's shoulders ached from remaining hunched over so long. Emily's attempts at breathing were more and more labored, and less often. By midday, she hardly moved at all.

"Emily?" Elijah called.

No answer.

"*Emily?*"

A soft moan slid through her lips. Her head drooped.

Elijah turned and leaned against his own tree. Exhaustion overtook him, and he slipped into an uncomfortable sleep.

When Elijah awoke, the sun was already starting its descent again. His stomach rumbled at him, caught in that horrible place between hunger and nausea. He looked up at Emily. Her head was still hanging forward, and her hair covered most of her face. The strands swayed ever so slightly because of a faint breeze.

She wasn't moving.

"Emily?"

She didn't answer. Didn't move.

"Emily?"

Still nothing. No moans. No wheezes. Nothing.

Elijah turned at the sound of footsteps and saw his father come round the tree with a shotgun in one hand and a hunting knife in the other.

Elijah was beyond fear at this point. Beyond hope. Beyond desperation. Beyond anything.

Except sorrow. He leaned against the tree again and wept, pressed his forehead against the bark and whimpered aloud.

Jeremiah stood over his son. He stared down at him a moment before looking up at Emily. He nodded—to himself, perhaps—and cut the ropes around her wrists with his knife. She slid lower, and the tendons and muscles in her hands ripped and tore, filling Elijah's ears with subtle, horrific snaps and rips he'd never forget.

Jeremiah pulled on Emily until her hands snapped free with an awful popping sound like a whip crack. She fell over his shoulder, and he laid her on the ground.

"She's dead," he said. Casual. Like she was no more than a rodent caught in a trap.

Jeremiah sheathed his knife and set the shotgun beside her. Then, he moved over to Elijah and withdrew a key. "You've a destiny, Elijah," he said, kneeling down and placing the key into the cuffs. "I hope you'll remember that."

In that moment, Elijah found that, in addition to sorrow, there were two other emotions he wasn't quite past, after all, anger and hatred. They coursed through his body like acid.

Once free, he lunged at his father's right leg. He caught him off guard, and the big man toppled to the ground with a painful grunt.

Elijah crawled over to Emily and spun round just as his father stood. He gathered up the shotgun, aimed, then squeezed the trigger. A tiny explosion shot from the barrel.

The bullet caught Jeremiah in the leg just below the knee. A portion of his pant leg and flesh beneath exploded, and bits of gore and skin shot out. He fell forward again with a scream and then growled with rage.

Elijah then turned his attention to Emily. Her eyes were half open, and the pupils stared out at nothing. Her lips were blue and parted as if she were trying to speak, but nothing would come out.

Elijah placed both hands on her head. Closed his eyes. Concentrated. He could hear his father's limbs scraping across the ground as he crawled nearer, but he ignored it. *"Please,"* he whispered.

But nothing happened. When he opened his eyes, Emily's lips were still blue. Her eyes were still half-open and staring. Still staring at nothing.

He wrapped his arms around her and squeezed. She offered no resistance. She offered nothing.

Nothing.

He buried his face in her shoulder and screamed through clenched teeth. *"Please! Come on!"* he cried. *"Come back to me!"*

But nothing happened. Emily remained cold and lifeless.

"I need you!" he cried. But she didn't hear. Would never hear.

Never again.

When Elijah opened his eyes, Jeremiah was just a few feet away. And still coming closer.

He laid Emily down, ever so gently, his eyes locked on her killer. Jeremiah halted, stared back. Elijah glanced at the shotgun, still resting on the ground by him, then back at his father. He was three feet away…close, but not close enough to overtake him before he picked the weapon back up.

His father knew that as well.

"Murderer," Elijah hissed through clenched teeth.

Jeremiah only stared back, gave no response. Only bared his teeth.

Finally, Elijah snatched the shotgun up again and aimed it at Jeremiah's face. Right between the eyes.

Jeremiah's eyes crossed—literally *crossed* like a cartoon character—and stared down the barrel. There was fear in his eyes. For the first time in his life, Elijah saw his father afraid.

"It doesn't matter what you do to me, son," Jeremiah said, looking up at his son again. "You still have a destiny."

"Screw destiny!" Elijah screamed.

He thrust his right foot forward and kicked his father's chin. He heard the man's teeth clack together, and he cried out, arched his back for one crazy half-second, and collapsed onto his back. Blood seeped from a fresh wound on his lip.

Elijah leapt onto Jeremiah, screaming like a crazed animal, and drove the butt of the shotgun into his face. It caught him on his right cheek just below his eye, and Elijah heard a loud crunch that he assumed was the bone underneath. He screamed and brought the gun down again on Jeremiah's mouth, knocking three teeth out and cracking a fourth in half. He continued driving the gun down again and again. Still screaming.

When he stood at last, Jeremiah's face was smeared with blood and gashes. It was already starting to swell, and he spit mouthfuls of blood into the air, which arced a foot or so above his face before splattering back down.

Elijah pointed the gun at what was left of his father's face. He bared his teeth, and his breath whistled in and out between them.

Do it! Kill him! He killed Emily! He killed Mom! No telling who else he's killed, either! Kill him! Just kill him!

He placed his finger on the trigger and started to squeeze—

Emily.
Mom.
Emily.
Mom.

But he stopped.

A tear, or what looked like a tear, trickled down from Jeremiah's eye. It danced and wove its way through the swellings and open wounds on his face, then dropped to the ground.

The remains of Jeremiah's bottom lip quivered, and a tiny, frightened whimper slipped from his mouth.

Elijah glanced back at Emily. Cold. Gray. *Do it! Just do it!*

He hated this man. He truly hated him. He was a murderer. He was a liar. He'd brought nothing to this world but pain. His entire life was a black splotch on the heart of humanity. His death would be a sweet release.

But something stayed Elijah's hand. A subtle twinge of a feeling he barely noticed but still couldn't ignore. Something—

He took a deep breath. Closed his eyes. Tossed the gun aside.

No. He wouldn't do it. Couldn't. Just...*couldn't.*

If he did, he'd be no better than his father, dealing out death and judgment to those he saw fit. Because he wanted it.

He refused to do that. Strange as it was, he didn't think Emily or his mother would want him to do that, either, to succumb to this frail, feeble, whimpering man at his feet.

He wasn't worth it. He never would be.

Leave him. Leave him be. To just lie here and bleed.

Elijah reached down, took the knife from Jeremiah's belt. His father jumped, brought his hands up in a weak attempt to shield himself. Another whimper escaped his lips. But he offered no resistance.

Elijah fastened the sheath to his belt, took one final look at his father. Then, he turned and walked away. He spared a final glance at Emily, whispered a final good-bye, then kept walking.

And he never looked back. Not once. The last sound he heard from his father was the strained sound of his breathing through split lips and a shattered jaw.

CHAPTER 32

"That's how I learned I couldn't raise the dead," Elijah sighed.

He took a bite of the ham sandwich Lori had made for him earlier. He'd been forced to live off whatever vegetables he could swipe from local gardens for the past couple of weeks. Cold, hard, raw vegetables. (Never mind what a nuisance "bathroom trips" were.) This was like manna from Heaven. It was—as far as Elijah was concerned—*glorious.*

"Jesus," Marcus whispered.

The three of them had taken seats at Lori's kitchen table while Elijah recounted his personal history. Neither Lori nor Marcus felt like eating. Of course, their diet for the past two weeks hadn't consisted of raw vegetables, either.

Mostly pasta and generic beef stroganoff. True American cuisine.

"And you've just been wandering the roads of America ever since?" Lori asked.

Elijah, still chewing a mouthful of ham, bread, and cheese, nodded. When he managed to gulp it down, he said. "Pretty much. Like I said, I'm just trying to find answers."

"And simultaneously on the run from your father," Lori added.

Elijah shrugged and drank from the glass of diet soda Lori had provided. "Yeah," he agreed, "but that's really only a small part of it. I'm just—looking."

Lori couldn't help but smile. "For God?"

Elijah nodded again. "Sure. If He's out there. And if I never find him, well, I guess I'll just die searching."

"That's dedication," Marcus said and raised his glass.

Elijah grinned and tapped his glass to Marcus's. "To dedication," he said, and took another sip. "But, as odd as this may sound, I don't really feel like I have to be all that dedicated. I mean, it seems everyone's looking for some—*purpose*—in their lives. You know, some *reason* to exist. And I guess I've got one."

"To just walk the earth in search of God?" Lori asked. There was skepticism in her voice, and she didn't bother hiding it.

Elijah nodded, but said nothing.

"And what if you don't find Him?" she prodded. "What if He's not out there?"

Elijah thought a moment, frowned, then shrugged. "Guess I'll never know if I don't keep looking." He grinned.

Lori sighed, but she couldn't help but smile. He was impossible. Just so *impossible.*

Elijah took a long gulp of soda and said, "Okay, well, history lesson's over. We need to get ready for our next step."

"Next step?" Marcus wondered.

"Chief Foster," Elijah told them. "He's been covering up my presence here since I 'vanished.' Under

Joshua's orders. We have to make that public, let everyone in town know their leaders are keeping secrets from them."

"Whoa, whoa, whoa," Lori protested and held up an exasperated hand. "And just how are we supposed to do that? It's not like anyone's going to listen to us."

"True, which means we'll have to *make* Greg Foster tell them," Elijah answered. "And we've got to move fast. Now that they're on the defensive, Joshua and his inner circle won't waste any time working out ways to deal with us."

"And how...how are you going to make him do that?" Lori demanded.

"I'll tell you on the way," Elijah said. He gulped down the last of his soda and stood.

Lori's eyes widened. "Now?"

Greg Foster heard his wife curse when the dishwasher door tumbled open and several dishes spilled out. Of course, Becky's version of *cursing* didn't actually involve curse words. No way, no how. He hadn't heard his wife utter anything in the way of foul language since menopause, and even that was just the once.

Greg sat in his recliner, feet up and remote at the ready. A glass of iced tea rested on a small table nearby, and ESPN commentators droned on about the latest happenings in the world of American sports on the widescreen plasma television they'd purchased not two weeks ago.

"Need a hand in there?" Greg called, really hoping she didn't, but not wanting to appear totally oblivious to her.

"No, I got it!" Becky called back.

She cursed again, *"Durn it!"* The dishes rattled. "How long since we emptied this?"

"Thought we emptied it last night?" Greg called back, his eyes still on the television. It was one of the final four games in the NCAA tournament. *The final four!*

"Huh-uh." More rattling.

Greg sighed. He wasn't sure if his wife was asking for his help without actually asking or not, but he suspected she was. He grunted as he leaned forward for the lever to—what would the word be, *decline?*—the chair. Then, he pushed himself out and headed for the kitchen.

He was interrupted en route, however, by a knock at the door. He stopped, one foot in the kitchen and one in the den, and directed his gaze across the kitchen, into the living room, and finally at the front door.

From where he stood, Greg could make out one person standing outside, but the front door only had the one window, and the artwork on it prevented seeing anything on the other side. So, there could've been more.

"You getting that?" Becky asked from the other side of the kitchen counter.

Greg frowned. "Sure." But who would come by this late? Granted, it wasn't the midnight hour or anything, but it was well past suppertime.

He trudged through the kitchen into the living room and took a moment to peer through the glass. Just one person. A girl, looked like. But that was as much as he could tell.

He grasped the doorknob, turned it, and pulled the door open. And he blinked once in surprise. Then again for—well, he didn't really know what the second time was for. "Lori?"

Lori managed a little smile in return. "Hi," she offered. "Umm—I hope I'm not bothering you showing up so late?"

"Don't be silly," Greg said, smiling. "It's not even 8:30, yet. Come on in."

"Thanks." Lori—a bit tentatively, Greg noticed—stepped inside.

She was a cute girl, Greg thought. Shame things didn't work out with Joshua. They would've been a good couple. Why'd they ever split up, away?

Lori wore long jeans, a light-colored blouse, and a denim jacket. Greg grinned a little. It felt perfectly fine out. He would've been happy to walk outside in a short-sleeve t-shirt, but Lori, like so many women in life, obviously got cold easily.

"Who is it?" Becky called from the kitchen.

"Lori, hon."

"Hi, Lori!"

"Hi," Lori called back.

"So what can we do for you?" Greg asked her.

"Well." She looked down, stuffed her hands in her coat pockets and bumped the tips of her shoes together. She chewed on her bottom lip. "It's about Elijah."

Greg's eyes widened. "Have you seen him?"

She nodded, still watching the floor. "Uh-huh. He stopped by my apartment earlier."

Greg took hold of her arm. His grip was gentle, but most definitely firm. It yanked her eyes up to his. "You should've called us."

She didn't answer. Not right away. Greg could almost see the gears turning in her head, could see them right through her eyes, churning and grinding as fast as possible to come up with a good answer.

"I want to know something, first," she said at last.

"No. Where is he?"

But Lori shook her head. "No. I want to know one thing."

Greg sighed, exasperated. But he didn't let go of her. "What's that?"

"Why are you covering him up? Why haven't you told the rest of the town about him?"

Now, it was Greg's turn to hesitate. Now, he did let go of her arm. The gears in his own head turned at a furious pace, desperately working to come up with a satisfactory answer, and fast.

Lori waited, saying nothing, silently telling him she was finished talking until he answered the question.

"We—we just felt it was in the public's best interests to keep this quiet for now," he said. "It's an ongoing investigation."

Lori frowned. "What kind of investigation?"

Oh, crap. "It's…just a general investigation, right now."

"But you're going to arrest him if you find him, right?" Now, Lori's eyes almost seemed to burn into his. "If you want my help finding him, I want to know what's going on."

Greg sighed. "I really can't say at this time, Lori. He may just be detained and asked to leave town, or he might be arrested and taken into custody."

"But why would you *arrest* him?" The tone of Lori's voice was becoming firm, demanding. "What's he done?"

"I think you know what he did, Lori," Greg said, mustering up some resolve of his own. "He attacked a police officer, stabbed him with a hunting knife."

"Blythe?"

Greg nodded.

"Is he okay?"

"He's fine, he—" Greg caught himself. Realized now what she was getting at.

"You know, don't you," Lori said.

"I—"

"You know, and I want you to admit to me you know." Lori took a step toward him. Lord, but she was bold. Had she always been this bold?

"Yes, I know. He—" Greg couldn't bring himself to say it out loud. Just *thinking* it was crazy enough.

"He can heal people, can't he?"

Greg nodded. "Yes."

"And he healed Blythe, didn't he?"

Aha! Now, Greg had some ammunition of his own. "Yes. But let's not forget that was *after* he stabbed him." He felt a triumphant smile trying to crawl onto his face, but he held it back.

Lori folded her arms. "So you think he's dangerous?"

Greg nodded. "Absolutely."

"Then, why haven't you made it public?"

Greg's jaw almost dropped. That's what she'd been playing at the whole time, to hear him acknowledge everything else, and then acknowledge that.

She'd cornered him, waltzed right into his own home and *cornered* him.

And he'd pranced merrily right into it for her.

Drat! Durn! The gears spun in his head once more, but they made less and less progress, just grinded on in his skull without any results.

"We—Joshua feels it would be best if we kept this quiet." He sighed.

"Josh wants it kept quiet?" She glared at him.

Greg stepped forward and tried to place his hands on Lori's shoulders, but she backed away. "You know he does. He's just acting in the best interests of the community."

"Is he?" She looked toward the front door. The usual contempt was in her voice.

What happened with those two? What went on between them that left Lori so bitter and angry? So—so *lost?*

For a painful moment that seemed to drag out nearly an hour, they both stood silent. Greg did the fidgeting this time. He looked down, dragged the toe of his shoe across the linoleum floor and swallowed. The only sound was the ongoing rattle of dishes in the kitchen.

Then, seemingly without warning, Lori headed for the door. Greg, startled, caught her by the arm and blurted, "Where are you going?"

"Back home." She pulled herself free and opened the door.

"Lori?"

She stopped, paused another moment, then half-turned back to see him.

"Are you going to help us?"

She stared at him for one more painful moment. Then, said, "No."

She shut the door behind her, leaving Greg alone in uncomfortable silence. He stared through the art-laden window, watching Lori's blurred silhouette moving away across the lawn toward her car.

He was startled from this when Becky peeked her head through the doorway behind him and yelled, "Okay, I'm done!"

CHAPTER 33

Lori was certain a police officer would already be waiting for her when she got home. Greg was sure to call someone to check her apartment yet again for Elijah. But there was no one. No cops, no Joshua, just an empty street.

Thank God for small favors.

She was about to head inside her building when a squad car rounded the intersection and eased toward her.

"Keep going, dickhead," she whispered. "Keep going."

The car slowed and stopped in front of her. It was dark, but Lori could see Cpl. Blythe sitting behind the wheel.

Should've figured it was too good to be true.

Lori's hands trembled at her sides, and her breath came in soft, jerky gasps. Despite her efforts to set her jaw, her bottom lip quivered like a baby.

Blythe. The bastard scared the hell out of her, and she hated him for it.

"Evenin', Lori," Blythe offered as he stepped out of the car, just as pleasant as you please. We're all friends here, after all, aren't we? It's not like I left a half-crazed town minister in your house the other night to scare the bejeezuss out of you? Oh no, ma'am.

"Hello," Lori managed.

"Heard Elijah stopped by your place today?" Blythe asked, shutting the door and heading toward her. He kept both hands on his hips. Was that supposed to be like some official stance of authority? Did they teach that at the academy?

"Yeah," Lori said. "He's gone now, though."

"You mind if I have a look?"

Lori sighed. "I'm sure it doesn't matter if I do. Come on."

She led Blythe inside the building and up the short flight of stairs, pulled out her keys and opened the door. She stepped aside as he shoved his way past, so he could get in first.

Lori rolled her eyes. This routine was getting old fast, and she tried her best to make sure that was all the expression Blythe ever read on her face. No way was she letting the bastard know about the lingering, icy terror creeping its way up her throat.

"Guess it's all clear," Blythe said. He'd be able to map out every room in her apartment if this kept up much longer.

Lori stepped aside from the door to let him pass. That's right, Corporal Ass-Clown. Just go right on out. No need to stay and chit chat. Just go right the hell out.

"You'll let us know if you see him again?" Blythe said once he reached the door. He stopped to look back at her, and Lori was convinced he could see the fear in her expression.

"Sure, whatever," she said.

"No, not whatever, Lori." He stepped back in. Stood just an inch or so inside her comfort zone, making her squirm. "Not helping could be deemed an obstruction of justice or harboring a fugitive. You don't want me to have to take you in, do you?"

Lori felt her knees quivering. "I told you he's not here, and I don't know where he is," she blurted.

Blythe nodded, smiled. "Fair enough." He turned and walked away. But just before he stepped outside, he called back, "Call if you need us, though?"

Lori nodded, and when Blythe turned she shut the door quick. *Click! Click! Jingle!*

She reached into her jacket pocket and pulled out the tape recorder she'd taken with her. She rewound it several seconds, then played it back:

"And he healed Blythe, didn't he?"

"Yes. But let's not forget that was after he stabbed him."

"So you think he's dangerous?"

"Absolutely."

"Then, why haven't you made it public?"

"....We—Joshua feels it would be best if we kept this quiet."

Her voice and Chief Foster's. Not exactly stereo quality, but it was there. Clear as day, or at least close enough to it, just like they'd hoped. Greg, in his own words, saying he was keeping Elijah's presence quiet on Joshua's orders, admitting they didn't want to tell the people in town there was someone roaming the streets who might be dangerous.

Or might be able to heal them.

Lori reached into her purse, withdrew her cell phone and called Marcus.

"How'd it go?" he greeted.

"Perfect," Lori said.

"So you got it?"

"I got everything."

Silence. Lori could almost picture Marcus nodding at the other end. "So, we're ready," he said.

"Ready as we're going to be," Lori sighed.

Marcus, Lori suspected, nodded again. "Okay. Try to get some sleep, okay?"

"Okay. 'Night."

"'Night."

She hung up. Next Sunday would be quite an occasion. She couldn't remember how long it had been. How many months? Or was it a year by now?

Well, either way, it didn't much matter, because after all this time, Lori was going back to church.

Could you say amen?

Elijah settled against a tree and looked to the sky. It was a clear night; the stars shone bright, and a near-full moon stared back at him.

He sighed. Back in the woods, back to foraging for food, back to cold, hard vegetables. Despite what so many activists might say, those were poor substitutes for a good bacon cheeseburger. *Real* poor substitutes.

But, once again, he had little choice. He couldn't be with Lori when she went to Greg Foster's house. It was way too risky, and it was pretty much a foregone conclusion police would scout her apartment once Lori told Greg he'd visited her there. Again.

Of course, this also left him out of the loop. Again.

He had no way of knowing whether or not Lori got Foster to admit to covering up his presence in Antioch, that he'd done it on Joshua's orders.

Those thoughts all ended with the suddenness of a hiccup, however. The sound of a footstep in the grass—a soft, faint rustle and squish—jerked Elijah's attention to the right.

The surrounding woods were almost opaque. He couldn't see anything. Nothing but blackness. Nothing. Nothing—

But then...something. A portion of the trees that were once visible suddenly weren't, as of some thick shadow blotted them out. Elijah saw the outline of—he couldn't be sure what, but it was there. Now that he'd seen it, he couldn't believe he'd ever missed it.

A flashlight beam suddenly exploded in his eyes. He clamped them shut and blocked the light with his arms, tried to stand and ward off whatever attack he knew was coming.

And knew he was already too late.

The footsteps came again, in rapid succession now. The intruder was charging. Elijah drew his arms away and squinted, hoping to catch a glimpse of his attacker. All he saw was the flashlight surging toward him. He reached for his knife, but his attacker reached him first.

The impact caught him in the abdomen, driving all the wind from his body. Pain wracked his guts beneath his bruised abdomen. His belly, which was still nice and purple this afternoon, exploded with pain. He tried to gulp down a mouthful of air, but his stomach would have none of it.

He was lifted up by the momentum and carried forward for what felt like a dozen yards before crashing to the earth. His attacker landed on top of him, once again driving his weight into Elijah's chest and sending more waves of agony coursing through his body. He tried to gasp again, but his windpipe remained shut.

Elijah scrambled out from underneath and tried to stand, but an unseen hand caught the heel of his foot and pulled it out from under him. He crashed down on his back, and his head thudded against the earth. His vision flared like a defective television on the fritz, and the night sky started to blur. His head began to throb.

He tried to roll over and stand again; but he still couldn't breathe, and his body was screaming at him for air. He only managed to flop over to his side like a dying fish and cough several times. At last, his airway opened, and he managed to gasp in precious oxygen.

He wheezed and tried to sit up, but something—*a boot?*—smacked him in the face like a mallet. He rolled the opposite direction onto his belly. His jaw throbbed, and his eyes started to water.

"—*Yezuss*," he gagged.

A powerful hand seized his scalp and pulled his head from the earth. "Now, now, mustn't take the Lord's name in vain," Frank Hollister's voice hissed. His breath was warm and damp against Elijah's ear.

Frank slammed his face back into the grass. For a moment, Elijah was certain the impact had crunched his nose, but, thankfully, when he touched his hand to it, he realized it was still intact.

Granted, it hurt like hell and was bleeding like a geyser, but, hey, at least it wasn't broken.

Frank's hand seized Elijah's wrist and yanked it from his face. He twisted it behind Elijah's back and wrenched it one good time until Elijah screamed. Elijah again reached for his knife with his free hand, but Frank caught it by the wrist and wrenched it, too, behind Elijah's back.

He heard the jangling of what could only be handcuffs, then felt the cold metal biting into his wrists.

Frank grabbed his scalp again, said "Stand up," and pulled him to his feet. He spun him around and punched him in the face. The man had to be almost sixty, but he hit like a truck. Elijah spun and doubled over. The right side of his face was on fire.

Frank pulled Elijah back and punched the other side of his face for good measure. Then, he threw him against the tree Elijah had planned to sleep against. He pinned him there with his forearm against Elijah's throat.

"You've been a real nuisance to this town, young man," Frank said.

He drove his fist into Elijah's gut, knocking the wind out of him and sending fresh waves of pain through his gut again. Elijah hunched over Frank's arm, and, for one crazy instant, he was certain he was going to pass out.

But Frank took hold of his shoulders and shoved him away from the tree. Elijah's legs felt like warm lead, and he very nearly fell on his face. Frank caught hold of his coat and kept him upright. He continued pushing, guiding Elijah in whatever direction he wanted.

"That's all over now," Frank said behind him. "All good things, and all that."

Elijah felt the imprint of Frank's boot on his ass just before he was shoved forward again, hard. He staggered several steps before stumbling and watching the ground rush up to his face.

CHAPTER 34

    The following events blurred together, like a cheap slide show trying to visualize the effects of a bad acid trip. Elijah was dragged through the woods—sometimes walking, sometimes not—until they reached a paved road. Frank tossed him in the back of a vehicle, but he couldn't be sure what kind. A truck? Or SUV?
    The route they took was also a mystery. Elijah kept fading in and out of consciousness, and even when he was conscious, he wasn't exactly firing on all cylinders.
    The entire right side of his face was on fire. He was pretty sure if he didn't have a shining black eye by now, he soon would. His nose had stopped bleeding, but it was still tender. He was lying facedown on the seat, and whenever the vehicle bounced or bumped, his nose thumped against the cushion and sent a wave of agony through his head. Several times he tried rolling to his side, but his equilibrium was shot, and his strength was almost nonexistent.
    His skull throbbed, and there was a lingering, dull ache in the back of his head. In the brief, precious moments of lucidity he enjoyed, he just hoped it wasn't a concussion.

Then, he was outside again. He couldn't remember the door opening or being dragged outside, but the cool air on his face told him he was no longer stashed in a vehicle.

Frank was dragging him along toward—oh, who the hell knew? His feet barely worked, and he fell at least twice. Frank caught him both times by the back of his coat collar and hauled him to his feet. Then, they were on their way again.

Have they caught Lori, too? Elijah wondered. *And Marcus?* Had someone else paid them a similar visit? Were they both waiting for him inside this place, bloody and broken?

Heal THAT!

A door was opening. There was a hallway inside, but the lights were out, and Elijah's vision was already like gazing through a tunnel. Frank didn't bother with the lights, only ushered his captive along. He kept his hands under Elijah's arms, and his fingers dug into his ribs like claws. His thumbs poked painfully into his armpits.

Another door opened, and this time light shined out. It was almost blinding. Elijah winced and grunted just before Frank shoved him into the room. He staggered, fell, and thudded on his side. He heard the door close, and then there were four faces staring down at him. Four fuzzy shadows.

"Catch you at a bad time?" one of them scoffed. Dean. Out of prison. And, from the sound of it, happy as a clown.

Dean—Elijah was pretty sure it was Dean, anyway—kicked him hard in the back. His foot *whumped* against Elijah's lower back, which jolted his guts and bit at his muscles. He lurched once and rolled onto his back in a feeble effort to shield it from another blow.

"Dean. Stop." Joshua's voice. Where on earth had Frank taken him?

"Get him up," Joshua said, and Frank's hands dug into Elijah's ribs once more. He forced Elijah to stand, which was getting more and more difficult. His knees were actually wobbling like a cartoon character.

Something—a fist, probably—slammed into his gut. Elijah lurched forward, tried to gasp for air, but only managed a pathetic whine.

"*I said, stop it, Dean!*" Joshua yelled.

There was a brief scuffle, and, from the sound of it, Elijah guessed Joshua shoved the young man across the room. He staggered back several steps before regaining his balance.

There was an uncomfortable silence as Frank unlocked the handcuffs, dragged Elijah across the room, and tossed him into a chair. Then, in one motion, he was behind Elijah and re-cuffing his hands behind the chair's back.

He managed to gasp a few breaths of air before Greg Foster spoke from the other side of the room. "You nearly killed one of my officers," he said.

Elijah didn't answer. His tongue felt thick and heavy in his mouth. He wheezed, trying his best to breathe normally again.

"And Nathan's in the hospital because of you," Dean added from wherever he now stood.

Elijah barely heard him. His head drooped forward. He stared down at his knees and felt a ribbon of spittle escape his lip and sink into his lap. The images blurred and grew dark.

Then, everything flashed back into focus when a firm hand struck him across the face. Elijah jerked upright again and groaned. Then, the same hand—it was Frank's—clamped on his nose, sending a shockwave of pain throughout his skull. He screamed and squirmed against his bonds, but Frank held firm.

"You don't get to lose consciousness, son," Frank told him. "Not 'till we're done."

Elijah kicked at him, but his legs had all the speed of a dying animal. Frank dodged him easily. He gave Elijah's nose a final squeeze before letting go and stepping back.

Spots danced in front of Elijah's eyes like a drunken carousel. He shook his head and blinked. The spots faded, but his vision was still blurry. He could make out a couch and a loveseat on the other end of the room.

Joshua stepped forward, leaving his deacons behind. He stared at Elijah for several long, awkward moments. His hand shot out and struck Elijah across the cheek, rocking him to the side so hard he was sure the chair might topple.

Then, Joshua's hands were on both arms of the chair, and he was nose-to-nose with Elijah, staring into his eyes. Elijah could feel the air from Joshua's nostrils on his face.

"Have you been sleeping with her?" Joshua said. His voice was just two steps above a whisper.

Elijah stared back at him, eyes wide. Had he been sleeping with her? Was that really the first thing on this guy's mind?

He couldn't help but grin. A small chuckle slipped from his mouth.

For all the man's posturing as a pious man of God, he was still just as obsessed with sex as the average teenager.

"Have you?"

Elijah shook his head and sighed. Unbelievable. Just unbelievable.

Joshua smacked him again. Elijah's head jerked back, and he stared into the preacher's eyes.

"Just what do you hope to accomplish here?" Joshua asked. "What are you trying to do? Bring down this work? Destroy everything we've built here?"

Elijah thought a moment, then smiled and said, "Thou sayest." He raised his eyebrows. Or at least, he hoped he did. His face was so battered, he couldn't be sure.

Joshua blinked. His eyes danced, and his head trembled. Elijah could almost see his face turning red. Give it a few more seconds, he thought, and steam would shoot from the man's ears.

Joshua jumped away with a growl and marched back to his cohorts. He stood there without looking back at Elijah for almost a full minute, saying nothing. His shoulders moved up and down, and Elijah could tell he was breathing through clenched teeth.

The others came round Joshua. Greg put a hand on his shoulder, but Joshua brushed it away.

"He doesn't leave this room," Joshua said.

Greg was the first and only to object: "But, J—"

"I *said*," and Joshua turned his rabid gaze on Greg, "he doesn't—leave—this—room."

Greg cowered back and nodded. "O—okay."

"I don't want him seen anywhere around town until after Sunday," Joshua told them. "Dean? Don't touch him. And I mean it."

Dean frowned, but nodded.

Then, Joshua turned and faced Elijah again. "You've shaken us up a bit, I'll grant you that," he said. "But what God has put together, no man should tear asunder. Come Sunday, we'll make your presence here public, and the entire church will know exactly who and what has been prowling around their streets."

Joshua narrowed his eyes and bared his teeth. "And after that, " he said, "you'll be begging us to send you out of this town."

Elijah spent two nights in that office, two nights bound in Joshua's chair. They'd tied his handcuffs to the base of the chair with rope, ensuring his arms remained locked in place and preventing him from standing. It wasn't long before his arms grew stiff, and the muscles in his shoulders protested. They were almost totally numb by nightfall.

Fate, in its own twisted way, smiled on him, though, and he lost consciousness just over an hour after Joshua and his posse left. He remained unconscious until late the next morning—which was Saturday.

By then, his face was a mess. His right eye was thoroughly blackened, giving his eye socket the semblance of a crater. The right side of his face was bruised and swollen. A handful of jagged cuts raced along the length of his chin around to his ear.

The left side of his face was somewhat less the worse for wear, but not by much. His right cheek flared bright red, and there was an angry gash just beneath his left eyebrow.

As for the rest of his body, the morning following his scuffle with Dean was mild by comparison. His entire chest ached; every breath was torture. And the spot Dean

had kicked on his lower back screamed at him whenever he moved—which, thankfully, wasn't much.
Not to mention his arms were sore as hell by then.

Lori and Marcus, however, knew nothing of this, and they went about their Saturday as if nothing was awry. Ignorance is bliss, after all.

Saturday just meant one thing for them: a busy night at work. It's common knowledge that restaurants are always busiest on weekends, and the people of Antioch loved their Saturday night pizza.

Janine showed up with her two boys. Right at 8:30. Regular as clockwork. *Stop throwing food at your brother, Billy. Jeremy don't blow in your straw.*

It was a clever strategy, Lori mused. Feed 'em late, and they'd fall right to sleep. Of course, Lori couldn't help but wonder how Janine put up with those boys in the hours leading up to that late dinner. Seriously, was there anything more obnoxious than two hungry grade-schoolers?

Except, like, maybe, two hungry teenagers?

Janine spent the majority of her time corralling Billy and Jeremy to their booth so they could stuff their faces with cheese and pepperoni and leave the other patrons alone. *Stay put. Both of you. I'm not kidding. Hey! What did I just say?*

Alas, poor Janine.

"Everything all right?" Lori asked her at a moment when Billy and Jeremy were content with shoving pizza in their mouths.

"I could use a refill, please?" Janine said and sighed. She had that slight but noticeable country twang in her voice.

"Sure thing." Lori smiled and took her glass to the back.

Marcus, his arms elbow deep in dishwater, was waiting for her. "What time do you want to leave tomorrow?"

Lori shoved Janine's glass under the soda fountain. "We should probably show up late. Like, maybe fifteen minutes after service starts," she said. "We don't want to attract any more attention than we're already going to."

"No kidding." Marcus withdrew four plates, set them in an adjacent sink, and hosed suds off them. "They'd probably plan an impromptu homecoming if we showed up early."

Lori groaned. She could just imagine. "Pick you up after ten, then?"

"It's a date." Marcus sunk his arms in the soapy water again.

Lori grinned and headed back out with Janine's refilled glass. Billy and Jeremy were still quiet, but that probably wouldn't last.

CHAPTER 35

Sunday arrived just like every Sunday should. The grass was green, the sky was blue and the sun shone high and bright. Just about any spot in town would've been perfect fodder for a postcard.

And yet, waking up was a real pain in the ass. Lori was jolted from sleep by the grating sound of her alarm clock. *Meep! Meep! Meep! Wake up! Meep!*

She wanted to smash the little bastard with a hammer, but she settled for just switching off the alarm.

With a groan, Lori threw off her covers and climbed out of bed. She'd slept in long, blue pajama pants last night. Kudos to Josh for making her afraid to sleep without clothes on anymore.

She hadn't slept all that well, either. Excitement and anxiety, intermingled, kept her stomach fluttering the whole time she lay in bed. She tossed and turned and, the rest of the time, just lay on her back, eyes closed and wishing she could stop thinking about tomorrow and just get some sleep!

The hot water helped a little. The sleepiness, though it did so grudgingly, left her eyes, and her limbs stopped feeling so much like lead.

She opted to wear gray pants and a red blouse. No skirts this morning, and no high heels, either. She didn't know what was in store, but, just in case she found herself on the run, she didn't want to wear anything that would slow her down.

She left home right at ten and arrived at Marcus' place exactly four minutes later. She honked once.

Marcus, who Lori figured must've been waiting right by the front door, emerged an instant later. He strolled out wearing black pants, a black button-up shirt, and a red tie.

He opened the passenger door and said, "You got the tape?"

Lori smiled and patted her purse.

"Rock on," he said, and slid inside.

Lori pulled back onto the road, then asked, "Heard from Elijah, yet?"

"Huh-uh. You?"

She shook her head. "Is he gonna' meet us there?"

Marcus frowned. "Dunno."

Well, didn't that just suck? Where the hell was he? Lori could appreciate how hard it was maintaining contact on Elijah's end (why oh *why* couldn't the man invest in a cell phone?), but this was really weak. They were pretty much venturing into the lion's den, and they were doing it with no plan.

Had things gotten too dangerous? Had Elijah felt he couldn't risk venturing to either Lori's or Marcus' place in the past few days? Had he been forced to keep laying low in the woods? Would he even be able to make it to the church today?

There were two entrances to the ChristPoint parking lot, and they were both bottlenecks. There wasn't exactly much they could do about it when nearly the *entire freakin' town* was coming to the place.

In the minutes leading up to service time, vehicles would file in, bumper-to-bumper, and be directed by ushers to their respective parking spaces. It was like visiting an amusement park

Lori and Marcus managed to skip all that. Every member of ChristPoint showed up right on time, every time, so the entrances were all but deserted when they pulled in around fifteen after. Not even a single straggler.

The massive parking lot spanned around the entire building, roughly seventy yards or so in every direction. Lori had to drive around the entire lot before she finally found a space in the very back.

She turned and looked at Marcus after removing her keys from the ignition.

"You ready for this?" he asked.

"God, no."

Marcus smirked, nodded, and opened his door. Lori did the same. *God help us,* she prayed. *Please let us be on the side of right.*

Though it was filled almost to capacity with vehicles, the church's parking lot was totally devoid of people. Lori and Marcus made the long trek around the building to the main entrance alone, and in silence.

Two door greeters met them at the entrance. Typical Sunday morning greetings: "Hello! Come right in! Good to have you this morning!" Lori and Marcus smiled, said "Thanks," and kept moving, hoping to keep as low a profile as they could.

It lasted about a minute and a half.

"Lori? Is that you?" The voice came from her left, and Lori recognized it right away. It'd been a few years, but she still remembered. Sonya. From the nursery. Lori closed her eyes and took a deep breath before turning around.

"It *is* you!" Sonya cried. She rushed forward. Her ample bosoms bounced back and forth beneath her blue dress like a pair of water balloons.

Before Lori could stop her, Sonya wrapped her arms around her and squeezed. Hard.

"It's so good to see you," Sonya gushed. "It's been so long!"

Lori tried to say, "Mh-hmm!" But all she managed was a strained squeak. Good God, if the woman squeezed any harder, she might fart!

Sonya finally released her and stepped back beside her husband (her *second* husband, Lori reminded herself), Jerry. "Jerry," she said, "you remember Lori?"

"Oh, of course," Jerry said and shot his hand out. "Nice to see you back."

Lori took it and smiled. "Thanks. Good to see you both."

Jerry looked over at Marcus. He didn't offer his hand. "Marcus, isn't it? Nice to see you, too."

Marcus nodded and smiled back. "Thanks. You, too."

"I see you guys are late, too," Lori said.

"Yeah," Sonya agreed. "My fault. Took too long getting ready."

Marcus took hold of Lori's hand. "Well, let's make our way inside before we miss anymore," he said, and tugged her toward the sanctuary.

"Good idea!" Sonya took hold of Jerry's hand and hurried along beside them.

"Oh, um, we'll probably sit in the balcony," Lori told them, thinking as quick as she could. "You know, since Marcus is new here."

"Aha, ok." Jerry smiled knowingly. "We usually sit up front. So, maybe we'll see you again afterward?"

"Yeah, sure, maybe," Marcus said, and yanked Lori's arm hard enough she almost fell over.

The song service was already winding down when Lori and Marcus took their seats.

"Glad I could be the bigger sinner, here," Marcus hissed.

"Get over it!" Lori shot back.

They sat high above the congregation in the back of the sanctuary. Even though the balcony wasn't deserted, there were a lot fewer people up here than down below. The soundboard was also located on the balcony. Two teenagers and a middle-aged gentleman manned the system. Pretty simple work, really, once you knew what did what. On the other hand, it was also tedious as all crap.

Lori remembered sitting in on a few soundboard lessons, in the event she might ever be needed there.

"All you gotta worry about is three things, Lori," an aging gentleman named Lloyd Froeman had told her. "House, monitor, and gain. House is what everyone in the audience hears. Monitor is what everyone on stage hears. And gain is how 'hot' the microphones are."

When he could tell the last sentence had confused her, Lloyd said, "That just means whether or not you have to stand right next to the microphone for it to pick you up or a few inches away. Got it?"

Lloyd really had been a sweet old man. A widower. Kids long gone. Whatever happened to him? The guy manning the board now was at least ten years younger. Maybe twenty.

Spare microphones lined the front of the board. Some of them, Lori knew, were still wired into the system. They weren't live at the moment, but they could be. It was just a matter of figuring out how they were numbered and setting the volume.

No problem, Lori figured. *Just hold the mike up to the tape recorder and push play.*

Yeah, sure, no problem. But just how was she supposed to do that without the pimple-laden sound crew noticing?

Meanwhile, the praise band had stepped back to allow one of the deacons—some man in his thirties Lori didn't recognize—to pray over the morning's offering. He raised one hand heavenward and said, "Oh, Lord, we thank you for this opportunity to give back to you after all the blessings you've given us. We ask that you'd bless this offering to help further your kingdom. Bless those that give and those that cannot. We ask this in Jesus' name."

And the congregation said, "Amen."

The band returned to sing a slower medley while ushers made their way through the aisles. From the corner of her eye, Lori spotted another usher making his way along the balcony aisles opposite her and Marcus. He handed an offering plate to an older lady sitting at the end of the pew, who placed her offering inside and passed it down the row.

Lori waited, all the while glancing back at the soundboard. When the plate reached her, she handed it off to Marcus, who handed it off to the next person.

Joshua sat in the pastor's chair—*his* chair—throughout the service. He rose and sang for the music, clapped and prayed at the appropriate times, but little else. Now, Lori saw, he stared ahead at nothing in particular. His fingers were clasped before his face, and his forefingers touched the tip of his nose.

When do we do this? Lori wondered. *When's the right time?*

Eventually, the ushers returned to the front, plates filled with the day's offering. They set them on the altar and returned to their seats.

And then, Joshua stood.

CHAPTER 36

Joshua hadn't noticed Lori and Marcus' arrival. In fact, he hadn't noticed much of anything. He spent the early part of the service thinking of Elijah, still locked in his office.

He wondered idly if the man's arms were asleep by now. After all, he'd been handcuffed with his arms around the back of a chair for over two days now. That had to hurt.

Then again, the man *had* attacked his church, seen to it that one of his deacons was hospitalized while another spent the night in jail. Elijah's suffering, Joshua decided, was righteous.

When the ushers started taking up the morning's offering, he couldn't help but wonder if Elijah could free himself. Could he escape his bonds? Could he be stalking his way toward the sanctuary right now? Ready to leap out at him like a demon from the depths as he prepared for his sermon?

Or would he return to Lori? At that thought, Joshua tensed his fingers, and his knuckles popped. Would he venture back to her apartment? To her bed?

Images of Elijah and Lori, naked and embraced, filled his head. Joshua imagined her arching her back, gasping, staring toward the heavens and rolling her eyes back as the climactic ecstasy surged through her body. He imagined Elijah's course fingers groping her body, taking hold of her breasts and squeezing.

Joshua gritted his teeth.

The interloper would never touch her again, never know her as Joshua had. He wasn't meant to. And his plans to somehow overthrow Joshua would never come to fruition.

Never.

When the ushers returned, he stood and looked out at the congregation. Still unaware that Lori and Marcus were among them, he stood and made his way to the podium.

This was it. This was his victory. He would tell them all of Elijah, why he was here, what he'd done, and what he hoped to do.

He would tell them everything.

Now, he stood before them all. Again. As he always had. Every service. No sermon this morning. No lesson. No, today was all about informing them, letting them know just what they faced as a church.

And what they should do about it.

"Good morning," he started. "I didn't prepare a sermon for this service. There's…there's something more pressing."

No one answered. No *Amen*'s, no *Preach it*'s. Only their rapt attention.

"I'm sure everyone here remembers Jesus telling his disciples that one day men would appear on the earth, professing to come in His name, but they were really just wolves in sheep's clothing," he went on.

He didn't smile. In fact, his expression was almost sad.

"Some would even heal the sick and cast out devils," Joshua said. "But on Judgment Day, God would tell them He never knew them. 'Depart from me, ye workers of iniquity.'"

At this point, unseen by Joshua, Lori was tensing. Whatever direction Joshua was taking, this morning's message nagged at her.

Joshua paused. He looked down a moment, chewed his lip. Then, he looked up again and said, "There is such a man in our community, and he's been here for a few weeks now, a man claiming he has the healing power of Jesus Christ…who's already seduced a handful of Antioch's residents. Of course, it's no one in *this* church."

Lori spun and seized Marcus' arm. He opened his mouth in a silent scream and stared at her, eyes wide. He pried his limb free before letting her say anything.

"*They caught him!*" Lori hissed.

Marcus took hold of her arms and whispered, "Calm down, sweetie."

"You be calm!" Lori snapped back. "We've gotta' do this. Now!"

"Okay, okay," Marcus agreed. "So how do we do that?"

"We need to get one of those microphones," Lori said. "And fast."

Joshua continued on with his speech—detailing how this stranger had attacked a police officer with a hunting knife—while Lori and Marcus hurried down to the soundboard. Lloyd's replacement was the first to notice them.

"One of the deacons needs you downstairs," Marcus blurted. "Uh, Dean, I think?"

Not-Lloyd frowned. "What?"

"Yeah, he said he needs to speak with you about one of the podium mikes," Marcus tried.

The two teenagers now spared a glance back. One of them gave Lori a second look.

"The podium mike's fine. What are you talking about?" Not-Lloyd was starting to look irritated.

Marcus shot Lori a desperate look. "Should've known that wouldn't work."

He went for broke. He leapt forward, pulled Not-Lloyd to his feet, gripped the man's groin with his right hand, and squeezed for all he was worth. Not-Lloyd started to scream, but Marcus clapped his left hand over the man's mouth to keep him quiet. He clawed at Marcus frantically, but Marcus ducked his head low and pushed him away from the soundboard.

Behind them, people were already standing. Lori could even hear the first steps of men marching forward to help.

So, she didn't have much time.

Marcus had pinned Not-Lloyd to the wall and was struggling to keep him there. The man was gripping Marcus' wrists with one hand and desperately pushing against him with the other

Both teenagers were staring at Marcus and their Sunday morning boss, mouths agape. Lori hurried forward and reached between them for a cordless microphone. She switched it on and told the one on the right. "Turn this up."

The boy stared. He managed a feeble, "Huh?"

Lori pointed at Marcus and bared her teeth. "Do it quick, before he rips them off!"

The kid jumped, and his hand shot to the controls. He shoved it up so high that feedback shrieked throughout the entire sanctuary. People grabbed their ears and ducked. Others yelled.

Lori clamped her hands over her ears and shut her eyes. The sound seemed to vibrate throughout her skull. She felt it in her teeth. Thankfully, the kid rebounded and pulled the controls down enough the feedback faded.

When Lori opened her eyes, she saw that Joshua had stopped his message. He stared up at the soundboard—at *her*—with wide eyes. The entire congregation had turned, as well. All of them, every single one of them, stared at her.

To her left, Marcus still struggled with Not-Lloyd, who was starting to cry. The men who'd first meant to help were still recovering from the audible shockwave that had just shaken the church, but that wouldn't last.

Lori uttered an "umm," then remembered the tape recorder in her purse. She reached in just as those footsteps resumed behind her, pulled out the little machine and hit PLAY.

"*Why are you covering him up? Why haven't you told the rest of the town about him?*"

"*We—we just felt it was in the public's best interests to keep this quiet for now. It's an ongoing investigation.*"

Joshua gaped at Lori, eyes wide, frozen and shocked. She was holding a microphone to a small tape recorder, and her voice and Greg Foster's were playing over the sound system. Some previous conversation the two of them had. About Elijah.

About *him*.

Lori's voice: *"What kind of investigation?"*

Greg's voice: *"It's—just a general investigation, right now."*

Lori: *"But you're going to arrest him if you find him, right? If you want my help finding him, I want to know what's going on."*

Greg: *"I really can't say at this time, Lori. He may just be detained and asked to leave town. Or he might be arrested and taken into custody."*

Joshua glanced down at the ushers. Several of them had already turned and were charging toward the balcony.

Lori: *"But why would you arrest him? What's he done?"*

Greg: *"I think you know what he did, Lori. He attacked a police officer. Stabbed him with a hunting knife."*

Lori: *"Blythe? Is he okay?"*

Greg: *"He's fine, he—"*

Lori: *"You know, don't you."*

Greg: *"I—"*

Lori: *"You know, and I want you to admit to me you know."*

Joshua tried to speak over the audio. "Lori?" he said. But his voice was barely audible. No one, save a handful, looked back at him. He tapped his ear-mounted mic a few times. Nothing. They'd turned him off.

Lori: *"He can heal people, can't he?"*

Greg: *"Yes."*

Lori: *"And he healed Blythe, didn't he?"*

Joshua stepped away from the podium and started down the aisle. He didn't run, but parishioners' faces passed by him in a blur.

The ushers were already ascending the stairs on their way to intercept Lori. He couldn't see it from his vantage point, but the soundboard operator was also managing to finally muscle his way free from Marcus.

Greg: *"Yes. But let's not forget that was after he stabbed him."*

Lori: *"So you think he's dangerous?"*

Greg: *"Absolutely."*

Lori: *"Then, why haven't you made it public?"*

Joshua stopped. The revelation rapped him across the face like a cold fist. He couldn't see Greg, but he was certain the man was probably sinking as low in his pew as he could right now. Head down, shoulders drooped like a scolded dog.

Greg: *"We—Joshua feels it would be best if we kept this quiet."*

And there it was. Lori's message. To the entire church. Spoken by the city's very own chief of police. Just as potent as any sermon.

By now, the ushers had reached the balcony and were converging on her. Joshua watched, unable to move, as Lori turned to flee. She tossed the cordless microphone at the first usher to fall on her.

Thunk!

Another shoved aside the near catatonic teenagers from the soundboard. Then, Lori, already struggling with the first usher, found another microphone and held it to the recorder. It repeated that one, damning line: *"We—Joshua feels it would be best if we kept this quiet."*

"Josh wants it kept quiet?"

"You know he does. He's just—"

The audio cut short. The usher at the soundboard looked back at Joshua, his mission accomplished. Further back in the balcony, two other ushers caught Lori by the arms. And another, alongside the now limping soundboard operator, held another person—Marcus. They all stared back at Joshua.

And the congregation followed their gaze. They too looked back to Joshua. All of them. Looking to him for answers to the questions Lori just hit them with. What just happened? What did it mean? What was going on?

But Joshua didn't have them.

CHAPTER 37

Elijah heard scuffling in the hallway just outside. His neck was stiff, but he looked up anyway. And it hurt like hell.

The door opened, and four men he didn't recognize muscled Lori and Marcus into the room. When she saw him, Lori gasped, "Oh my God!"

Dean, Frank, Greg, and Joshua followed them into the room. There was still no sign of Nathan. No doubt he was still recovering. The four of them marched into the office and stood around Elijah while the other four men—ushers, Elijah guessed—forced Lori and Marcus onto the sofa.

Both of them stared at Elijah, reminding him his face must look every bit as bad as it felt.

"What's the consensus?" Elijah heard Joshua mutter.

"Hard to tell at this point," Frank answered. "No one said much."

Even with the ushers standing between them, Elijah could see Lori staring back at him. *We did it*, she mouthed slowly. A smile started crawling across Elijah's face, but he stopped it. It was a sure way to get his ass kicked.

Again.

"Well, I guess now we know for sure the three of you have been conspiring against us," Joshua said, and walked around Elijah to stand between him and the others. "I'd hoped Lori was better than this, but I guess I was wrong."

"Guess so," Lori said behind him.

Joshua turned and stared at her. "I just can't understand this. Why? Why would you do this? It'd be different if we were criminals or—"

"Aren't you?" Marcus interrupted.

Joshua bit his lip a moment. Then, continued. "If I'm not mistaken, no one on this church's staff ever attacked a police officer with a hunting knife."

"And how's that officer doing, by the way?" Lori demanded.

Joshua glared at her. His eyes were hard. "And what about Nathan Riley?"

Lori and Marcus both started to answer, but Joshua stopped them.

"Don't give me that 'Dean did it!' nonsense," he snapped. "We all know Elijah attacked Dean and tricked him into attacking Nathan."

Joshua marched forward and took hold of Lori's shirt in his fists. He yanked her to her feet while the startled ushers looked on, bewildered. This was moving in a direction none of them expected.

"Why are you doing this to me?" Joshua spat at her through clenched teeth. *"Why? I loved you, Lori! You know I did! Why would you do this?"*

He shook her hard enough her arms flailed and her head bobbed. Her hair thrashed like an epileptic rock star. She gripped his arms to try and steady herself, but he only shook her more, demanding again and again. *"Why?"*

It was useless, but Elijah struggled against his bonds anyway. Two firm hands—Dean's and Frank's—clamped down on his shoulders.

Marcus leapt to his feet and gripped Joshua's arms. "Let go of her," he yelled before one of the ushers pulled him back.

Joshua threw Lori onto the sofa and turned away from her. He moved back to Elijah and slammed both hands onto the arms of his chair. He brought himself nose-to-nose with Elijah and stared into his eyes.

"You've turned her against me," he hissed. "Just like you hope to turn this entire church against me. But it won't work."

Elijah said nothing. He only stared back. That wild rage he'd seen before now burned like candles in Joshua's eyes. It was all focused right at him.

"I didn't get to this morning," Joshua continued. "But tonight, I'll tell the people everything. And no waiting until sermon time, either. This time we'll open the service right up with an announcement about you, about *them*—" he pointed at Lori and Marcus, "—and about what you've tried to do here." He took a breath, paused, then went on. "This is *my* church. These are *my* people. It's *my* town. What God hath put together, *no man* shall tear asunder."

He jerked away and looked at the ushers. All four of them fought to remain composed, to keep the fear that lurked just beneath their eyes from surfacing.

"Leave them here," Joshua told them, pointing at Lori and Marcus. "And none of this leaves this office. Go on home."

The men nodded and scurried out.

When they were gone, Joshua turned to Greg. "I don't suppose you have anymore handcuffs?"

Greg, who looked about as comfortable as a cheerleader in prison, shook his head. "No."

Joshua nodded. "Okay. Put them in your car, and take them to the jail."

Greg's eyes shot wide open. "What?"

"You heard me. I want them locked up. Now."

"I can't do that!" Greg whined.

"Yes, you can, and you will!" Joshua shouted at him. "Throw them in with a cell full of criminals, if you have to. But I want them locked away. I don't want them showing up in this church again today."

The three deacons ushered their prisoners through a backdoor. Outside, a squad car, driven by none other than Cprl. K. Blythe himself, had just pulled up. He hurried around to open the backdoor for his soon-to-be passengers.

Elijah was tossed in first, and none too gently, either. He hit the seat shoulder first and growled as fresh pain stabbed his arm. He muscled himself upright again and—with some less-than-gentle prodding from Blythe—scooted over to the door.

Marcus went in next. They didn't bother tossing him, but they did shove him inside hard enough to bump his head on the ceiling once or twice.

Just before Lori would've been shown inside, Joshua stepped between her and the car. "Last chance, Lori," he said.

Lori glared at him for roughly a second and a half before rolling her eyes and climbing in next to Marcus. Then, she turned and stared out the door at Joshua.

Blythe hesitated. He waited for some indication from the church's pastor, but Joshua only stared back at her. He finally shook his head and turned away, headed back inside the church.

Blythe closed the door and headed to the driver's side. Greg climbed into the passenger seat beside him. Within moments, they were heading away from ChristPoint.

On their way to jail.

"You know this is wrong," Lori said to Greg.

"We don't have a choice, Lori," Greg answered.

"We haven't committed a crime," Lori insisted.

"How about criminal mischief?" Blythe countered. "Public disturbance?"

Lori hesitated, but Elijah answered for her. "Those are misdemeanors," he said. "They don't merit jail time. Or...*this*." He moved so his battered face was visible in the rear view mirror.

"Heh, I would've done that for *free*," Blythe chuckled.

"You're not under arrest," Greg said, turning to look into the back seat. "You're just being detained until this evening."

"Until Josh can convince the entire town Elijah's the devil, and we're under his influence," Lori countered.

Greg started to answer, but stopped.

"This isn't how a city government is supposed to operate," Marcus chimed in. "A preacher isn't supposed to call the shots."

Greg pointed an accusing finger at him. "Now, you know Pastor Hutchinson has done more for this town than anyone else. He's united the people under one banner, brought us together for a common purpose."

Marcus leaned forward, his face almost pressed against the divider, and glared at Greg. "And just what the hell is this common purpose?"

"The same purpose every church has," Greg answered, not backing down. "Serve the Lord with all your heart and all your mind and all your soul!"

"And you need Joshua to do that?" Marcus countered.

This time, Greg hesitated. Then, Blythe banged on the divider with his elbow. "That's enough talking," he ordered. "Stay back, and shut up."

Marcus fell back with a sigh. He fumed through his nostrils for several seconds, then turned to look at Elijah.

Elijah leaned close and whispered, *"Make sure and tell Lori. When we stop and they take us out, follow my lead and do exactly as I say when I say. We'll only have one chance at this."*

CHAPTER 38

They couldn't let themselves be taken into the jail. Elijah was certain of that. The moment they stepped inside the building, they were finished. Outside, on the other hand, with only Blythe and Foster to deal with, they had a chance.

A slim chance—*real* slim—but still a chance.

Meanwhile, something gnawed at him. His knife. The bastards had taken it from him the night Frank hauled him into Joshua's office, and he hadn't seen it since. He wanted it back, even if it was for no other reason than to be certain *they* didn't have it.

That wasn't all Elijah wanted. He also meant to take Blythe's car.

He felt his companions' eyes on him, and he turned to look back. They both gave the slightest of nods. *We're ready.*

Elijah didn't nod back, just stared back long enough to make it clear he got the message. Then, he turned his attention back to the front seat. He leveled his gaze at Foster, who frequently cast nervous glances back at him.

Keep him nervous, Elijah told himself. *Keep him on edge.*

Blythe weaved his way through the downtown streets and finally brought the squad car to the backdoor of the city's jail. It was in a long, narrow alley just wide enough for the car doors to open. There was a single security camera mounted over the door.

"End of the line," Blythe said, and climbed out. Foster followed him.

Elijah felt his friends' eyes again, but didn't look back. When the door opened, he followed Blythe's hands guiding him out of the car, but once he'd planted his feet on the pavement, he rammed the back of his head into the man's face. He felt Blythe's nose crunch against the top of his skull. Both men stumbled back and toppled.

Foster managed to yell out a dismayed "*Hey!*" just as both men hit the pavement. Blythe roared. Elijah fought to make sure the man stayed beneath him and looked into the squad car, where Marcus and Lori still sat and stared.

"*Come on!*" he screamed.

They both blinked almost in unison and hurried outside. Foster, who stood rooted beside the car, finally thought to reach for his pistol, but Marcus intercepted him as his hand reached the holster. They both struggled for several agonizing seconds until Lori stepped in, wormed her hands around Foster's pistol, and yanked the weapon away.

"Lori, what are you doing?" Foster demanded.

She pointed the gun and screamed, "*Shut up!*"

He did.

Elijah rolled off Blythe and scrambled to his feet. Then, Lori aimed the gun at the injured corporal. "Don't forget, he's still armed," Elijah told her. He turned to Marcus. "Quick. Move the car in front of the door."

Marcus glanced at the car a moment, then understood. As he hopped in to the driver's seat, Elijah headed for the chief. Foster took two nervous steps back as Elijah, his hands still cuffed behind his back, stumbled toward him.

"L-look, young man," Foster stammered. "I am a police o-officer. What you—all th-three of y-you—are doing is a felony."

Elijah didn't stop until he stood nose-to-nose with the man. He held his gaze a moment longer, then said, "Who has the keys to these cuffs?"

Greg blinked, hesitated.

"I said—"

"He does," Greg sputtered. He pointed at Blythe, who was still clutching at his nose. A steady stream of blood flowed over his mouth and chin onto his shirt.

Elijah turned and walked back to him. *"You'll spend the rest of your lives in prison for this!"* Blythe spat at him as he crouched nearby. Elijah felt speckles of warm blood hit his face.

The jail door banged against the squad car, and Elijah could hear the guards inside yelling. For the moment, their blockade was holding. "Keys," he said to the injured corporal.

Blythe hesitated at first, as if daring him. Elijah made a show of looking back at Lori, who still had the pistol pointed at the fallen man. "I don't know how good a shot she is," he said, then looked back at Blythe. "But this close up, I'm not sure it matters."

At that, Blythe growled and yanked the keys off his belt. Elijah turned, and Blythe slapped them into his hand, making sure the edges dug into his skin.

"Thanks." Elijah stood and walked over to Marcus, who now stood beside the car. He handed the keys off, and after trying several times, Marcus found the right one and release Elijah's hands for the first time in days. It was all he could do not to let out a sigh of absolute relief.

"Now what?" Marcus asked him.

Elijah gestured for Marcus to help him with Blythe. "Stand up," he told the man.

Blythe growled through bloody teeth, but he obliged. Elijah stepped forward and held out his hand. "Give me the gun."

Blythe cast a quick glance at Lori, who kept her pistol trained on him, then looked back at Elijah. *"You're gonna' pay for this,"* he hissed, baring his teeth.

He pulled the gun from its holster and held it out. But when Elijah reached for it, Blythe turned it and fired at Lori.

The gunshot exploded in Elijah's ears and echoed throughout the alley. He leapt forward and pried the gun from the man's grip. He spun Blythe around and threw him into the side of the cruiser. Foster was yelling, but Elijah barely heard him. Blythe grinned back at him, a truly ugly sight with two rows of bloodstained teeth.

Elijah held the pistol just beneath Blythe's chin and chanced a look back at Lori. She was still on her feet, but she was staring at the gaping hole in the front of her blouse. A crimson stain was fast expanding from the center. Her legs gave out, and she fell to the ground.

Elijah jerked his attention back to Blythe and screamed, *"Why did you do that?"* He took hold of the man's shirt. *"Why?"*

Blythe didn't answer. He spat a mouthful of blood, which splattered on Elijah's cheek. It was thick and warm.

What was wrong with this man? What made him do this?

Hell with it. Elijah muscled Blythe into the backseat of the squad car and slammed the door closed. Then, he rushed over to Lori.

Marcus was already at her side. "She's not breathing," he said. His voice trembled. Tears were building up beneath his eyes, ready to spill down his cheeks at any moment.

A second squad car appeared at the other end of the alley and sped toward them, lights blazing, but no one paid it any attention.

Oh, God, please! Elijah placed his hand over the wound in Lori's abdomen. Warm blood oozed through his fingers and coated his hand. And beneath that, he could feel a gaping hole in her belly the size of a baseball. The blood flowed in steady pulses, pumped by a heart unaware it was speeding along toward oblivion.

He closed his eyes.

Please!

Please, God!

Nothing. Lori's blood was warm, but Elijah could almost *feel* her body growing cold. Still no breath. No pulse. No movement.

Nothing.

"Please, Lori?" Marcus' voice. It cracked when he said her name. He was weeping. Elijah heard the intermingled sorrow and panic in his strained voice. "Don't leave me." He sniffled.

The flow of blood slowed. Unfortunately, Elijah had no way of knowing whether that was good or bad. Blythe had punched one beast of a hole in her. For all he knew, it could've been slowing because there was almost no blood left.

Elijah's eyes stung, and he realized he was beginning to cry, as well. *Please, Lori. Don't leave us.* He felt a tear slip through his eyelids and fall.

Still nothing.

Had he lost his gift? Was it truly a blessing from on High, and the Almighty had taken it back because Elijah dared to oppose one of His ministers? Was this how God repaid him?

Or was it just too late? Was she already dead?

Those thoughts ended when Lori gasped in a lungful of hair. Her hand shot up and clutched Elijah's shirt, startling his eyes open. She stared back at him and continued inhaling as much air as possible. She coughed twice and spit up mouthfuls of blood both times, but the color was returning to her face. Beneath Elijah's hand, her belly grew warm again.

"*Oh, thank you, God!*" Marcus wailed. He leaned forward and buried his face in Lori's shoulder. He wailed again, his voice only slightly muffled by her blouse.

Lori's breathing slowed, relaxed. Then, she twitched and pushed Elijah's hand away from her stomach. "That tickles," she sighed, her voice a soft whisper.

Elijah smiled, and he felt another tear escape his eye. It trickled down his cheek, leaving a cold trail behind. "You okay?" he asked.

She nodded. "Think so." When Marcus pulled away, she looked down at her chest and said, "But I should probably change clothes."

"Probably," Elijah agreed.

"What just happened here…?"

The three of them turned their attention to the policeman now standing beside the squad car that arrived moments earlier. Sgt. Darren Morris, Elijah saw. "She was shot," he said, and started helping Lori to her feet.

"By who?"

Lori's arms were draped around Marcus and Elijah's shoulders, but she managed to point back to the squad car where Blythe sat next to Foster.

"But now you're…you're okay?" Morris stared at the bloody hole in her blouse.

"Yeah." Lori pulled hers arms to herself and stepped back from her companions, standing on her own weight. "I think I am."

"But—?"

"Bit of a long story," Elijah said, stepping forward and placing a hand on the man's shoulder. "Tell me. You attend ChristPoint?"

Morris hesitated a moment, then shook his head sheepishly. "No." He seemed to blush. "Only guy on the force who doesn't."

Lori grinned. "We need to talk."

CHAPTER 39

Just about an hour later, Joshua sat alone on the hood of his car. He stared at the ground, his hands—still wearing gloves—hanging between his knees. Blood dripped from a nasty wound on his right arm.

He was escorting Nathan home from the hospital just over an hour ago when he'd received word of some sort of incident at the jail. Elijah, Marcus, Lori, Greg, and Blythe were all missing, and apparently a police officer named Morris had vanished with them.

This was supposed to be a happy day. Nathan was returning home, and Elijah would finally—*finally*—be put in his place.

Naturally, Nathan was ecstatic to be back home. He'd spent days confined to a hospital bed in critical care, and he couldn't wait to relax on his own sofa again. *Ironic how much we appreciate the simple things when they're taken away,* Joshua mused and smiled.

Doctors had inserted metal rods into his ankle to repair it. They told him to stay off it until well after the rods came out—likely four to five weeks. Rehabilitation was going to be a long and arduous process.

But Nathan had a wonderful wife, Katherine, who would look after him and see to his every need. Katherine was the epitome of a loving woman, ready to care for her injured husband in whatever way he needed. And, despite her age, she was still a striking woman. Her hair was long and blonde, her features soft and gentle, and she was still in excellent shape.

Joshua smiled and sighed. He longed for that. He'd hoped Lori would fill that gap in his life, but it appeared that wasn't to be.

He looked up at the comfortable, two-story house before him. Nathan and Katherine's house. He'd parked in the driveway.

Just moments before, Katherine had asked him to keep an eye on Nathan while she ran to the drug store to pick up her husband's medication. And, of course, Joshua agreed. He wasn't just Nathan's pastor; he was his friend.

Nathan had lain down on the sofa, and Joshua found something on television he liked, some old movie on cable starring the legendary Clint Eastwood Joshua didn't recognize. Nathan was plenty eager to see it. He'd always loved westerns, especially the "spaghetti westerns" that starred Eastwood. "Give the Duke his due," he'd once told Joshua, "but the Man With No Name's the best cowboy that ever lived."

He'd never even noticed Joshua putting the gloves on.

Joshua had wedged a pillow beneath Nathan's head, and then—

Joshua blinked, and fresh tears slipped from his eyes.

Then, he'd withdrawn Elijah's knife from his pocket and slit Nathan's throat. Ear to ear. The blade was still in its leather sheath when he pulled it out, so he'd had to move fast before Nathan realized what was happening.

And he had.

But Nathan still hadn't managed to scream before the blade cut through his neck. He'd only been able to stare in shock as the blood poured down his front and soaked the couch.

His eyes. Joshua sniffled. He'd seen betrayal and horror in those eyes. *How could you do this to me*, they'd demanded. *Why did you do this?*

But it was necessary. It had to happen. There was no other way.

After receiving word of Elijah's escape, Joshua begged God for an answer. He'd beseeched Him for direction, for guidance, for a path. How could he prove to this town and its people that Elijah was a roaming vagabond? How could he reveal to them the true sinister nature of Antioch's strange visitor?

And, for the first time since Elijah walked into Joshua's life, God had answered. Finally, after all this time. At long last the Lord paid heed to His desperate servant.

What Antioch needed was a martyr: someone to die so that others would live, to prove that Elijah was no healer. That he was, in fact, a killer.

After Nathan's eyes had glazed over, Joshua held the knife to his arm, clenched his eyes, gritted his teeth, and sliced a giant gash in his flesh. Then, he stepped outside to call the police.

He could already hear the faint wail of sirens in the distance. He concealed the knife in his car; for some reason, he felt he might still need it.

Now, the town would understand that Elijah was to be feared. Not him.

He remembered the looks in everyone's eyes this morning after Lori played the tape. They resembled the look in Nathan's as he died. They all wondered if he could be trusted, if he could lead them.

I can, he told himself. *I can.*

"You can't be serious? You want to go *back?*" Marcus shouted.

Elijah smiled. "I have to. We all have to."

"The hell I do!" Marcus folded his arms and glared back. "We barely got out of there alive, and now you want us to go back—into the lions' den—for the *second* time today?"

Elijah nodded. "Yes."

Darren, their latest accomplice, leaned against the driver's side door of the squad car, arms folded, listening. They'd pretty much brought him up-to-date at this point, on Elijah, on Joshua, and on ChristPoint.

They'd parked the car well off a paved road in the county. The chances of anyone venturing out this way were slim, but Darren kept his eyes on the road just the same.

I've probably just lost my job, he thought and smirked. *Insubordination. Conspiracy. Accomplice.*

The legal terms tumbled through his head, bouncing around like loose change.

But that's okay, he supposed. *So be it.*

Darren had long taken issue with the Rev. Hutchinson and his religious stranglehold on Antioch. The man was practically an unofficial mayor with a lifetime term of office. Hell, Antioch's *real* mayor, a squirrelly little man named Howard Crass, hadn't made any decisions on his own in years.

Darren had never been big on religion. It just wasn't his thing. He could never bring himself to pray to a God who essentially demanded worship from humanity under the threat of eternal hellfire.

He'd been raised in a church, went with his parents every Sunday until he was eighteen, but he figured he stopped believing around the age of twelve when his grandfather died.

The old man had suffered from dementia for years. He needed to be reminded who each of his family members were every day. In the last six months, nurses had to bathe him and wipe his ass.

Hard to understand a God who'd allow that to happen in a man's final years.

Despite his skepticism, though, Darren had no problem with people of faith. He didn't pretend to understand it, but he'd always been able to admire the strength many people drew from a belief in something greater than themselves.

Until Joshua rose to power. The good Reverand wasn't interested in spreading God's message; he wanted everyone to listen to *his* message. And *only* his message. The only strength he was interested in was his own.

With each passing year, there were fewer and fewer people left to stop the man. Darren spent his life as a relative recluse. He'd tried a few times for a transfer, but nothing ever materialized. So he'd continued living and working in Joshua's shadow.

But now, with these people—with *Elijah*—it looked like there just might be a way.

Elijah. Who was this guy?

"And what do you think, Lori?" Marcus was asking.

Darren caught the kid casting wary glances his way in between sentences. He still didn't trust him, likely viewed him as "part of the establishment," or something like that.

Which was fair enough. After all, he *was*.

"I don't want to abandon my family," Lori said.

"You barely talk to them!" Marcus insisted.

Lori clenched her fists and screamed, "*I don't care!*"

"Guys," Darren broke in. "I'm the new guy here, so you don't have to pay any attention to me. For whatever it's worth, I can see where Marcus is coming from here. You," he pointed at Elijah, "just spent three nights cuffed to a chair. And you," he pointed at Lori, "were just shot. In fact, you *should* be dead right now."

He paused, letting that sink in. Then, he said, "But if there was ever a time to bring Joshua down, this is it. After that stunt you guys pulled this morning, the entire church is questioning him. There'll never be a better moment to stand before the entire congregation and show them once and for all what he really is."

Lori nodded and leveled her gaze at Marcus, who shook his head and sighed. "Fine," he said "Fine. Let's do it. But if I end up dying, I'm gonna' be super-pissed."

Darren smiled. He liked these guys. "So what's your plan?" he asked.

"I'll tell them," Lori answered. "Everything."

Elijah placed his hand on her shoulder. "You sure you can do that?"

"You guys have any better ideas?"

"They sure as hell won't listen to me," Marcus agreed.

Elijah turned to Darren. "Can you get us in?"

Darren nodded. "I think so. We may have to get creative if Joshua's gotten nervous and surrounded the place with cops, though."

"He won't do that," Lori said. "He wouldn't want his church to look *scary*. It doesn't mean they won't be there. It just means they won't be in uniform if they are. But I can probably get us into some less-traveled hallways."

"Then, we go in together," Elijah told them.

So this is it, Darren thought. He'd entered this game late, but this looked like the final play. These kids just might have a real shot at dethroning the mighty Rev. Hutchinson.

He actually felt a little excited.

It evaporated when he heard the car's radio announce a citywide manhunt for Elijah in connection with the slaying of Nathan Riley.

CHAPTER 40

"*He killed Nathan?*" Greg Foster squawked.

Joshua nodded. "Sometime this afternoon. Probably after he and the others escaped."

"But—he just—" Greg collapsed onto an empty pew. He, Joshua, Frank, and Dean had gathered in the sanctuary in the hour before evening service. Greg looked up at Joshua, still in shock. "He never seemed to have it in him."

"You should've seen him in my apartment," Dean said.

Greg shook his head. He was still reeling from everything that had happened today. One of his officers, Darren Morris, had taken off with Elijah, Lori, and Marcus just over an hour ago. After watching them lock Greg and Blythe in their own squad car, Sgt. Morris invited the fugitives into his own car and drove away.

He'd witnessed Elijah *heal* Lori of a gunshot wound with his own eyes. It was amazing, absolutely amazing. The girl was dying, dying right in front of him, and then, she was walking around like nothing happened.

She should've been on her way to the morgue.

"You think they'll come back or make a run for it?" Dean asked.

"I think they'll be back," Joshua answered, "probably to interrupt tonight's service just like this morning."

Greg didn't hear them. He was processing the time frame of Nathan's death. The coroner hadn't announced a time of death yet—those details hinged on an autopsy—but Joshua reported it to the police station less than an hour ago. He told them he'd stayed with Nathan in the house while Katherine went out for groceries, and Elijah broke in and attacked them. He even had a nasty wound on his right arm to prove it.

But Darren left with him? Certainly, Darren was disobeying direct orders by helping Elijah, Lori, and Marcus escape, but would he actually stand by while Elijah killed someone?

And even if Darren did go along with such a thing, that would mean they had to rush over to Nathan's house in order to kill him, then flee the city.

"Greg?" Joshua's voice.

Greg shook his head, blinked. "I'm sorry, what?"

"Can you provide security for tonight's service?" Joshua asked. "Civilian clothes only, though. I don't want people to see squad cars lining the entrance when they come tonight."

"Uh—yeah—sure."

It didn't add up. It just...*didn't*.

Elijah's knife. He didn't have it. They'd taken it from him the night Frank hauled him in. They'd never given it back. In fact, the last person to have it was—

Greg's breath caught in his throat. *No.* He looked back at Joshua. No, it wasn't possible.

Joshua was going over their plans for the night. Frank and Dean were to remain near the back of the sanctuary, at the main entrance. Police officers would be scattered around the sanctuary, along with a handful of ushers. *Vigilance* was the key.

"Greg?" Joshua again.

"Yeah?"

"You stay with your wife during the service, but stay in contact with all your officers. Keep a radio handy, but only use it when absolutely necessary." He looked at the others. "We will *not* live in fear.

Elijah sat up front with Darren for the ride back into town. Lori and Marcus rode in the back. None of them spoke.

The sun had just crept below the horizon, and the sky was darkening. Venturing back into what Marcus considered "enemy territory" was already a grim task, but the recent announcement of Nathan Riley's death cast an even darker shadow over the whole thing.

It was a stark reminder of what the stakes were.

Marcus had been the first to voice his suspicions. "It was Joshua."

No one argued with him.

"But I don't get it," Lori ventured. "Why would Josh kill Nathan?"

No one answered at first. Nathan's death was so unexpected. It was hard to come up with anything.

"Is he just getting desperate?" Darren offered. "His last try at making the town afraid of Elijah?"

"It's possible," Elijah agreed. "We've backed him into a corner. I imagine he can feel himself losing his grip on the town. He's running out of options."

"Which makes him all the more dangerous," Darren said.

Elijah nodded. All too true.

"So what's our plan, exactly?" Marcus asked.

"Confront him," Elijah answered. "In front of the entire congregation."

"That's it? Tell me that's not all we're going to do."

"Well, we're not going to just march in through the front door, if that's what you're worried about." Darren looked at Marcus through the rearview mirror and grinned.

"Oh, sure, that's a load off my mind." Marcus rolled his eyes. "But can't you just arrest him? Or something?"

"No offense, but how am I supposed to do that when the chief of police is wedged face-first up his butt?" Darren raised an eyebrow at the mirror.

"So that's it, then?" Marcus sounded impatient. "We're just going to sneak into the sanctuary in the middle of his sermon and call him a liar?"

"Crude, but yes," Elijah said. "We can't force people to see him for what he is. They have to make that choice themselves."

"And if they don't?"

Elijah raised his eyebrows and sighed. "We should probably keep an eye on the fire exits, just in case."

Joshua knelt alone in his office and prayed while the congregation milled into the sanctuary. "Hallelujah," he said aloud. "I praise your name, Jesus. I thank you for all you've done for me, and I ask you to continue to strengthen me tonight as I carry out your work in this church."

He would address everyone at the opening of the service. There would be no waiting to be interrupted mid-sermon this time. No, he would make certain his people were well aware of the danger they faced.

"Elijah—he's a wolf in sheep's clothing, Lord," Joshua prayed. "He threatens this church, this town, this entire great work that you have wrought."

No, Joshua would stop him. With God's help, he would stop him. Elijah would not tear down what he'd spent his life building. *What God hath brought together, let no man tear asunder...Mark 10:9...*

Joshua leaned back and raised his hands heavenward. His eyes remained closed, and he cried, "*Oh, Jesus, I thank you for your many blessings! I praise you for who you are! Hear my prayer, oh God! Hear your humble servant! Guide my path! Guide my hands! Guide my words!*"

He heard the faint sound of the piano in the sanctuary. It was nearly service time. He needed to go and be with his people. He placed his right hand over his heart, where he'd sheathed Elijah's knife. "If he comes at me tonight, I'll be ready, Lord," he breathed.

He stood and clasped his hands before his face for one final moment. "Help me beat him, Jesus," Joshua whispered. "Help me to cast him aside and save this church. I ask this in your name. *Amen.*"

He wiped his eyes and headed for the sanctuary.

CHAPTER 41

The parking lot was full. Naturally.
Darren weaved Blythe's squad car around the outer rim of the massive church's parking lot. He and the others kept watch for any sign of police, ushers, or anyone else who might be out patrolling the area.
There was no one.
Probably doesn't want guards roaming around the outside of the church, Lori figured. *Sends a bad message.*
"I don't suppose you've got a key to the back door?" Elijah asked.
"Actually." Darren grinned. "You guys are in luck tonight. I swiped Chief Foster's keys, and he *does* have a key to the back door."
"Praise the Lord," Marcus sighed.
Darren didn't bother searching for a parking space. He stopped the car at the rear entrance—the same one Elijah, Lori, and Marcus were hauled out of just hours before—and everyone filed out.
Darren checked his pistol. Full clip. Safety off.
He was about to slip it in his holster when Elijah touched his arm. He looked back and was more than a little startled at Elijah's piercing gaze. "Leave it," he said.
"Huh?"

"The gun," Elijah said. "Leave it."

"Are you nuts? The entire police department is probably in there, and they're ready to arrest all four of us on sight. Not to mention, they *will* be armed."

Elijah shook his head. "I don't care. No guns."

Darren stared back, not believing. But still he reached into his holster and pulled out the pistol. He handed it to Elijah and shook his head. "This is a mistake," he said.

Elijah considered a moment. Then, he took the clip out, emptied it one bullet at a time until it was empty, put the clip back, and returned it to Darren. "Threaten all you like," he said. "But no shooting."

Darren took the gun back and stared. Was this guy serious?

"No one dies," Elijah told him. "Not tonight." He looked at Lori. "Not even Joshua."

Darren nodded. Fair enough. "You know the layout of this place, right?" he asked Lori.

"Every hallway, every staircase, every door," she answered.

"Okay then." Darren pulled out Foster's keys and fumbled through them until he found the right one. He unlocked the door, turned the doorknob, glanced around at everyone one last time, then pulled the door open.

And found himself face-to-face with a stupefied teenager.

The boy couldn't have been more than fifteen years old. He was short and skinny, with blondish hair that fell over his ears like an old mop. His hand was held out as though to turn the doorknob, but now it just hung frozen in the air. He stared up at Darren with wide eyes. His mouth hung open like it was about to say something—*anything*—but the words just wouldn't come out.

"*Crap!*" Darren hissed and clamped a hand over the kid's mouth before he could scream. He checked the hallway inside (empty) and yanked the wide-eyed youth outside.

Darren shoved the boy none too gently against the wall, hand still clamped to his mouth. The others gathered round, boxing the horrified kid in without any hope of escape.

"Perfect," Marcus spat. "So, what do we do with him?"

"The car," Elijah said. "Lock him in the back. Best we can do right now."

"Hey, chin up," Darren told Marcus as he dragged the kid toward the squad car. "Now there's one less usher to deal with."

He tossed the teen in the car and slammed the door shut before he could make any noise. The boy banged on the window with his fist a few times, then leaned back and started kicking.

Thud!

Thud!

"That gonna' hold him?" Marcus asked.

"Should," Darren said. "All he's gonna' do is wear himself out and probably give himself a sore foot." He looked at Marcus and grinned. "He'll probably scuff things up a bit, too, but, hey, it's not my car, anyway."

Joshua stepped to the pulpit and looked out at the congregation. They were all here, every single member. No doubt they all wanted answers to the questions raised this morning. They deserved answers, and Joshua was going to give them.

"For those who haven't heard the news, yet," he began, "Nathan Riley is dead."

There was a collective gasp among the audience. Clearly, several people *hadn't* heard, yet

"He was murdered in his own home just moments after he was released from the hospital." Joshua paused. This was heavy news, and people needed time to digest it all. "And Elijah is the one who killed him."

The four of them, following Lori's lead, stuck to less used hallways and managed to avoid any more obstacles. They followed a hallway that ran underneath the sanctuary, and Joshua's muffled message bled through the ceiling at them.

"This place is a fortress," Darren said.

"It's Joshua's monument," Lori sighed. "His testament."

"How much farther?" Elijah asked.

Lori pointed ahead to another doorway. "Through that door. Then we'll turn left and go up some stairs and be in another hallway that runs along the front of the sanctuary. There's a pair of doors that lead right on stage."

"Some of you might wonder why we kept Elijah's presence here quiet for so long," Joshua continued. "That's a fair question. And, I'll be honest, it might've been a mistake on our part. On *my* part."

He moved away from the pulpit, stepped down from the platform, and walked into the midst of the congregation. His people.

"The fact is, we didn't know who or—or *what*—we were dealing with," he said. "He attended a morning service not long ago. Some of you may remember? He stayed with an old friend of mine for several days, and then he left."

He continued on, heading down the aisle toward the back of the sanctuary, where Dean and Frank stood guard at the rear entrance.

"Then, he attacked Corporal Kent Blythe, stabbed him in the chest with the same hunting knife used to kill Nathan this afternoon. Corporal Blythe? Would you stand so everyone can see your shirt?"

Blythe, who sat in a pew midway down the aisle, stood. His uniform was cleaned, so the bloodstains were gone. However, the large hole remained. He pulled it open as best he could to show the entire congregation.

"Thank you." Joshua motioned for him to sit again. "But this is where things got...*weird*. Just seconds after stabbing Blythe, Elijah turned and...*healed him.*"

There was another collective gasp.

Joshua's words were audible through the walls now.

"*That slimy son of a...!*" Marcus whispered.

"Careful there, buddy," Darren said. He clapped Marcus on the shoulder. "You'll get yourself struck by lightning."

Elijah placed a finger to his lips, shushing them both. He turned to Lori, who pointed to a set of double doors. They were wooden, with narrow windows.

"Those lead right on stage," she said.

Elijah and Darren crept over to them and peered through. At first, they wondered if they were looking through the right doors. Joshua's pulpit was there, but it was empty. Then, they caught a glimpse of him in the distance, walking among the congregation. They could also just barely make out the edges of shoulders on either side of the door, which meant two ushers or two police officers were guarding it.

"In the book of Matthew, Jesus said 'Beware of false prophets, which come to you in sheep's clothing, but inwardly they are ravening wolves," Joshua declared, his voice rising. "Many false prophets will appear and deceive many people. The Bible says they'll perform great signs and miracles—just as Elijah has done—to deceive even the elect."

Joshua turned and made his way back to the platform. His words came faster now. His movements were more animated.

"Mark my words," he declared, "this Elijah *is* a false prophet! And woe unto those who fall under his spell! Amen?"

"*Amen!*" the audience cried.

"You take that guy, I'll take this guy," Darren said.

"I take which guy, you take what guy?" Elijah asked.

Darren started to answer but stopped when Elijah grinned. "Not funny."

"You're right," Elijah agreed. "Let's not waste anymore time. One three?"

Darren nodded. "One. Two."

"*Three!*"

CHAPTER 42

Joshua, now just several paces away from the platform, stopped at the sight of Lori marching toward the podium. Behind her, Elijah, Marcus, and the police officer who joined them held the two guards watching the door back. He glanced around the sanctuary, sending a silent message to the other plainclothes officers in the sanctuary: *Get them!*

Lori screamed, "*Hold it!*" Her loud and frantic voice reverberated off the walls and echoed throughout the sanctuary. She was momentarily halted at the sight of a dozen men hurrying toward the stage to cut her off. Joshua, who stood less than ten feet away from her, only stared.

Lori set the microphone aside and said, "Elijah didn't kill anyone, Joshua. You did."

Silence.

The men rushing the stage stopped behind Joshua. Several glanced at him, awaiting orders. Joshua did nothing.

"Didn't you?" Lori demanded. "You've had his knife ever since your men locked him up in your office three days ago. And you used it to kill Nathan to implicate him."

Joshua turned back to the congregation. His face was grave. "Just like I said." His voice was sad. "He's performed great signs and wonders, but, underneath it all, he's a *wolf in sheep's clothing!*"

The congregation's gaze danced back and forth between Joshua and Lori.

"Elijah's not a false prophet," Lori countered. "He's not a *prophet* at all. He's just…going through life looking for answers. Just like the rest of us."

Joshua turned back to her. His expression had turned cold. "I've heard enough of this. Arrest them!"

The men rushed forward and flooded the stage. Behind Lori, Elijah let go of the guard he and Marcus were holding and raced to her side before the men could reach her. It made little difference. They were grossly outnumbered.

Members of the congregation stood as the spectacle unfolded. Chaos erupted. Half a dozen men laid hands on Lori and Elijah and forced them to their knees. Moments later, Darren and Marcus were also dragged forward.

Marcus thrashed wildly and managed to wriggle himself free. He charged at Joshua with three ushers chasing close behind. He grabbed the preacher by the shirt and screamed, *"Stop lying to them!"*

Confused and frantic voices from the congregation filled the sanctuary. Marcus spun and tossed Joshua into a nearby pew. A moment later, he was on him again, thrashing him madly.

"Stop this, Joshua!" he screamed. *"Stop—"*

Elijah's blade flashed out from Joshua's coat and sank into Marcus' chest, piercing his heart. Marcus' words caught in his throat, and he stared down at the blade with wide eyes. Joshua, with equally wide eyes, stared back at him.

Both men were surrounded by pandemonium. No one around them witnessed Joshua's deadly attack.

But Elijah did.

"*No-o-o!*" he screamed. He struggled against the guards holding him, but their grip held firm. "*Let me go! Let me go to him!*"

Marcus staggered back, eyes wide. He glanced at the knife in his chest for all of three seconds before dropping to the ground.

"Let go of me, you bastards!" Elijah bellowed.

The sanctuary grew quiet, save for Elijah's protests. The silence worked its way to the back of the room like a wave. Soon, no one spoke. They only stared, horrified at the scene unfolding before them.

"Let him go," Joshua breathed. "Now!"

Reluctantly, the guards holding Elijah released him. He shoved them aside and leapt off the platform to Marcus.

But Marcus' eyes were already glazed over. Already empty. Elijah placed both hands his bloody chest. "*No,*" he whispered. "*Please, no!*"

He closed his eyes, felt the tears escaping them and concentrated.

Come back, Marcus!
Come back!

The sanctuary was silent, save for the hushed whispers of those in the back who couldn't see, begging to know what was happening.

Elijah took hold of the knife and yanked it from Marcus' chest. Blood arced through the air, following the blade's path, and spattered on the carpet. The crimson liquid oozed from the fresh wound and saturated the front of Marcus' shirt. Elijah placed his hand there, closed his eyes once more.

Work!

Work, dammit, work!

Nothing. Marcus grew cold. His complexion paled. His skin grayed.

Elijah didn't bother fighting the tears that spilled down his cheeks. He sniffled. "Please, Marcus?" he whimpered.

But Marcus never responded.

Elijah leaned over him and wept, buried his face against his friend's shoulder and wailed. The agonizing sound echoed throughout the otherwise silent room.

No one spoke. Not Lori. Not Darren. Not Joshua. Nor the entire congregation. All watched in silence. Only the sound of Elijah's anguished cries filled the sanctuary.

Then, he leaned back, sniffled several times. For a moment, he could only caress the top of Marcus' head, running his fingers through his hair. At last, he lowered his hand and gently closed his friend's eyes.

Closed them forever.

It was several moments before anyone spoke. The shock of what had happened closed their throats, sealed their mouths and rooted them in place.

Joshua found his voice first. From behind Elijah, he said, "Heal him!"

Elijah turned to look at the him. There was a small crimson stain on the front of Joshua's shirt where Marcus' blood had spattered. His eyes were frantic, wild. "*Heal him!*" he demanded.

Elijah stood and shook his head. "I...can't. It's too late."

"*Heal him!*" Joshua screamed. He raced forward and gripped Elijah's coat. "*That's what you do! Heal him!*"

Elijah felt fresh tears escaping his eyes. He held Joshua's gaze and shook his head. "He's dead. I can't heal that."

Joshua shook him. Violently. "*I don't care! You can't let someone die in my sanctuary! You have to heal him! You have to...*"

He broke off and rushed to Marcus' side. He placed one hand on Marcus' head and raised the other toward Heaven. "In the name of Jesus Christ," he declared, "I command you to rise up and walk!"

Nothing.

"*Rise up and walk!*"

Elijah looked up and around the sanctuary. Several women were crying. Even some men struggled to hold back tears. He looked back to the platform where the ushers held Lori. Her face was a mask of horrible pain. Tears streaked down the sides, and her mouth was open in a silent wail.

Elijah marched forward and glared at the two men holding her. "Let. Her. Go."

They did.

Lori rushed to Marcus' side, knelt down, and cried. Beside her, Joshua continued beseeching God to resurrect her friend. "*Rise and walk! I command this in Jesus' name! In Jesus' name! In Jesus' name!*"

Lori shoved him away. "*Stop it!*" she screamed. "*You're the one who killed him! Why do you think God would listen to you?*"

Joshua stared back at her. Fresh tears were in his eyes. He turned, saw Elijah staring down at him, and howled. He crawled up to the platform, moving like a wild animal, with burning lunatic fury in his eyes. He raised the blade overhead and charged, meaning to drive it deep into Elijah's heart.

Elijah caught him overhead by the wrist and held him there. The church and guards still watched in paralyzed silence as the two men staggered about the stage.

"*You've ruined everything!*" Joshua howled. Spittle shot from his mouth and hung from his lips in thin ribbons. "*You've ruined me!*"

Darren started forward to help, but Elijah hollered, "Stay back!"

They spun around, and Joshua pushed Elijah into the pulpit. It toppled and fell from the platform onto the floor below. Those seated on the front row gasped and fled just before it smashed on the ground a few feet away.

"*I'll...I'll* kill *you!*" Joshua snarled.

They bumped into the platform chairs reserved for the pastor and honored guests. The pastor's chair tilted a foot or so, but managed to maintain its balance.

Joshua and Elijah stumbled to the floor. Elijah landed on his back, and Joshua landed on top of him. They both squawked but continued their struggle. Joshua raised the knife overhead again and drove it down toward his enemy's neck.

Elijah caught it just inches from his throat. The point of the blade danced crazily as he fought with Joshua for control of it.

Joshua bared his teeth. Pure, unadulterated hatred burned in his eyes.

Then, the sound of a heavy impact exploded throughout the sanctuary, and Joshua toppled over. The knife slipped from his hands and slid across the platform floor.

Elijah looked up at Lori, who stood over him now with a heavy Bible. She was panting, tears still in her eyes.

Elijah crawled over Joshua and retrieved his knife before the pastor could recover. As he did so, he heard Joshua whisper, "Kill me."

Elijah stared at the man. He lay on his back, his head turned, his eyes closed. Tears seeped out from between his clenched eyelids. "Kill me," he whispered again. "Please?"

But Elijah only shook his head. "No one else dies tonight," he told Joshua. "Not even you."

He stood and wrapped his arms around Lori. She leaned into his embrace and buried her face in his shoulder. She continued weeping, her tears soaking a portion of Elijah's coat.

"It's okay to cry now," he told her, then glanced at Marcus' body. "He deserves that much."

The paralysis that held everyone in place seemed to fade. Hushed whispers broke out. Feet shuffled.

Darren made the first real movement, making his way down the aisle to Joshua. He reached down for the man and said, "Joshua Hutchinson, you're under arrest...for the murder of Marcus Colley."

Joshua reeled on him. His eyes were almost comical, bulging from his sockets like enormous orbs. His lower lip trembled, and he inhaled a deep, ragged breath before screaming. His voice reverberated over the sound system and rattled the walls. Several windows cracked. Everyone in the room—including Darren—clutched their ears and doubled over.

Joshua rolled away and jumped to his feet. He stared back at Darren for a moment while the man recovered. His face had the look of a lunatic demon. A single string of spittle hung from his mouth.

"No!" he hissed though clenched teeth. *"No!"*

He turned and ran down the aisle—the congregation parted to let him pass—toward the rear entrance. He burst through the doors, raced through the empty foyer, and charged out into the night.

Darren yelled after him and gave chase, but his equilibrium hadn't quite recovered. His ears still rang, and he stumbled into a mass of people clutching their heads.

"Someone...!" he croaked. *"After him!"*

The police guarding the rear entrance, still covering their own ears, didn't hear.

"You idiots! He's getting away!" Darren shoved against the people surrounding him. Several stumbled aside, but he met another wall of people behind them.

One of them was Cpl. Blythe.

The cool night air bit at Joshua's skin. He weaved his way through the parking lot, making his way to his car.

No one called after him. The night was silent. Dead silent. Everyone was still inside the sanctuary. They were all under Elijah's spell now. All of them.

He screamed again and slammed into the side of his car. His upper torso caught the impact, and pain wracked his chest and arms. He cried out.

But no one answered.

He fumbled in his pocket for his keys. His hands shook violently, so he had trouble getting hold of them.

Once they were out, it took several tries just to insert the key into the lock.

Lori sank to the ground, still sobbing. Elijah sank with her. He kept his arm around her, and she leaned into his shoulder, burying her face against his chest. They remained there for several minutes, oblivious to the chaos around them.

Lori started when a gentle hand touched her shoulder. *Marcus?* she thought for one crazy moment. But she knew better.

She pulled away from Elijah, turned and looked up. It was her mother. Tears lined her face, and she sniffled, but otherwise she was the most beautiful thing Lori had seen all night.

A moment later, her father appeared beside her mother. He placed a hand on his wife's shoulder and gazed down at his daughter.

The couple knelt down and wrapped their arms around their daughter.

When he finally got the door open, Joshua looked back at the church. Everyone was still inside. They weren't coming. They were still inside.

With *him.*

He raced to his car, threw the door open, and leapt inside. He cranked the ignition and sped out of the parking lot. He drove down ChristPoint Drive—named for the church (*his* church)—into town. Save one or two cars, the streets were deserted. Everyone was at church.

(*His* church.)

With Elijah. *With Elijah!*

Why, God? Why is this happening?

The vehicle zoomed through the city, barely stopping at intersections, until it finally passed the city limits and continued on. Joshua squeezed the steering wheel and held his foot to the gas pedal as hard as he dared.

While Lori and her parents reunited, Darren leapt at Blythe. He dove at the man and caught him at the midsection. Blythe grunted and, caught totally unprepared, was carried into the air by Darren's momentum. He landed hard on his back, and Darren's weight bore into his chest, driving the wind out of his lungs.

Darren rose up, reared his fist back, and punched the downed man hard in the jaw. Blythe's head bounced back and struck the floor. His eyes crossed for a moment and probably would've blacked out, but Darren slapped him once across the face to bring him back.

"I'm out of handcuffs right now," he said, "but you're still under arrest."

Finally, Joshua reached the interstate and drove west. He screamed again and pounded the steering wheel with his fist. He pressed his foot on the gas pedal, pushing the car well past the speed limit.

I've failed. Lord, I've failed...

CHAPTER 43

The manhunt for Elijah was called off, and a region-wide manhunt was issued for John Joshua Hutchinson. His car was located a week later at a truck stop near Louisville, but the Reverend was gone. No one at the station recognized his description, either.

The search continued for several weeks, but the effort dwindled when no further evidence of Joshua's whereabouts surfaced.

When police turned their attention from him to Joshua, Elijah was once again free to stay with Lori.

"Marcus' funeral is the day after tomorrow," she told him the night following Joshua's disappearance. "His family's handling everything."

They were eating a light dinner in the apartment's tiny dining room—vegetable soup with yeast rolls—sitting across from one another at Lori's little table.

"I haven't met them, yet," Elijah said.

"Neither have I," Lori sighed. Her voice was grim. "They disowned him years ago. Ever since he came out. They haven't said a word to him since."

Elijah stared at his bowl. "Poor guy."

"Don't feel too bad for him," Lori said. "He wouldn't want that. He made it on his own just fine." She grinned. "He really was a tough little S.O.B."

At that, Elijah grinned, as well. "Was he?"

"Oh yeah. As soon as they kicked him out, he got his own place, found a job. And he did it all on his own terms. He never asked for help from anyone."

Elijah nodded. "I'll miss him," he sighed. "I didn't know him long, but I'll miss him."

"Me too." Lori's voice cracked, and she covered her mouth. She felt the tears coming, but she fought to hold them back.

Elijah hurried around the table and wrapped his arms around her. "It's okay," he whispered.

"No, it isn't!" she cried. She leaned back, looked up at him. "He was my rock!"

Elijah nodded. "I know. But you have your parents back, now?"

Lori looked away and sniffled. She wiped her eyes and grunted. "Yeah. Yeah, you're right." She looked back at him. "That's something, isn't it?"

Elijah nodded, smiled. "You're much stronger than you give yourself credit for," he said. "You stayed here for years, hoping one day you could get your family out from under Joshua's thumb. Despite all the pain it caused, you stayed."

He brushed away a single tear that started to trickle down her face. "And now you have," he continued. "And they're going to need you. To be *their* rock."

Lori's face tightened, and she buried it in Elijah's chest.

Elijah went with Lori to Marcus' funeral two days later. Marcus' parents—James and Ellie Colley—stood in silence by their only son's casket. It was, in Lori's estimation, quite possibly the most awkward arrangement she'd ever seen.

James Colley's face was hard as stone. He betrayed no emotion to anyone, least of all Lori or Elijah. He shook their hands and offered only the briefest of nods to both of them.

Ellie managed a small, appreciative smile, but little more. "Thanks for coming," was all she said.

Lori and Elijah stood beside the casket a few moments, looking on Marcus one last time. The morticians did a fair enough job of making him presentable, although Lori thought he looked more than a little ridiculous wearing a suit and tie. "*I've never seen him wear one in his life,*" she hissed.

The turnout was also small. Lori and Elijah were the only two friends to attend. The funeral chapel, a cozy little room with about eight pews lined up in two rows, was littered with only a smattering of well-wishers: people neither Lori nor Elijah had ever met. "Probably his parents' friends," Lori said afterward.

The visitation lasted only an hour. There was no service. In fact, the Colleys never cast a final glance at their son as attendees sealed the casket and wheeled it from the room.

Afterward, they had the body cremated. And neither Lori nor Elijah ever learned what became of the ashes.

In the weeks that followed, Greg Foster stepped down from his position as chief. He did it as quietly as possible, with little, if any, announcement of his departure. The local news entities only managed to break the story the day before his resignation. Which was just as well. His tenure was considered by many to be a disgrace. He returned home to his wife. They stayed in Antioch for another year or two before finally packing up and heading south to Florida.

Dean also left. He headed to Louisville, hoping to find a significant business opportunity in the big city. His father was good friends with the president of a major bank there, and he arranged a prominent position for his son.

Frank Hollister didn't go so quietly. He'd invested all his remaining years in Joshua and his church, and now both were gone.

Neighbors grew anxious when Frank didn't leave his home for almost four days. They eventually called in the police, who forced their way inside with a battering ram. The first thing to hit them was the smell, the harsh stench of death and decay that attacks a person's nostrils like needles and makes his eyes water. The point man cursed and covered his face before venturing into the house.

They found Frank, dressed in his U.S. Marine uniform, hanging from the ceiling in his bedroom. He'd fashioned a homemade noose from a rope. His skin was already purple, and his swollen tongue hung from his mouth.

He didn't die easy, either, doctors said. He died from asphyxiation rather than a broken neck, and lacerations beneath his chin indicated he'd possibly had second thoughts and tried to fight his way out in the moments before he lost consciousness.

As for ChristPoint, it seemed most people viewed it as *unholy ground.* It disbanded shortly after the violent departure of its pastor. The building sat empty.

But religion proved to be just as resilient in Antioch as the rest of the world. Less than a season after the church's closure, individuals started gathering in homes throughout the city, holding their own private services, gathering congregations of their own. The old churches began reopening their doors by the following spring.

South Street Pentecostal Church, one of the few small ones that hadn't been transformed into a furniture store, was the first to reopen its doors. A bright, young pastor—Bro. David Yates—took charge of the new congregation, promising Holy Ghost-filled, Bible-fulfilling services.

Lori, who actually knew David Yates as a regular customer at J.D.'s, took particular comfort in the man's significant lack of ambition, at least, as compared with Joshua's. He told her days before reopening the church while eating dinner, "I'm not out to save the entire town, just the ones who want to be."

South Street was also joined by a handful of new churches that hadn't existed before ChristPoint. Faith Harbor. House of Worship. Christians In Action.

And then, before long, the larger churches also returned. Most of the old buildings were still intact, even though some were strewn with antiques and used sofas.

First Church of the Nazarene was probably the first large church to reopen, although the pastor of Northside Bible Baptist—which opened the same day—might argue. The Nazarene Church insisted they opened their doors a good half hour before Northside. Northside said the opposite.

In the years to come, the initial rivalry evolved into a partnership of sorts. Both churches worked together on youth activities and charity events. But they still sponsored their own baseball teams every summer, just to keep the "feud" alive.

EPILOGUE

Elijah never witnessed these events firsthand. He departed Antioch long before any of it happened.

He left only days after Marcus' funeral. That morning, he showered after Lori left for work, relishing the hot water for what would probably be the last time in days. Then, he dressed and gathered his clothes.

He returned to J.D.'s Pizzeria just before sunset. It was Wednesday, so the place wasn't all that busy. There were just five patrons in all, a mother and two boys at one table and an elderly couple at another.

Lori, now an assistant manager, stepped out from the kitchen to greet him. "Get you a table?"

Elijah smiled and shook his head.

Lori nodded. "You're leaving, aren't you?"

"Yeah."

"I figured you were," Lori said. "I'm really glad you stayed for Marcus' funeral, though."

Elijah nodded. "He deserved it."

"Wherever he is now," Lori sighed, "I hope...I hope he's happy."

Elijah took her hand. "I think he is."

"Oh! Wait here!" Lori held up a finger and ran back into the kitchen. She came back with a brown, cardboard box that Elijah guessed was roughly a foot long. "Here."

Elijah, still smiling, narrowed his eyes at the package. He pulled the top off, then shot his attention back at Lori.

"It's not the same one," she told him. "Police are keeping that. But it should do."

She'd given him a hunting knife with a leather sheath. It was almost an exact replica of the one police had confiscated as evidence in Marcus and Nathan's deaths.

"Like you said, it's dangerous on the road," Lori said.

Elijah strapped the sheath to his belt and covered it with his coat. Behind him, the single mother scolded her two boys: *"Stop throwing food at your brother, Billy! Jeremy, don't blow in your straw!"*

"Thank you," Elijah told Lori.

She stepped forward and wrapped her arms around his neck. She squeezed hard for several moments.

"You remember when I told you I still believed in God?" she asked. "Well, I still do. I don't know what He's got planned for you, but I'm convinced He brought you here."

She let go and stepped back.

Elijah thought for a moment, then said, "Maybe…"

Lori approached him again, leaned forward, and kissed his lips. She placed her hands to his cheeks and held him there until he kissed her back. He wrapped his arms around her and placed his hands on her back.

The boys in the booth stopped bickering and giggled.

Elijah pulled her close, clearly relishing the embrace of a woman. When Lori finally pulled back she said "I wish you could stay."

Elijah brushed his hand across her cheek and nodded. "Me too," he whispered.

They released each another, and Elijah turned for the door. He opened it (*doo-dah!*), stepped outside, then turned back. "You know," he said, "Joshua, what he preached, it wasn't wrong. Faith. Hope. Belief. Those are all wonderful things. *Important* things.

"Whatever you do, don't lose hope. Don't lose faith. Just because of him."

Lori smiled. Damn him. He could still make her do that whenever he wanted. "Will we ever see you again?"

Elijah shrugged. "Who knows? The world's full of surprises. But, you—you and this town—I think you're gonna' be okay."

He smiled at her and turned to walk outside. He crossed J.D.'s parking lot and returned to the road. Lori watched him through the window as long as she could before returning to her customers.

Elijah spared himself a final glance back at the restaurant. It sat quiet, peaceful, a small business operating in a small town, serving small town customers. Each day would be much like the one before. Despite the incredible changes facing Antioch, J.D.'s—and so many places like it—would continue. Life would go on. As it always did.

Elijah turned back to the road and resumed his journey, continuing down the highway, deserted save the occasional car zipping past. He looked to the sky and noticed the sun setting in the west.

He grinned. "Well...that's funny."